Monsoon Rising

DAVID LEE CORLEY

DAVID LEE CORLEY

DEDICATION

Dedicated to my mother, Patricia Ann Corley. Yes, that's right, my mom. Without her love and support I never would have found the courage to write. So, she gets it, the dedication for my first novel even though it's too scary for her to read. Seriously, she watched the movie 'Psycho' and didn't shower for a year.

DAVID LEE CORLEY

CHAPTER 1

The nomad sat in a Bangkok coffee shop sketching on a napkin with a pen. He was a peculiar man. Unlike the other westerners wearing shorts and t-shirts the nomad wore freshly pressed slacks and a long sleeve shirt with the collar buttoned up and loafers. It was unusual attire for the hot and humid weather of Thailand. The coffee shop was another Starbucks-wanna-be on the fourth floor of Terminal 21, a mega mall built for rich Asians and the *farang*— Thai slang for a westerner. The air buzzed with conversations, some in Thai most in English. The nomad was oblivious to it all like an island in the stream.

The nomad finished his napkin drawing and took a moment to admire it. The drawing was a cognitive illusion. The bare branches of a tree on closer inspection became the arteries and muscles of a woman. Below the branches was a self-portrait of the nomad sitting in an overstuffed chair drawing. Creation occupied his mind. His need was rising like the thirst of a runner approaching the end of a marathon. He knew that soon there would be work to be done but for the moment he was at peace. Peace is what he wanted most. Stillness.

A Thai waitress cleaning tables nearby glanced over at the drawing. "That very good" she said.

The nomad looked over at her expressionless. He studied her chubby face and overly tight uniform. Too many customer leftovers stolen from the plates she bussed.

"What is very good?" he asked.

"Photo."

"It's not a photo. It's a drawing."

"Yes. Drawing. Very good."

"Is it your vast experience in the art world that makes you qualified for such a judgement?"

"I no understand."

"No. How could you possibly?"

He crumpled the drawing and stuffed it into his empty cup. He could feel the disappointment on her face as she returned to bussing tables. The nomad rose from his table and left.

The nomad felt at ease as he descended the mall's 4-story escalator to the street level. He studied the shops and restaurants as he glided downward. He liked the restaurants in mall. They were clean unlike the dirty little family restaurants and street food that so many of the Thai enjoyed. Bangkok was growing on him. It had the energy of a big city but with Thai hospitality and an abundance of beautiful women. He liked that there were no hard and fast rules in Bangkok. Nobody cared who you were or what you had done in the past. You could be anything or anyone in Bangkok especially if you had money. The Thai respected money. Some worshiped it. Most Thai worked two jobs plus a hustle on the side just to survive in the city but it was better than back-breaking work on a rice farm and a lot more exciting.

The uniformed guards at the entrances to the mall saluted all farang patrons as they entered and exited. It was a show of respect to the westerners but the nomad felt like they were saluting his superiority— their way of saying that he was in control and theirs to command. He always gave them a little salute back encouraging his little army to keep up the good work.

The nomad exited the air-conditioned mall. It was dark and humid outside. The hot air hit him like a sauna. He immediately started sweating through his shirt and ruined the ironed creases on the sleeves. It annoyed him. He liked to look neat and clean. He was not like the others. He stepped around the concrete slabs that covered the sewers hidden below the sidewalk. He had learned through experience that the slabs were often cracked all the way through. If one was not careful, he could end up with a broken leg covered in shit. The smell of human waste mixed with the aromas of street vendors frying chicken in boiling vats of oil and roasting pork satays over compact charcoal grills. Like most farang who spent more than just a few weeks in the country, the nomad had grown accustomed to the smell and at times it even made him hungry.

He ducked under loops of electric wire hanging down from the power poles that serviced the apartments stores and restaurants packed tightly along the streets and down the alleys. In Chiang Mai after a light rain, the nomad had seen a man knocked off his feet after he brushed up against two live wires. He had watched with interest as the man lay in the gutter with his eyes rolled back in his head and his body twitching with mini-convulsions. The man was still unconscious when an ambulance rushed him off to a hospital. Later in his hotel room the nomad had researched death by execution on Google and watched several YouTube videos including an unruly elephant named Topsy put to death by electrocution on Coney Island. Death in all its forms was a curiosity and he found humor in the black and white footage of Topsy's demise filmed by Thomas Edison's movie company.

The nomad walked past a teenage girl sitting on a blanket breast feeding her baby. She raised a well-used 7-11 cup as he passed and her sad eyes looked up trying to make contact with the rich westerner. He was not there to solve the world's problems but he liked giving money to the destitute. It was God-like deciding who would survive another day and who would succumb to Darwin's law. He dug out the coins from his pocket and dropped thirty baht into her dirty cup. It was not enough to make a difference in her life but it would give her enough for a chicken satay or a small bowl of noodles. She and her baby would survive another day thanks to him.

The nomad joined a throng of pedestrians crossing Ratchadaphisek Road, an 8-lane street that snaked its way through Bangkok like a femoral artery. He knew it was always better to cross with a crowd. There was less chance of getting run over or clipped by a scooter. Tens of thousands of cars and *tuk-tuks*—motorized tricycles with open air passenger cabs—chocked the streets as scooters weaved in and out taking up every spare inch of pavement. It was surprising that anything moved in the city, but it did and fairly well considering nobody obeyed traffic signals or stayed in their lanes unless a policeman stood in the middle of the street issuing tickets. The driver in front had the right of way. That was the custom and custom usually mattered more than law in Thailand.

Heading north on the opposite side of the street, he zigzagged through the crowd and past the sidewalk bars that served watered-down shots of Johnnie Walker Black to one or two customers at a time. He turned onto a side street resembling a mini Las Vegas with its colored neon and blinking bulbs. The street was called Soi Cowboy and was one of Bangkok's many adult playgrounds.

Prostitution was illegal but the law was more like an inconvenient speed bump when it came to making money in Thailand, especially when the money came from foreigners. An attractive go-go dancer could make five times what she could make as a line-worker in a factory or as a shop-girl working in the mall. She could support her parents and her children and still have money left over for nice clothes and the latest smart phone. She would never go hungry as long as men wanted her. And if she was lucky, she would find one or two farang boyfriends to support her or even marry her before her looks gave out.

The nomad strolled past several go-go bars with names like Raw Hide, Toy Bar, After Skool and Doll House. Thai boys slapped their handheld signs advertising cheap beer and 5 for 1 shots. Go-go dancers between sets wore that night's themed lingerie and wrangled passing men by grabbing their arm and pulling them toward the front door of the club. Inside the clubs most of the girls danced with little enthusiasm and bored expressions and often chatted among themselves ignoring the customers until the mamasan scolded them and smacked them on their pussies, tweaked their nipples and pulled their hair. If the girls objected they would be immediately replaced. Most danced topless with one or two completely naked depending on the bar owner's attitude toward risk and the time of night. A surprise inspection from the local police could bring hefty fines for naked or topless girls and even shutdown the bar if the proper bribes had not been paid. Spotters warned the girls when it was time to suit up. As soon as the danger passed, the clothes came off and the party continued.

The nomad crossed the street to Suzie Wong's, a go-go bar known for its beautiful dancers armed with foam tubes used to whack passing customers on the back or themselves on the ass if a customer was so inclined. The music inside was old-time rock and roll, a favorite of older farang with thick wallets and blue pills marked with a V. Two Suzy Wong dancers grabbed the nomad's arms and pulled him toward the entrance. At first he cooperated but then stopped when he heard, "You wanna get nailed?"

He turned back to the outdoor bar across from Suzy Wong's and saw a very attractive dark-skinned bargirl holding a hammer and standing next to a log set on end. Her smile showed off her white teeth. The nomad knew that bargirls made their money getting customers to buy them lady-drinks which were the same as regular drinks but cost 50% more to cover the girl's commission. He knew that bargirls were usually cheaper than the go-go girls if he wanted to take her back to his hotel. Seeing the danger of losing a potential customer, the Suzy Wong girls pulled at the nomad more forcefully and turned him around and pulled him toward the club entrance. He turned back to give the bargirl another look. Her face had full lips, a little nose and sculpted cheekbones and her skin was dark and smooth. She was a beauty and knew it and stood smiling and confident. Probably from Isan. Most of the working girls came from the province of Isan in Northeast Thailand.

The nomad knew she could easily be had by just pulling out his billfold. But he wanted more than that. He wanted her to like him. To want him. In his younger days the nomad went for girls who suffered from lack of confidence and could be manipulated easily. But after a few years, he evolved. Now he liked a challenge. He pulled away from the Suzy Wong girls. They cursed him as he stepped over to the bargirl.

"Hi. You're a frisky one" he said.

"What fisky?" she said.

"Frisky? It means playful."

"You like payful?"

"I like you. You have a cute little nose."

"Thank you. What your name?"

"I am David. You?"

"I Buppha."

They shook hands.

"What does it mean, Buppha?"

"It mean flower" she said. "Where you from?"

"United States."

"America?"

"Yes. America. Where are you from?"

"Surin."

The nomad knew the small city of Surin was in the Isan province near the Laotian border and the primary source of rice for all of Thailand.

"A farm girl?"

"Yes. Family grow rice."

"You are very confident for growing up on a farm."

"Yes. Farm."

"How old are you?"

Asking personal questions such as a woman's age was considered polite in any introductory conversation in Thailand. She held up two fingers followed by six fingers.

"Twenty-six?"

"Yes. Twenty-six."

"Do you have children?"

She looked confused.

"Babies? Do you have babies?"

"Yes. One."

He looked down at her belly. There was no vertical scar from a Thai-style c-section or loose skin below her bellybutton. She was probably telling the truth about only having one child. He had no objection to mothers as long as they remained tight.

"Boy or girl?"

"Girl. She eight."

"I bet she is a beauty like her mother."

She struggled to understand most of what he said. Like most bargirls, her English was limited and she wanted to change the subject so she didn't look stupid. "You want to play?" she asked motioning to the log standing on end.

"Always."

She tapped the point of a six-penny nail into the log with her hammer. "First one to finish nail buy drink" she said.

"Okay."

She raised the hammer ready to strike.

"Wait. I'll take that nail" he said and gestured to her nail knowing that she probably placed the nail's tip in the sweet spot of the log. He took the hammer from her hand. "...and I go first."

"You play before?"

"Once or twice."

He unbuttoned his cuff and rolled up the sleeve. He hit the nail squarely and drove it an inch into the log.

"You strong" she said. She glanced at the long scar on his muscular foreman. "You get hurt bad?"

"Bad? No. Not really. Do you have scars like this?"

"Like this no."

"Good. Your turn."

She tapped in another starter nail and struck the nail squarely. It went in but not as far as his. He took the hammer and swung at his nail and missed. "Shit" he said.

She giggled. He turned in anger but caught himself. He smiled and handed her the hammer. She swung again and hit her nail squarely. She was consistent and that was the key to the game. The men always used brute force while the bargirls used compliments and consistency.

An hour later, she had six half-finished beers on her side of the table. She took a final swing at her latest nail and drove it until the head was flush with the log.

"Well done" said the nomad and motioned to the bartender to bring her another beer.

"No more beer. My teeth floating."

"It's 'my back teeth are floating.'"

"Thank you for correcting me. My back teeth floating."

"Okay no more beer."

"Maybe we could play something else?"

"Okay. What do you have in mind?

"Maybe you take me to hotel and I fuck you good."

"That sounds interesting."

Again she didn't understand him. His vocabulary was beyond her.

"Yes?"

He looked her over once again. Her face was without

a serious blemish. However, experience had taught him the hard way that things in Thailand were not always what they seemed. "You're not a—"

"—ladyboy?" she said. She pulled open her shorts and allowed him to have a peak. He nodded his approval. Thai women were clean and bathed two or three times a day.

"Do you know how to swim?" he said.

"I swim little" she said.

"Good. Let's go to my hotel. It's got a pool and I'm hot."

"Yeah. You hot. You pay bar fine. Okay?"

"How much?"

"Eight hundred baht."

"Okay. And you? How much you cost?"

"Short time or long time?"

"Short time for now but we'll see where the night takes us."

"Twenty-five hundred baht short time."

The nomad glanced up at the security camera covering the bar and saw that they were aimed directly at him. "Okay but I have a good idea."

"What good idea?"

"What time does the bar close?"

"Two o'clock."

"Why don't you meet me at two o'clock outside my hotel. I can give you the 800 baht bar fine and the 2500 baht. You'll make more money. Maybe you do a little extra for me."

"Okay. I like. But no say anything to other girls so I no get in trouble."

"Of course."

Elevator doors opened and Buppha and the nomad walked out into a foyer. A sign on a door read Pool. She twisted the doorknob. It was locked.

"Fuck. It locked" said Buppha.

"It's okay. I have a key" said the nomad. The nomad slammed his foot into the door. It didn't open. He tried again and again until the lock gave way and the door swung open.

"You bad boy."

"Only if they catch me."

They entered the dark indoor pool room and the air was still. The moonlight through the windows illuminated the water. Buppha looked for a light switch.

"No. Leave it dark" he said.

The nomad moved up behind her and kissed her on the back of the neck. She turned and pulled off his shirt revealing his heavily scarred chest, abdomen and arms. She pulled back startled.

"It's okay. It doesn't hurt now" he said.

She kissed several of the scars on the chest. He closed his eyes and moaned. He liked this girl. She was smart and knew what he wanted. She moved off and teased him pulling off her clothes. The nomad's eyes studied her naked body free from scars. She was perfect and worthy of his passion. He pulled off the rest of his clothes revealing even more scars on his buttocks, genitals and legs, some from cigarette burns and others from cuts and gashes. One long scar was from a cracked fibula that had broken through and ripped the skin. Naked, Buppha touched the water with her toes.

"It cold" she said.

"I'll keep you warm."

The nomad dove in and disappeared beneath the dark water. Buppha waded into the shallow end and kept one hand on the side of the pool. She was not a good swimmer. The nomad surfaced behind her. He gently folded his arms around her like a mother holds a child on a winter day.

"It's okay. I've got you."

He gently pulled her from the side. Apprehensive she turned around and wrapped her arms around his neck. They moved into the deep end of the pool. The nomad treaded water for the both of them. Buppha relaxed a bit. He would keep her safe.

"There you go. You can trust me. I've got you" he said softly.

As they approached the opposite side, she again reached for the side. The nomad again moved up behind her and took her other hand and placed it on the side so she could hold on to the wall with both hands. She felt his erection on her buttocks.

"You use condom?"

"Yes" said the nomad.

The nomad placed his hands over hers and thrusted gently against her. She let out a moan. The nomad thrusted again more firmly. Her face flinched.

"Wait. Slow. I not ready yet" she said.

The nomad thrusted again and again harder and faster.

"No. Stop. It hurt."

He didn't stop. She began to panic and kicked him in the knee. He pushed away in pain.

"Fucking bitch" he said.

She was a fighter. He liked that but she must be controlled and punished for the kick. It was the only way she would learn. He disappeared below the surface. She held onto the side of the pool and pulled herself hand over hand toward the shallow end. Her feet searched for the bottom. The nomad surged out of the water behind her and came down on top of her back. His teeth bit into her shoulder. She screamed in pain. He thrashed his head back and forth and his teeth dug deeper until finally he pulled his mouth away leaving a golf-ball-size hole in her shoulder. He released her and spat out a hunk of flesh into the water. Blood flowed from his mouth and mixed in the water around him. Again he submerged below the black water.

She stared at the hole in her shoulder and watched it fill up with blood. She could not grasp what had just happened or what was about to happen. She looked around at the black water. The nomad was not in sight. She took a breath and pushed herself under the water. Her feet found the bottom of the pool. She scrambled for the shallow end. Her head bobbed out of the water and she looked back at the blackness. No sign of the nomad. She turned back toward the stairs and watched as the nomad rose from the dark water between her and the pool steps. She stopped frozen in fear. The nomad reached out and gently placed his hands on her arms and lifted her up.

"No. Please."

The nomad opened his mouth wide and his teeth descended onto her face. The water thrashed as she struggled. Her screams muffled into guttural grunts. The water calmed. The nomad rose from the water and spit something out of his mouth. An object plunked into the water and bobbed to the surface. It was her little brown nose.

The nomad sat calmly on his hotel room balcony looking out at the city lights below. It was just before dawn. He felt full and at peace. Eventually, the authorities would find the girl's body where he had hidden it and the search for her killer would begin. By then he would be gone. But there was no need to hurry now. He was still safe. And then it hit him—a bolt of pain seared through his brain. The pain left as quickly as it had come. *Just ignore it* he thought. *It'll go away.*

The pain hit him again stronger. He quickly moved into the bedroom and pulled his toilet kit from his luggage bag and fished out a plastic container and opened it. Inside was a plastic statdose pen and one replacement cartridge. The other cartridge had already been used and discarded. He placed the remaining cartridge in the pen and shot himself in the wrist. After a few moments, the medication to took affect and his face relaxed. His peace had returned. The electrical storm in his mind was gone. It was going to be okay.

He wanted to close his eyes and sleep. Even the slightest attack drained him of all his energy. Maybe he would lay down for a few minutes. No he thought. It's time to go while it is still quiet before the hotel's day staff arrives. There was work that still needed to be done.

He put the statdose pen back in the plastic container, the container back in his toilet kit and the toilet kit back in his luggage bag. He pulled out his wallet and removed his prepaid credit card. He also pulled out his passport and his phone. He moved back out to the balcony and sat down. He bent the credit card back and forth until it snapped in half. He threw the pieces into the ashtray on the table. He ripped out the photo page of his passport showing his photo and his assumed name—David Mitchell. He methodically tore each page of the passport into four sections and placed them into the ashtray. He pulled the sim card from his cell phone and placed it in the ashtray. He stomped on the cell phone breaking the glass and frame then threw the useless remains over the balcony into the alley below. He broke open a disposable lighter and poured the fluid into the ashtray taking special care to thoroughly soak the photo page of his passport. He used the remains of the lighter mechanism to ignite his passport photo page. He let it burn completely and dropped the flaming photo page into the ashtray, igniting the rest of the evidence. He left the ashtray contents to incinerate and exited the balcony and walked back into his room.

He opened a pouch in his luggage bag and pulled out five passports. He selected one of the passports and opened it to the photo page. Inside was a prepaid credit card with a name matching the passport—Kyle Tanner. He slid the credit card into his wallet and his passport into his jacket pocket. From another pocket in his luggage bag, he pulled out a compact electric screwdriver, a matchbook and a can of lighter fluid. He slid all three it into his jacket pocket. He pulled out a cigarette and placed it behind his ear and zipped up his bag.

He moved back onto the balcony and emptied the ashes of his mini-evidence bonfire onto a piece of tinfoil and neatly folded it up and slipped it into his backpack. He moved back into the room and searched the trashcan. He stuffed the loose garbage into his backpack. He pulled out the can of lighter fluid and squirted the drapes and the bed. Using another lighter, he set the drapes alight and the room quickly became engulfed. He exited the room with his backpack and luggage bag. The nomad knew that the fire would not destroy all his fingerprints and DNA but this was Thailand and the police and fire departments were seriously under staffed and under equipped. There was little chance they would even bother looking for an arsonist once the fire was out.

In the hallway, the nomad disappeared down the stairwell just as the fire alarm sounded. At the bottom of the stairwell, the nomad set his luggage bag by the door and opened the door leading into the lobby and took a quick peak. The front desk staff scurried around trying to figure out if there was a real fire or if it was a false alarm. Guests gathered in the lobby demanding an explanation. In the confusion, the nomad with his backpack slung over his shoulder slipped into the back room behind the front desk.

Inside the back room, video monitors displayed the different views of the hotel's security cameras. The nomad searched and found the computer controlling and recording the security cameras. He pulled the removable hard drive from the computer along with five others sitting on a nearby rack and dropped them into his backpack. He pulled out the can of lighter fluid and squirted the computer with fluid. He pulled out the book of matches and the cigarette behind his ear. He lit the cigarette and placed the burning cigarette on top of the match heads and folded the cover closed. In a few minutes the cigarette would burn down and ignite the match heads. He placed the homemade incendiary device at the base of the computer next to a gathering puddle of lighter fluid. He zipped up his backpack, slung it back over his shoulder and exited the back room. In the lobby the nomad mixed with the other guests and waited.

Inside the backroom the incendiary device ignited. The computer went up in flames. Smoke poured out of the back room. Guests panicked and ran into the street. The remaining staff ran for fire extinguishers.

The nomad slipped behind the front desk and opened a file drawer. He searched through the copies of passports with the attached admin forms until he found his own. The passport copy clearly showed his photo and his name—David Mitchell. He pulled it and stuffed it into his jacket pocket and squirted lighter fluid into the file. He moved to the hotel computer, pulled out his electric screwdriver and removed the screws from the back panel and removed the computer's hard drive and dropped it into his backpack along with the other hard drives. He squirted lighter fluid into the computer. The computer shorted out starting another fire. He left the desk and walked back to the stairwell and opened the door. He grabbed his luggage bag and exited the hotel as the fire trucks pulled up.

The nomad walked down the street and over a bridge above a storm canal. He looked around to see that he was truly alone and unzipped his backpack and dumped the hard drives and the loose garbage from the room trashcan and the tinfoil holding the ashes into the water below. His trail was now erased. *It is going to be a fine day* he thought as he moved off in the early morning light.

CHAPTER 2

Billy Gamble woke staring at the ceiling of a very small room. It seemed more like the inside of an oversized coffin than an actual room. There was no door in the room but there was light bleeding through a cloth screen down past his feet. His head hurt and his lips were chapped. He was fairly sure he wasn't dead but he wasn't prepared to swear on it. *Where am I?* he thought fighting a growing feeling of vertigo. *Taipei? No.* He remembered leaving Taipei two weeks ago. It wasn't Taipei. *Seoul?* Billy sniffed the cool damp air. *No kimchi.* Everything and everyone in Korea smelled of kimchi—a fermented cabbage made with onions and ground red peppers. It wasn't Seoul.

He closed his eyes trying to focus as his head throbbed. It was a wicked hangover. *What did I drink last night? Last night...?* In his mind were blurred images of flashing neon, green laser beams and Asian showgirls with their fists pounding to the music while dancing on robots. *Robots? Yeah robots. Lots of chrome-skinned robots dancing and a panda bear riding a cow and Mothra spewing sparks while carrying a gorilla in its talons. Mothra?* It hit him. *The Robot Restaurant. I'm in Tokyo.* His mind cleared a bit and the vertigo faded. It made sense now. He came to Japan after Taiwan. He was still far from home. The micro air conditioner on the wall above his head hummed. It reminded him of something. He closed his eyes and remembered...

Barbwire hummed from a hard wind. The Grand Tetons of Wyoming towered over a small homestead. A twenty-year-old pickup sat covered with two feet of fresh snow, its rocker panels and fender wells rusted from too many long winters. A school bus with snow chains and a plow welded on the front pulled to a stop on the road. Two boys exited the bus and cut themselves a new path thru the snow. One boy headed for a shed while the other headed for the house.

A young Billy entered his father's wood shop and closed the door against the wind. For a woodshop there was a definite lack of power tools. Handmade gigs, well-aged chisels and wooden hand-planners with their varnish long worn off hung from the ceiling and on pegboards. It was the kind of stuff people collected as antiques and displayed in local bars and restaurants not anything anyone used anymore. His father stood over a homemade workbench. A wood vise gripped a table leg. He used an old-fashioned hand-drill to auger a hole in the top of the leg.

"How was school?" asked his father.

"Boring as shit."

"Watch your mouth. Mother doesn't like you to swear."

"Sorry, Pa."

"Come 'ere."

Billy walked over to the bench. His father pulled the auger bit out of the leg and wood chips fell to the floor covered in sawdust.

"Blow."

Billy blew into the hole and purged the remaining wood chips and sawdust. His father handed him a bottle of wood glue and a hand-carved wooden dole.

"Three drops. No more no less."

Billy let three drops of yellow glue fall and pushed the dole into the hole. It was a tight fit. Billy knew what came next and picked up a wooden mallet.

"Light taps" said his father.

Billy tapped lightly until glue oozed out of the hole past the sides of the dole. His father handed Billy a rag.

"Quick like a rabbit neat like a barkeep."

Billy used the rag to carefully clean up the excess glue.

"Make good and sure ya get it all or the stain won't take."

"Why don't ya just use big screws? They're faster."

"Faster ain't better. This table'll be strong for years. Maybe even a lifetime."

The young Billy nodded. His father took a sip from his Coleman thermos of maybe coffee, maybe something with a little more kick. It depended on the weather and his mood.

"You got chores 'fore supper."

"Can't I stay awhile longer?"

His father gave him a "What do you think?" look. Billy didn't need to be told twice especially when the second tellin' was usually accompanied by his father's boot. He exited the woodshed and closed the door tight behind him.

It was twilight. The sun's warmth was gone and the temperature dropped like a pinecone from a tree. Billy and his brother Lowell waded knee deep in the snow carrying a bale of alfalfa between them. Billy's jacket had a patch sewn on the side where Lowell had torn it climbing under a fence before it was handed down to Billy. Nothing was wasted in their family. Nothing. Billy fell and dropped his hook in the snow along with his end of the bale.

"Get your ass up, Buttface" said Lowell.

"I'm trying" said Billy.

"Try harder, Shithead. It's colder than a witch's tit out here."

"My dick's freezing."

"How would you know? You ain't got a dick."

"You ain't got a dick."

"Bigger than your little pecker."

"Shut up."

Billy swung the hook into the side of the bale and lifted up his side again. The boys entered a barn. Eight appaloosa horses with long winter coats were tucked into separate stalls and restless for their supper. One of the horses, a sorrel mare with three socks and a white powdering on her buttocks, whinnied.

"Shut the fuck up, Snowdrop. We're coming" said Lowell.

"Yeah we're coming, Snowdrop. Shut the fuck up" said Billy.

The boys dropped the bale in the center of the barn. Lowell grabbed a pair of wire cutters hanging from a nail and snipped the wires holding the alfalfa together. The alfalfa bale fell apart into square flakes. When Lowell put the cutter back on the nail, he reached up and grabbed a hidden pack of cigarettes and a matchbox.

"You feed 'em. I'm having a smoke" said Lowell.

"Pa catches you smoking in the horse barn again he's gonna—"

"He ain't gonna do nothing cuz your yapper ain't gonna say shit."

"Gimme one."

"You're too young to smoke. It'll stunt your growth."

"I don't care. Gimme one. I'm cold and it'll warm me up."

"Okay. When you're done feeding 'em."

Lowell struck a match on the zipper of his jeans and lit a cigarette. He tossed the burning match down to the wooden floor next to a small pile of dry hay and started a fire.

"What the fuck, Lowell?"

"Shut up, dick-less."

Lowell unzipped his fly and peed on the little fire and extinguished it. Billy pulled the bale apart and tossed a flake into each horse's stall. Billy walked back to Lowell and held out his hand for a cigarette.

"You're 'bout as useless as tits on a bull. Ya ain't done, shit-for-brains. Ya gotta give 'em their grain or they'll freeze to death."

"They're in a barn. They ain't gonna freeze to death."

"Maybe not but you still gotta feed 'em their grain. It's like dessert to a horse. They gonna get all pissy if ya don't give it to 'em."

Billy walked over to a large plastic barrel and opened the lid and gave each horse a scoop of grain mixed with molasses on top of their alfalfa. The horses snarfed it down like kids eating candy. Billy walked back over to Lowell and put his hand out for a cigarette. Lowell dropped the pack to the wooden floor. Billy bent down to pick it up. Lowell turned and farted in Billy's face.

"That'll keep you warm" Lowell said running out of the barn. Billy picked up the pack. It was empty.

Billy sat by the fire in the family room. He was halfway finished assembling a 2500-piece puzzle. Billy didn't look at the box lid that showed a picture of an underwater reef filled with coral fish and a shark. Instead he studied the edges of each loose piece and studied the edges of the assembled pieces. In his mind he measured distances between the farthest edge of each piece and searched for matching patterns, not the color of the printed image on each piece like normal children. He assembled the puzzle quickly. His mother called him to dinner.

Billy sat at the dinner table with his family making a volcano out of his mash potatoes and gravy. The phone rang. Billy glanced at Lowell sharing a worried look. His mother answered it and handed the phone to their father interrupting his meal. His father listened and his expression darkened.

"I see. Well thank ya for calling, Pete. I sure appreciate it. Louise'll be down tomorrow to pay for anything missing. Be sure and say hello to Betty for us. You have a good night."

Billy's father hung up the phone and sat back down at the table without saying a word. Billy gave his brother an even more worried look. His father finished his supper in silence.

Billy and Lowell in their white underwear stood silently in the bathroom with their pants down around their ankles. Their father entered the bathroom and closed the door and turned to his sons.

"You steal baseball cards from Henderson's five and dime?" asked their father.

"No. Ol' Pete hates kids. He's just trying to get us in trouble" Lowell said.

His father nodded and turned to Billy.

"That true?"

Billy stood motionless, petrified. After a long moment he shook his head. Their father pulled off his belt and doubled it up in a loop holding the buckle-end in his hand.

"Billy, you first."

His father lowered the toilet lid and sat.

"I'm sorry, Pa."

"Yes ya are. Now get 'em down."

Billy pulled down his underwear and leaned over his father's lap.

"We don't steal in this family."

His father struck Billy three times leaving three long red welts on his butt and upper thigh. In tears Billy pulled his underwear up and moved off to one side. He watched his brother pull his underwear down and assume the position.

"This is for stealing."

His father delivered three licks with his belt. His brother started to rise but his father stopped him and pushed him back down.

"And this is for lying."

His father delivered even harder blows. Whack— whack—whack—

Billy watched with tears running down his face as his father struck his brother again and again. Watching was always worse than the belt. The lesson was learned by both.

Billy blinked. His memory was over. This wasn't home, of that he was sure. He glanced at the time on his iPhone—6 a.m. He had slept in and it was time to get up. His room was a hotel capsule—the exact width and length of a single bed. There was a small shelf to hold personal belongings, a reading light and a single electrical outlet. That's it. No frills. Cheap but efficient. His roommates, mostly Japanese businessmen sleeping off a night of boozing at their favorite Izakaya, had already started their day. Hungover but reliable—that was the Japanese way. He unplugged his phone charger and grabbed his toilet kit and towel and slid to the end of his bed and opened the cloth shutter that served as a door.

Shit he thought. He had forgotten he was on the top bunk. He climbed down the stairs until his bare feet touched carpeted floor. He slid the complementary slippers on his size 13 feet and his heels stuck out over the back edge by a good two inches. Not even close. He kicked off the slippers and walked past the double-stacked capsules lining both sides of a long room. Billy was wearing the terrycloth sleeping garments issued by the hotel for all guests. They were the largest size available, but still road up to his shins.

He entered the white tiled bathroom. *Spotless. The Japanese are the cleanest people on the planet* he thought. He set his things on the counter and moved to one of ten urinals to start his morning routine. A Japanese man walked up to a urinal near Billy and looked down with disgust at Billy's bare feet.

"Them slippers they give me didn't fit" said Billy.

It didn't help. It was a breach of etiquette. The man moved off to the privacy of a toilet stall.

"Sorry. I didn't mean to—"

Too late. The man was gone.

"Ah to hell with it" Billy said to himself. "Not like I missed the bowl and peeped on the man's britches."

Billy finished up and entered the shower locker room, stripped off his sleeping wear, placed his things in a locker, locked the door and slipped the waterproof key band around his wrist. He was buck naked like the other men without even a towel to cover his private parts. That was the Japanese custom when entering a public bathing area. Naked.

He walked into the shower room. There were twenty shower stalls against the walls. He sat down on a short plastic stool in front of a shower head on the end of a flexible steel hose. There was a nice arrangement of complimentary shaving cream, razors, shampoo, conditioner and body gel on the shelf in front of him. He turned on the water and rinsed himself off. The Japanese were overly attentive about soaping up and scrubbing every inch of their bodies before entering a sento, a Japanese public bath. Billy failed to see the point. He turned off the water and stood up and walked over to the pool-sized bath.

Four Japanese men were already sitting in the steamy water. The temperature gauge on the wall read 40 degrees Celsius. Billy stepped in slowly. The water was hot. He was concerned what would happen when his balls hit the water. He looked around at the other men now staring at him. *Too late to back out now* he thought. He stepped farther into the bath and submerged his body, creating a mini tidal wave. The water was barely tolerable. He relaxed and leaned back against the wall. He grabbed a small bamboo bucket and scooped up some water and poured it over his head. He let out a whoop. Another breach of etiquette. He didn't care. The other four men got out and left the uncultured American alone in the bath.

"Be glad I didn't pee" said Billy.

Eve Donoghue stood in front of the Capsule Value Hotel for Men. She checked the address on her list of hotels. More than half the hotels were crossed off and it was still a long list. She walked to the front door and entered the hotel. She immediately took off her shoes and put on a pair of slippers provided by the hotel and set her shoes on the rack in the entryway.

Billy was dressed except for shoes when he exited the men's locker room. He turned into the shoe storage area across from the front desk and caught a glimpse of Eve as she entered the lobby. He was intrigued by seeing a white woman close to his age and took a second peek as he unlocked his locker and removed a pair of hand-stitched Lucchese boots made of calfskin with lemonwood pegs in the soles. The boots were well past due for a resole but he didn't trust anyone outside the U.S. to do it. They'd just have to wait.

Eve approached the receptionist and they exchanged bows.

"Do you speak English?" Eve asked with an Irish accent.

"Yes. A little" said the receptionist.

Irish Billy thought. I wonder how she likes her whiskey?

"I am looking for this man" said Eve and pulled a photo from her satchel.

Billy glanced around the corner and saw the Irish woman holding a grainy headshot of his face blown up from his Wyoming driver's license. *Oh shit* he thought and ducked back behind the row of lockers. The receptionist studied the photo. Eve saw a hint of recognition in her eyes.

"Do you know him?"

"What he do?"

"Nothing. His uncle died and left him a large inheritance. You know—money."

Bullshit Billy thought. He had two uncles, one an alcoholic used car salesman lucky to make rent each month and the other a farm equipment mechanic crushed to death eight years ago when a tractor fell off its cinder blocks. He knew why she was after him. He had stolen $4.2 million and the insurance company that was forced to pay the claim wanted its money back.

"Oh that good for him" said the receptionist.

"Aye, very good" said Eve. "I want to find him and tell him. Give him documents to sign so he can get the money."

Billy grabbed his boots and slipped back into the Men's locker room.

"Have you seen him?"

"Yes. He staying here."

"He's staying here?"

"Yes."

"Is he here now?"

"Yes. I think he still here. Not leave yet. You want I send someone get him?"

"No. I'll wait here until he comes out. I don't want to disturb him."

Eve sat in a stool that gave her a good view of the entire lobby. She pulled out her mobile and dialed.

"Detective Chiba, it's Eve Donoghue. I found him. Capsule Value Hotel at 1-2-7 Kabukicho. Aye. Four uniformed officers should be enough." Eve hung up the phone.

Billy opened his locker and pulled out his luggage bag. He pulled his boots over his white socks and spotted an exit sign in Japanese and English on the side wall of the locker room. He moved toward it then burst through an exit door into an alley with his wheeled luggage bag in tow. He vanished into Tokyo's morning commute. He was lost in the crowd. He was safe.

CHAPTER 3

Billy walked out of Starbucks at Narita International and sipped his black coffee while studying the crowd. By this time, the passport he used to enter Japan had been reported stolen and he needed another one to leave. He immediately eliminated the Asian faces and focused on white males similar to his own age. He didn't worry about hair color or length or color of eyes or even the size and shape of the nose lips and ears. He could change all that with contacts and prosthetic makeup. He didn't worry about weight. People lost and gained weight all the time. It could easily be explained away. Billy was interested in a biometric match. He measured distances and relationships between eyes, nose, mouth and ears. You can't fake those. It's what computers measured. It's what experienced border guards focused on.

Billy was a super matcher, a term coined by customs and intelligent officials. He could match biometrics visually. It was a very rare talent. Super matchers were highly sought after by governments as potential intelligent and immigration analysts. Billy had been approached in high school after taking the SAT. An intelligence recruiter interviewed him and asked if he would be interested in working for the US government. Billy was intrigued but his family needed him on the ranch since his brother had joined the Marines. His parents were struggling financially to keep up with the mortgage. It was a battle they would eventually lose.

Billy's original passport had been compromised several years ago when Interpol issued a Red Notice on him. He always checked the Interpol website before traveling between countries. And one day there is was. He still carried his original passport tucked away in a hidden pocket on the inside of his left boot. He could still use it to check into hotels. But he didn't dare try to cross a border with it. For that Billy needed another passport. A clean passport. Airports were the best place to find them. If someone had just exited immigration, he knew their passport was valid. He couldn't afford to make a mistake, not if he wanted to remain free.

Like most airports Narita International Terminal was exhausting. Long lines. Bored children running amok. Too many people with too much luggage. All this worked to Billy's advantage. Dozens of chauffeurs, hotel hostesses and junior company managers lined the rail at the immigration exit and each held a sign with the name of a passenger—some in Japanese most in English. Billy studied the passengers as they filed past. His doppelgänger didn't need to be an exact match. Just close enough to get past the busy immigration officials. He spotted a man similar to himself in height and age. He had a small scar on his left cheek. *That was a plus* thought Billy. The man slipped his passport into his oversized wallet filled with bills that looked Australian and slipped the wallet into his jacket pocket. Australians spoke English. That was another advantage and he could easily fake the accent. Billy picked up his bag and followed the man.

The Aussie moved to a currency exchange kiosk and exchanged some of his Australian dollars for Yen. Billy moved up behind him and set his bag down right behind the man's legs. The Aussie finished and turned and stumbled over Billy's bag. Billy caught him and kept him from falling.

"Whoa there big fella" said Billy.

The Aussie regained his balance. "Thanks mate."

"No problem."

"American?"

"Canadian actually. I take it you're Australian."

"Very good."

"The mate gave you away. You heading into Tokyo?"

"Yeah."

Billy pulled out his wallet and dug for some cash to

41

exchange. This was a total bluff. Japan was a tight country when it came to finance. You needed a passport to exchange currency and Billy didn't have one that he could use.

"I was gonna to take the train but if we split a taxi it'll cost the same and we can avoid the rush hour crush" said Billy.

"Sounds good" said the Aussie and gestured to the exchange kiosk. "You need to exchange some money?"

"Ya know what, I've got enough to get to my hotel. I'll do it there."

They both picked up their bags and headed off to the taxi stand.

In the taxi the Aussie took off his jacket and laid it on his lap.

"Whereabouts in Canada you from?"

"Calgary originally. Now I hang my hat in Vancouver. Great city if you like jazz. You?"

"Perth. Good city if you like blonds."

"I do if they're tall."

They shared a laugh. Billy pointed out the Aussie's window to a giant electronic billboard displaying the latest condominium development in overly bright LEDs.

"Will you look at that. Imagine what it costs in

electric bills to run that thing 24/7."

The Aussie looked out the window and Billy slipped his hand into the Aussie's jacket and pulled out the man's wallet. He removed the passport then slipped the wallet still filled with cash back into the jacket pocket all in one smooth move without the Aussie noticing.

"Probably more than my mortgage. But it's all right. Average couple only has one kid and lives in a shoe box. The Jippos are loaded. They can afford it." said the Aussie.

The taxi driver gave the Aussie a nasty look in the mirror.

"Sorry mate."

The taxi pulled into a hotel. The Aussie grabbed his jacket and searched for his wallet. Billy put his hand out to stop him.

"I'll get it. After all I almost killed you with my bag."

The Aussie again reached for his wallet.

"Don't be silly man. You saved me from an embarrassing spill."

Again Billy stopped him. "I tell you what. Let's meet up for a drink later at that bar in Ginza you were telling me about."

"Musashi?"

"That's it! You buy the first round."

"Probably be cheaper to pay my half of the taxi but all right. Eight?"

"I'll be there."

They shook hands. The Aussie stepped out and grabbed his bag from the driver.

The driver climbed back in and turned to Billy.

"Cerulean Tower?"

"Ah no. I need to go back to the airport. I forgot my wife."

Billy crossed the airport ticketing area and entered a toilet. He pushed his way into a stall and closed the door and lowered the toilet seat and sat. He opened the Aussie's passport and studied the photo. He unzipped his bag and pulled out a mirror and three contact lens containers each labeled with a different eye color. He put in blue contacts and changed his eye color to match the eye color on the passport photo. He retrieved a pair of plastic gloves and slipped them on his hands and removed several containers of temporary hair color and rubbed a dark brown into his hair. He used a red eyebrow pencil and a dab of rigid collodion from a small bottle to recreate the discoloration and uneven skin texture of the small but noticeable scar. He used his iPhone for a selfie and compared it to the Aussie's passport photo. Even though they had been trained not to focus on facial blemishes Billy knew the eye of the immigration officer would be drawn to the scar as the most noticeable facial feature. It was far from perfect but was in the ballpark. He was a westerner in an Asian country. Just as all Asians looked alike to westerners, so westerners all looked alike to Asians.

Billy approached a female agent at Japan Airways' ticket counter.

"How may I help you?" she said in good English.

"Do you have any flights available to Singapore?" Billy asked with an Australian accent.

She checked her terminal.

"Everything is booked today. I do have a few seats available tomorrow morning."

By now the Aussie had probably discovered his passport was missing. It would take the Aussie 4-6 hours to get to his embassy, wait in line and fill out the proper forms and report his passport lost or stolen. It would take the embassy staff another 4-6 hours to register the passport as a missing or stolen document in INTERPOL's STLD database. Billy figured he had about 8-12 hours to get into another country and through immigration using the Aussie's passport. Billy had a rule about not visiting a city twice. It was a sure way of getting caught. He allowed himself one exception.

"Ah no. How about Phuket?"

"Thailand? Let me check. I have one seat left on the five o'clock through Bangkok but it's first class."

"That'll work."

"Cash or credit?"

Billy pulled out his wallet. He knew it was not uncommon for any foreigner to pay in US dollars since it was the most commonly traded currency in the world and it wouldn't raise any suspicions.

"Cash. US dollars."

"Okay. The ticket will be $2822."

Billy looked like he had just been punched in the gut.

"You do know I am renting the seat not buying it?"

"You don't fly first class much do you?"

"Not much. I'll take it."

He pulled a wad of bills from his money clip and counted out the required amount and handed it to the agent.

"Do you always change your plans so easily?"

Red flag Billy thought. *She suspects something.*

"My wife just served me with divorce papers this morning. I don't care where I go. I just need to get away."

"I'm sorry. I didn't mean to pry. I'm sure Phuket will be beautiful. Passport?"

Billy handed her the Aussie's passport. She glanced at the passport photo then at him then back at the passport photo.

"Blue" she said.

"What's that?"

"Your eyes…pretty color."

"Oh. Thank you."

She keyed his passport number into her terminal and handed back his passport.

"Any baggage?"

The pilot announced the aircraft would be landing soon. Billy sat back in his overstuffed chair. *Yep first class* he thought. *Cushy.* Normally he didn't like to get spoiled. He thought it made him weak but this was an extenuating circumstance. The waitress came by with the last call on champagne. Billy didn't much like champagne or wine for that matter but he figured he had paid for it and believed in getting his money's worth. He let her refill his glass and slammed it down in one gulp and had her refill it again. He leaned back and looked out the window.

Below the sea was dotted with limestone islands that shot straight up out of the water. Most of the islands were small and covered with vegetation. A few had coves that offered tourists the dream of their own private beach. Approaching in the distance was a dark green peninsula with miles of shoreline. Hundreds of fishing boats spaced far enough apart to keep their nets untangled pocked the light green water along the coast.

On the southwest tip of Thailand surrounded by the Andaman Sea was Phuket, a beach town overloaded with seafood restaurants, t-shirt shops, tattoo and massage parlors. The Thai were famous for their massage. It's firm and slightly painful at times but not bone-cracking like Swedish massage. If you were male your female masseuse would usually ask you to flip onto you back then rub the front of your thighs until you got a hard-on at which time you would be offered a hand-job for only 500 baht.

Billy liked Phuket. He liked Thailand. It was the opposite of where he grew up in Wyoming except for the people. They were good, honest and hardworking. And the Thai were tough too. Last time he was here he had watched a Thai woman arguing with a man. There was a motorbike laying on its side in the middle of the street like it had been pushed over. From what Billy could gather the man wanted to sell her motorbike to make rent and she wasn't hearing of it. When he finally had had enough, the Thai man hauled off and hit her full on with the kind of punch that would have dropped most men for good. She fell. Billy knew better than to get involved in a Thai-to-Thai argument but he didn't like seeing women get hit either. Before he could get between them the woman got back up and slapped the shit out of the man until he finally ran off leaving the motorbike. Billy respected that kind of tenacity. Sometimes you had to fight for what was yours.

Billy waited in a long line with hundreds of other foreigners at the Phuket Airport immigration portal. He scanned the immigration kiosks and studied the officer behind each. He was looking for a young woman, but not too young. He didn't want someone new who would be anxious to impress her boss. A woman, especially a Thai woman, would be less likely to challenge a man. He needed someone efficient that focused on moving people through her kiosk. He found what he was looking for at the far end of the hall. Her line was moving quicker than the others. When his turn came up he moved toward her kiosk and the short line in front of it. A line manager waved him to another line, but Billy continued, ignoring the line manager. The line manager stepped in front of him and pointed to the other line. Billy pointed to the line that he wanted but the line manager was having none of it. He was drawing attention from the supervisors and that was the wrong thing to do in immigration. Billy got in the line selected by the line manager.

He studied the officer tending the kiosk. It was an older man and he was meticulous and took his time reviewing passports. *Shit* thought Billy. I could fake illness and run to the bathroom and hope for a better officer next time. He had already raised a fuss and they might ask for a medical inspection. He didn't want that. The sooner he got out of here the better. He decided to go for broke with the line he was in. Conformability was the key to making it past. He was just one of thousands who would check through this kiosk today. His turn came and he stepped up to the kiosk and handed the officer his passport and arrival form and departure form and stepped back and put his feet on the foot marks painted on the floor and looked into the computer camera mounted on the end of a thin metal tube. The officer looked through the stamps already in the passport and studied the passport photo and studied Billy. Billy stared into the camera. If the camera moved up or down it meant he was having his photo taken which was the final step of the process before stamping.

"You not have address of hotel where you stay" said the officer. The officer was asking questions and that was a bad sign.

"I'm sorry. I don't have it. But it's the Expat Hotel in Patong."

"Which? There are two."

"Oh, ah…the one closest to the mall. I think they call it Patong Center Expat Hotel."

"You have reservation?"

Billy didn't have a reservation but he knew it would draw more attention if he said so. "Yes."

The officer scribbled something on Billy's arrive card.

"How long will you be in Thailand?" said the officer.

"Three weeks."

"And then where?"

"Back to Perth, Australia."

"Do you have a ticket back to Australia?"

Billy didn't, but he knew he could be denied entry without a follow-on ticket.

"Yes. It's electronic. I can look it up if you wish. It'll just take a few minutes."

Billy pulled out his iPhone and pretended to search for the ticket. The officer took a long look at Billy and studied him like a biologist studies a specimen in a jar. Billy could feel his stare. He knows thought Billy. If he calls over a supervisor I'm fucked.

"No" said the officer.

Billy looked up from his iPhone and watched the camera tilt up to adjust for his height. The officer took his photo and stamped the documents and handed the departure form and the passport back to Billy.

Billy exited the immigration hall and took the escalator down to baggage claim. He was in the clear and was now allowed to stay in Thailand for 30 days. He could extend for another 30 days if he wished by paying a small fee. That was 2 months and longer than he had stayed in any country for the last 3 years.

CHAPTER 4

A mini-van pulled up in front of the Expat Hotel and Bar. Billy had cleaned off the makeup and hair tint and removed his contacts. He stepped out and collected his bag from the driver at the rear compartment. He tipped him 50 baht which was a little over a US dollar. Billy liked to tip. He knew most Thai salaries were barely enough to survive on each month so even a small tip helped. It pissed him off that most Europeans and Australians didn't tip. It wasn't their custom. He thought it a poor excuse and rude.

The Expat bar on the ground floor was open on two sides to let in the occasional breeze. The bar was decorated with 70s rock and roll album covers—Santana, Kiss, and Metallica. The back wall was lined with photos of smooth female asses in thongs. The six HDTVs mostly showed futbol and rugby games with the occasional motorcycle race or ultimate fighting match. The HDTVs were strategically mounted on the walls along with four security cameras. It was a guy's bar and proud of it although a surprising number of woman also liked to hang out with their boyfriends. The hotel's front desk was tucked into a corner and usually empty. The bar staff checked in the guests.

A scream rose from the hotel bar. *Here we go* Billy thought.

"Mr. Billy" said Noi, a young Thai woman with hair tinted red. She managed the hotel and bar. Everybody loved Noi and her cat Tougtong—a short-haired tan and white calico. Noi adopted Tougtong when he started following her from the outdoor market where she bought her dinner every night. Tougtong would eat whatever scraps he was offered then take a nap under the bar counter while Noi worked. Eventually Noi started cooking him fresh fish in hopes of putting some weight on him. Noi dressed Tougtong in tiny striped t-shirts mostly pink and white. It was humiliating but he didn't seem to mind as long as Noi kept feeding him fresh fish served in his very own plastic bowl. Tougtong was the luckiest cat in Thailand.

"You no text me you coming" said Noi.

"Well I wasn't comin' this mornin'."

"You no like Noi anymore?"

"You know I do. Why do ya think I came? I couldn't

keep away."

"Oh Mr. Billy. You smooth talk. You have reservation?"

"Ah no. You got room?"

"If no have I kick out someone."

"No need for that. I'll be just fine sleeping with Tougtong under the bar."

"Last time you here you promise take me to Khao Phing Kan."

"What on this side of hell is a Koy-fin-can?"

"James Bond Island."

"Oh yeah. I reckon I remember something about that."

"You take me yes?"

"Girl you best be naked if you're gonna start asking for things."

"Oh I like."

"I bet you do."

Noi picked up his bag and started for the hotel.

"I got that girl."

"No I have. You long trip. Old man need rest."

He slapped her on her tight ass.

"More please" she said.

Life could be a lot worse thought Billy. They entered the bar and two more bargirls ran up and gave him a hug. Pla with a new set of breasts that her farang boyfriend bought her and Muay more Chinese-looking than Thai but slender like most Thai.

"You ring bell Mr. Billy?" said Muay.

"Christ Muay. I haven't even unpacked."

She frowned.

"Oh hell. Might as well get things started."

Billy gave the colorful rope hanging from the bell over the bar three good tugs. The girls and the other patrons cheered.

"Tequila?" said Noi.

"Ya gotta ask?" said Billy.

The girls counted the customers and filled the shot glasses required and placed them on a tray along with little dishes of salt and lime wedges and passed the tray around the bar. When everyone had a glass Billy rang the bell again and everyone cheered and slammed down their tequila. Billy was back.It was late afternoon. Sunlight poured through the hotel room shears. Billy rolled off Noi both sweating and breathing hard.

"Lord girl. Ya gonna wear me out the first day."

"You no like?"

"Well yeah but my peter's gonna fall off if you keep at it the way you're goin'."

"What peter?"

"My dick."

"Good. I need new toy."

"Nasty girl."

"Yes but you like nasty."

"I like you. That's for sure. You're different from most girls."

"How I different?"

"Well for starters you're a lot more ornery."

"Yes I horny."

"Not horny. Ornery."

"Not same?"

"No. Not same."

"What ornery?"

"It means stubborn."

"What mean stubborn?"

"Oh lord. This could go on all day. Forget I mentioned it."

"You take me to James Bond Island?"

"Yes I take you to James Bond Island."

"Then we stay overnight in hotel on Koh Phi Phi?"

"Ya'll 're pretty pushy for being as short as you are."

"Go dinner and dancing?"

"Yes. Stay over. Go dinner and dancing."

"We make love in ocean at night?"

"I don't know about that one. There's sharks."

Noi frowned.

"Okay. I'll risk it. We make love in ocean."

"…at night?"

"…at night…with the sharks."

Noi climbed on top of him and started to grind him again. "I excited."

"I see that. You're gonna break me you know that."

"I think you cowboy. No break easy."

"Everyone's got limits."

She ground even harder. "You no want?"

Billy rolled over on top of her.

"Mmmm…I think you want" she said.

It was night. Billy walked out of the elevator and through the bar. Noi was busy with other customers and Billy knew better than to disturb her beyond a wink and a nod. Noi took her job very seriously and wanted to set a good example for the other girls. In private she was playful and loving, but in public she was all business and focused on her customers.

A water tanker was parked on the side of the hotel. The Expat Hotel along with the other hotels in the area was not connected to the city water. Every two weeks or whenever the water turned brown from sediment, a private water tanker hooked up a heavy hose to a pipe that emptied into a storage tank on the roof of the hotel. The drivers of the water tankers were paid per delivery so no time was wasted on chit-chat with the bar staff. Billy stepped over the tanker hose and avoided several streams of water leaking from the coupling.

Billy finished a wire transfer at a Western Union office and walked out onto the busy street. An English couple stood on a street corner and waited for the light to change. The light changed to red but the scooters and tuk-tuks just continued to race past as if nothing had happened. *Welcome to Thailand* Billy thought. Like the Thai Billy jaywalked and dodged the oncoming traffic like a game of Frogger. The key was not to look at an approaching vehicle. If he made eye-contact, he would lose the right of way and the driver would race past. It was not the law but like many things in Thailand, it was the way things were done and it was best to go along and get along.

Billy entered the Patong Night Market—a popular place with backpackers and locals to pick up a cheap meal. Portable restaurants with plastic seats and tables lined the main thoroughfare. Roasted seafood was always a big hit but you could get fried chicken, pork satays and little pancakes with quail eggs plus any type of Thai food. Sanitary conditions were not ideal with the occasional rat raiding the trashcans and scaring the shit out of the tourists but most everything was fried or roasted so the heat killed any lingering bacteria. The pavement was slippery with grease that popped from the fryers and mixed with soapy runoff from the dishwashing buckets.

Behind the restaurants were rows of vendor stalls selling dresses, shoes, bras and panties made in the Bangkok factories and shipped by the truckload to Phuket. This was where the bargirls and go-go dancers shopped. Lucky girls brought their farang boyfriends, usually two to three times the girl's age but with fat wallets. Five hundred baht could get you three panties, two bras and a pair of jean shorts that left little to the imagination. Cheap but sexy.

Billy watched an ice cream vendor fold chunks of broken Snickers bars and bits of marshmallows into a pile of vanilla ice cream laying on a stainless steel slab super-cooled by dry ice. The vendor used a wide putty knife to scrap the ice cream from the frozen surface and chop it up into a fine mixture and splay it flat again and cut it into five strips and scrap it into rolls. It was more a show than a necessity but it seemed to work given the size of the crowd watching. Billy didn't have much of a sweet tooth but he was tempted. He moved on.

Billy walked past the fruit shake vendors and picked out a half dozen pork and chicken satays from a BBQ stand.

The vendor laid the raw satays on a sizzling grill and the aroma of chard animal flesh rose in the smoke. Ain't no bacteria gonna live through that thought Billy.

Billy glanced at a passing farang in his late 50s. He was overly tanned and wearing khaki shorts and hiking boats and a military rucksack stuffed to the hilt with a bed roll and a sleeping bag tied to the top. An old-timer. He would sleep at campsites or in the jungle to save money. There were younger farang with backpacks at the night market too but they were usually college graduates spending their gap year traveling until lack of funds forced them to return to their home countries and start their careers. This old-timer wasn't like them. He had given up on the dream of a house with a mortgage that would never be paid off and a BMW in the garage. He had gone nomad. Homeless and alone traveling the world forever making money by selling handmade jewelry or working as an under-the-table mechanic or picking up the occasional handyman job until he could no longer swing a hammer. The old-timer pulled the change from his pocket and counted it. It was mostly coins which weren't worth much in Thailand.

Is that me in twenty years? thought Billy. *There but by the grace of God go I.*

Eve sat in the airport hotel lounge nursing a whisky and a bowl of wasabi-flavored soybeans. A group of Japanese businessmen sat in a booth nearby laughing just loud enough to be annoying. A Japanese cover band belted out 80s pop hits in something that sounded vaguely like English. Her phone buzzed. She looked at the caller's name and took a deep breath before answering it.

"Hang on" she said. She moved to back of the lounge where it was a little quieter. "I had him. He must have slipped out while I was waiting for backup. Someone might have tipped him off. I'm not making excuses. He's good. You know that. I've gotten closer than anyone else but it's still going to take time."

Her phone chimed from an email notice. "Hang on a minute. I think I just got something."

She opened the attachment to an email. It was a copy of a Western Union wire transfer. She zoomed in on the originating Western Union office—Jung Ceylon Mall Phuket Thailand.

"He's in Phuket Thailand" she said. "I don't know. It's gonna take time. What do you want me to do? It's a beach resort so there are lots of hotels, maybe four or five hundred. I think we can eliminate the luxury resorts and the American brand hotels. Too many American guests. He wouldn't risk the chance of running into someone that could recognize him even if it is a long shot. Yeah, I'll catch the next flight."

She hung up and walked back to her seat at the bar. She gestured to the bartender to give her one more round. A Japanese businessman gestured for the bartender to put her drink on his tab and he sat down beside her.

"No thank you" said Eve.

"I cannot buy you a drink?" said the businessman in good English.

"Nope."

"Why not if I may ask?"

"There are three reasons a man offers to buy a woman a drink in an airport hotel bar. First he thinks she an easy lay. I'm not. Second he thinks she is a prostitute. I'm not. Third he is a cop that thinks she is a prostitute and is trying to set her up. And I'm not that stupid. So you see no matter who you are you're shit out of luck."

"And what if the man just wants to have a nice conversation with an attractive—"

"Fuck off."

The man moved off. The bartender sat her drink down. She pulled a hotel booking app on her phone and keyed in Phuket—2716 hotels were available.

"You gotta be fucking kidding me" said Eve to no one particular.

CHAPTER 5

It was morning and already hot and humid. Billy and Noi walked to the end of the pier with a group of tourists. Most were farang with a few Chinese and Koreans. Billy wore shorts and sandals and felt out of sorts without his boots but he didn't want to get them wet with the salt water. They waited their turn and climbed aboard a double decker cruise boat with twenty plastic kayaks stacked and tied onto the stern deck. The top deck was covered with a wooden roof and open on the sides to let the breeze in. They sat in the middle giving themselves a good view. Noi was excited. She had lived in Phuket for over five years but had never been to the islands all her customers talked about.

It was a sunny day with only a few clouds in the sky. The tour boat made its way out to a calm sea. In the distance was the Phang Nga Bay archipelago—a shallow bay with 42 sheer limestone islands. It looked primordial.

The cruise boat stopped in a bay in front of a small beach. Billy had paid extra to visit the Muslim fishing village on the Koh Panyee Island. Noi and Billy climbed into the long tail boat that would ferry them to the island. They took their seats on a bench next to a Chinese woman. Billy sat on the side with Noi sitting in the middle. He knew that Noi didn't swim and would be afraid of the sea if it got rough. Noi immediately put on one of the orange life preservers. The boat pilot shouted something in Thai and pointed to Billy.

"He want you sit in middle" said Noi. "Say you too heavy. Tip boat."

"You gonna be okay sitting on the side?"

"I be okay. But I fall in you save okay?"

"Done."

Billy switched places with Noi. The pilot cranked up the small block engine mounted on a long steel shaft with a propeller on the opposite end. Billy thought it was a strange looking contraption but it worked well when the pilot lowered the propeller into the water and goosed the throttle. The boat sped away from the cruise ship at a good clip. The boat bounced on the waves and salt water splashed up hitting them in the face and cooling them down.

The long tail pulled up to a floating pier and they

climbed out. The pier rocked with each passing wave and scared Noi. Billy put his arm around her and led her off the pier onto a stable wooden boardwalk built on pylons. The boardwalk led to the Muslim village.

Noi used her phone to take a selfie of her and Billy in front of the island mosque built in the shadow of a sheer cliff covered with vines and roots. She would post the photos on her Thai Facebook page when she got back to the hotel so her children and brother could see where she had visited. This was a big moment in her life. It was something that most Thai would never do.

The Muslim families who lived in the village were mostly fisherman. In the morning they would go out in their long boats and fish the archipelago. In the afternoon when it was hot they farmed fish, shrimp and crab in floating net-like cages supported by lengths of bamboo bound to plastic buoys and anchored to the shore. The tourist shops that sold the same crap you could buy in Phuket were staffed by the Muslim women with their heads covered in hijabs.

On the opposite side of the island Billy watched with interest as the village carpenters made long tail boats by hand using the same tools his father had used.

"You like boat?" asked Noi.

"I like wood. My father was a carpenter."

"He build boat?"

"No. Furniture mostly. You know like chairs and tables."

"He teach you?"

"What he could."

"I never know my father. He leave when I little. Your father good man?"

"Good man? He was a hard man. He didn't talk much but when he did it was usually something worth remembering."

"Your father still alive?"

"No. He died a few years back."

"You miss him?"

"I suppose."

Billy moved off and Noi followed.

The long tail boat caught up with the cruise boat already anchored in the bay of Ko Ping Kan known by the farang as James Bond Island. The pilot maneuvered his boat into the shallows. The passengers climbed out into the gentle surf and waded into shore. Noi kept her life preserver on until she was safely on the beach. The small island was packed with tourists. It was one of Thailand's bigger attractions.

They made their way to the back of the island. Noi took more selfies of her and Billy in front of the famous Nail Island. It was a limestone karst rising out of the water from a thin base that gave tourists the impression of a rocket ship being launched at sea. It was made famous and given its nickname after the filming of the James Bond movie The Man with the Golden Gun.

Noi wore her life preserver and sat in the front of a large kayak. Billy sat in the middle and a Thai guide sat in the rear paddling. The guide maneuvered the kayak through a long sea cave. Billy and Noi laid down on their backs to keep from bumping their heads on the limestone ceiling. The cave led out into a lagoon hidden within the island. Wild monkeys hung to vines and branches along the seventy-foot cliffs that surrounded the lagoon. Noi pulled a small bundle of bananas from her backpack and tossed a banana to one of the monkeys. Billy glanced back at the guide shaking his head. The guide knew what was about to happen. The monkey stuffed the banana with the peel still on into his mouth and jumped fifteen feet onto the front of the kayak where Noi sat. Noi screamed.

"Monkey bite. Monkey bite" she said.

The guide slapped his paddle on the water next to the monkey but the monkey didn't flinch. The monkey grabbed for the bunch of bananas in Noi's hand. She pulled away refusing to surrender the bananas. Billy watched as seven more monkeys dropped from their vines into the water and swam toward the kayak. *I didn't even know monkeys could swim* thought Billy.

"Give 'em the damn bananas" said Billy.

"My bananas. No monkey's" said Noi.

Billy watched as the monkeys swam closer. "I'll buy

you more" said Billy.

Billy grabbed the bananas from her hands and flung them into the water in front of the swimming monkeys. The monkey on the kayak jumped in the water and swam to where the bananas were now floating. The monkeys fought for the bananas screeching and biting each other.

"Christ all mighty you'd think they 'as made of diamonds."

"Bad monkey" said Noi.

The guide paddled away.

Billy lay awake next to Noi as she slept. They were back in his room at the hotel. She was snoring in a cute way. Tougtong slept curled up at her feet. Noi showered with Tougtong every night to keep him clean. He liked it. The water cooled him down. But Billy had rules. Tougtong was locked in the bathroom whenever they had sex. Billy didn't like the way Tougtong watched and occasionally bit at their toes moving under the sheet like a mouse. The room was mostly dark with only a thin shaft of city lights coming through the drawn blackout curtains. There was always some noise in Phuket no matter where you were or what time at night. Motorcycles raced with blown-out mufflers. Drunk Thai girls shouted at their drunk farang boyfriends. Cats fucked. After a while it became white noise.

Billy thought about the Irish woman he ditched in Tokyo. Who the hell was she? How did she find me? Am I getting careless? Even if she was with INTERPOL she couldn't track my passport. I haven't used my real passport in years. It wasn't the passports was it? Or was it something else. No. I'm just being paranoid. That's got to stop. Paranoia slows ya down and gets ya caught. Just keep moving and you'll be okay. No city more than a few weeks. Never the same city. So why the hell are ya in Phuket again, Billy?

For Billy, the Expat was the closest thing to a home and Noi was the closest thing to family he had had in years. But home and family were dangerous. Still he couldn't help himself.

Just a week he thought. *No harm in a week.*

A loud thud like something heavy had dropped caught Billy's attention. He heard it again. He felt around on the nightstand until he found something cold that he hoped was his iPhone. He pressed the button that brought up the screen with the time and date. It was 4:15 a.m.

People oughta have more respect of sleeping hours he thought.

Two more thuds and a yell. No. Not yelling, more like shrieking. Someone was angry. Noi stirred. Billy didn't want her to wake. She had to go to work in two hours and needed her sleep especially after the workout he gave her last night. Another thud. Noi raised her head.

"What that?" said Noi.

"Never you mind darlin'. I'll take care of it. You go to sleep."

Noi's head hit the pillow. Billy reached for his pants on a chair beside the bed. He walked to the door and opened it and peaked out into the hallway. Another thud and more shrieks.

It's a Thai thing Billy thought. Don't be an idiot. Stay out of it. It'll blow over.

More load thuds and shrieks in Thai.

Maybe not he thought. Can't hurt to have a look.

It was coming from the stairwell. Billy followed the noise down the stairs to the next floor. He peaked around the stairwell corner and saw a tall shapely woman kicking the shit out of a door and cursing in Thai at someone inside the room.

Billy sat down on the stairs thinking. Let it go Billy. It's not your business. He heard the woman crying in-between her kicks and cursing. *Probably a fight with her farang boyfriend* Billy thought. *Still none of your business. Go back to bed.* But he couldn't. He swung around the stairwell so he faced the woman. She didn't notice him and continued to pound on the door.

"Hey" Billy said. "People are trying to sleep and your carryin' on ain't helpin' none."

She turned and said "Fuck off" in a low husky voice.

Her voice surprised Billy. She was a he. Ladyboys were common in Thailand, especially in places like Phuket where foreigners came to experience something different than what they could find at home. Ladyboys were different. This ladyboy was particularly attractive with a nice face and long black hair and dark legs that disappeared into a white mini skirt and large breasts behind a silk blouse.

She has some style thought Billy and then corrected himself. *I mean he. A little heavy on the face powder but I reckon that goes with the territory.* The ladyboy used his fists to pound on the door.

"You're going to hurt yourself" said Billy.

"I no give fuck." The ladyboy reverted back to kicking the door and crying.

"What's the problem?"

The ladyboy stopped kicking and turned to Billy. "He not pay me."

Now Billy understood. The ladyboy was hooking men as they stumbled drunk out of the Bangla go-go bars. He got this guy to bring him back to his hotel and after a blowjob the ladyboy sprung the truth on him when he pulled down his mini skirt. The ladyboy threw a fit hoping the embarrassed customer would pay him to go away. It was a scam of sorts. It happened a lot in Thailand. But this time it wasn't working.

"How much?"

"3000 baht."

"You're expensive."

"I worth it. I already give him a blow job."

"Spare me the details."

Billy walked up to the door and knocked lightly. "Hey buddy?" said Billy through the door.

"Who the hell are you?" the customer said through the door.

"A neighbor who likes his sleep. Let's wrap this up. You got a nice blow job before…your surprise. So give him 1500 baht and call it a ni—"

"No. He owe me 3000 baht" said the ladyboy.

Billy was growing impatient. He turned to the ladyboy. "There is a good chance someone has already called the police and if they haven't I will."

The ladyboy shut up. Billy turned back to the door. "So where are we at?"

"Fuck off! I ain't give that thing a dime" said the customer.

"He's gonna keep kicking in your door until you pay him or the cops haul his ass away. Either way, you brought him here so the hotel is going to hold you liable for whatever damage he causes. Do you know how much a door costs?"

Silence. The ladyboy was growing impatient. Billy motioned for her to wait. The door opened and a man's hand popped out giving Billy 1500 baht.

"Nice doin' business with ya" Billy said. He handed the money to the ladyboy.

"You should tell a guy" the man said to the ladyboy through the crack in the door.

"Fuck off you pussy" said the ladyboy.

"Good night" said Billy. He grabbed the handle and closed the door before things could escalate again. Billy walked to the elevator and pressed the down button.

"Can I walk ya out?" Billy gestured to the elevator as the doors opened.

"Maybe we go to your room?"

"Not gonna happen."

"You not know what you missing."

"I am sure you are very special."

The ladyboy walked into the elevator. Billy followed him. The doors closed.

Billy eased his hotel room door open and closed it quietly and pulled off his pants and climbed back in bed with Noi. She stirred and glanced at her phone for the time. She climbed out of bed.

"Where ya going?"

"I have to feed fish before go to work."

"You have fish?"

"Yes 300 fish."

"Three hundred?"

"Yes. They swim in big bowl in my backyard. They small."

"I would hope so. Doesn't Tougtong eat them?"

"No. He only like cooked fish. But he like to play with them."

"I bet he does."

"I talk to my fish when I feed them. I tell them how my day."

"And what do they say?"

"They fish. Fish no talk."

She leaned over and kissed him. He pulled her closer. She pulled away.

"Later" she said.

She walked out. He missed her already. Billy wondered if maybe he did something wrong. He didn't always catch the nuances of Thai culture and was prone to putting his foot in his mouth. He would never do anything to hurt her on purpose. He knew that leaving would hurt her, but there was nothing he could do about that. He had to keep moving. It wasn't an option. It was just a matter of when.

CHAPTER 6

A cue ball slammed into a rack of 9 balls scattering them around the purple felt table. Billy played alone at the only pool table in the hotel bar. He had a hand-crafted stick that screwed together in the middle. He had picked it up from a Filipino man selling cues on the beach in Boracay. It was the only luxury he allowed himself besides his boots. He powdered his left hand from a bottle of baby powder and rubbed the excess powder on the cue's shaft to make it slide easier and chalked the tip while studying his next shot.

A side-cargo tuk-tuk pulled up outside the lobby bar. The driver hoped off and pulled two large ice bags out of the sidecar and walked into the lobby and behind the bar. He opened the floor ice chest that kept three hundred bottles of beer cold and poured the ice on top of the bottles until no more ice would fit. He moved to the second ice chest and poured in another bag of ice. He took the empty plastic bags and tossed them into the tuk-tuk. He wrote out a receipt for the two bags of ice and brought it to Noi. Without exchanging any words Noi opened the bar cash box and took out 300 baht. Noi paid the iceman and their eyes met. The iceman glanced over at Billy playing pool then back at Noi. His eyes condemned her. Noi motioned with her head for the iceman to leave. He walked out and climbed onto the tuk-tuk and drove off.

The tuk-tuk dodged a taxi that pulled up in front of the hotel. The nomad stepped out of the taxi, paid the driver and pulled his bags from the trunk and walked into the bar and over to the front desk. Billy studied the nomad's face. He measured distances between his eyes, nose and mouth. He was a good match for Billy. His height and weight were about right too. Noi stepped out from behind the bar and approached the nomad.

"You check in?" said Noi.

"Do you have a room?"

"We got penthouse. Big room, big TV and kitchen. Same floor as pool. Everything else sold out."

"Okay. I'll rent it."

"How many night?"

"One week if I find it satisfactory."

"You like. Very nice." Noi checked the room schedule. "Yeah that good. Credit card?"

"No. Cash."

"Thai baht?"

The nomad nodded.

"Good. Passport?"

The nomad handed her his passport. Billy glanced over at the passport's dark blue cover with gold letter that read United States of America Passport. *I might be able to get back into the States with that* thought Billy. *I could go home.* Noi opened the passport to his photo page and made a copy.

"You have nice eyes" said the nomad.

"Thank you."

She scribbled down the passport number on a form and handed the form to him to fill out the rest.

"Name, address and phone. I fill out the rest. You give us email we send you newsletter with photos of bargirls and parties."

"Can you have someone bring up my bags?"

"They don't do that" said Billy. "It's just the girls. No bellhop."

"Are you the owner?" said the nomad.

"Me? No. Just a guest."

"Do you always listen to other people's conversations?"

"I was tryin' to be helpful. Didn't mean to offend."

Tougtong rubbed up against the nomad's leg. The nomad jumped. "Jesus!" said the nomad.

"It's just Tougtong. He's the bar cat" said Billy.

"I thought it was a rat."

"We no have rat here. Tougtong eat them." said Noi.

"Yeah Tougtong'd eat anything that don't eat him first." said Billy.

"You stay here a lot?" asked the nomad.

"When I am passing thru. Rooms are clean, beer's cheap and the staff is nice."

"Passing thru?"

"The Expat's kind of my home base when I'm in Southeast Asia. This your first time to Phuket?"

"Why do you want to know?"

"No reason. Just curious."

"Just curious?"

"Sorry didn't mean to pry."

"Then why are you sorry?"

Billy took a moment to study the nomad, unsure if he

was for real or just joking. "I think we may have gotten off on the wrong foot."

"Why do you think that?"

"I'm Billy Gamble" said Billy offering his hand.

The nomad looked down at Billy's hand then up into Billy's eyes. "That's an interesting name...Gamble." The nomad shook Billy's hand.

"I'm Kyle Tanner."

"Nice to meet you."

"Why is that nice? You don't know me."

"Yeah. That's true. I don't. Not much for niceties, are ya?"

"No. They are lies disguised as manners."

"I reckon there's some truth to that."

"If I choose to spend my time talking with someone, I want to know what they really feel and think not their superficial bullshit."

"Disappointed much?"

"Continually."

"I bet."

"You're good."

"Good?"

"At billiards. I saw you playing when I came in. That's a nice cue you have."

"Oh. Thanks. I picked it up in Boracay. A Filipino carpenter makes them and sells them to tourists on the beach."

"What are you playing?"

"9-ball. But actually I'm just practicing. You play?"

"Pool? No. I've never had time to learn the game."

"I believe you're the first person I have met that hasn't played pool."

"You meet many people?"

"A fair amount. I'm not sayin' it's a bad thing. Just that most people wouldn't admit it."

"What's the point of lying about something as mundane as pool?"

"No point. Well if you ever want to learn, the rules are pretty easy and shootin' just takes a little practice."

The nomad nodded.

"Mr. Kyle your room ready" Noi said.

The nomad walked back over to the reception desk and took the card key from Noi.

"Floor eight" said Noi.

"Same as the pool" said the nomad.

"Yes pool same floor. Breakfast come with room. No charge."

"Is your kitchen clean?"

"Yes. No bugs."

"Does the cook wash his hands?"

"Cook woman. Yes wash hands after pee. Very safe. No get sick."

"Then I will have breakfast here."

"Seven to 10 in morning. Free coffee too."

The nomad studied Noi like a butcher who sizes up a side of beef.

"Do you swim?"

"Me? No swim."

"Too bad."

The nomad picked up his bag, moved to the elevator and pressed the call button. When the elevator doors opened, he took a moment before stepping in. He turned back to Billy practicing his break at the table.

"Maybe one of these nights you could teach me how to play pool?"

"Sure thing" said Billy.

The nomad entered the elevator. Noi moved up beside Billy.

"Darlin' I think that boy's a couple sandwiches shy of a picnic."

It was night and hot and the air was still. The nomad sat on a restaurant patio. Overhead fans whirled creating a false breeze. The waitress brought a hamburger and fries and set them in front of the nomad and walked off to take an order from a Korean couple. Few Thai dined in the same restaurants as the farang. The Thai didn't like western food and the cost for a meal was usually double or even triple what a Thai restaurant charged. He opened the bun and pressed down on the patty checking its wellness. It was stiff. He cut a V in the patty with his knife. The meat was solid gray. As the waitress passed his table, he held out his arm blocking her way.

"I asked for a medium-rare hamburger."

"Yes. That medium."

"No. I asked for medium-rare. It should be red in the center. Bloody. This is well done."

"It good."

"It is not what I ordered. Take it back and have them cook me another medium-rare."

"Manager make me pay if I take back."

"Then you should eat it."

The nomad rose and walked out of the restaurant without paying the bill. He walked down the side street lined with portable shops and passed a vendor selling realistic pellet guns, stun guns and other weapons. He stopped and studied a display of knives. He picked a small curved knife. The blade and the wood-carved handle was in the shape of a C. He pulled it from its leather sheath.

"That karambit. Like tiger claw. From Indonesia" said the knife vendor.

The nomad slipped his index finger into the ring at the bottom of the handle and whirled the knife around catching the knife in his hand as if drawing it from a concealed position.

"It small. Blade very sharp. Good for fighting" said the vendor.

"Yes. And other things I would guess" said the nomad. "How much?"

"One thousand baht."

The nomad pulled out a 500 baht bill and held it up.

"Seven hundred fifty best price" said the vendor. The nomad set the knife down and started to walk away and put the bill back in his pocket.

"Okay. Okay. 500" said the vendor. "You want I wrap it?"

"No. I will carry it." He paid the vendor, picked up the knife and put the leather sheath in his pocket.

"No let police see. They take."

"I doubt that" said the nomad and walked away

flipping the karambit around his finger and catching it.

The nomad crossed a busy intersection and walked onto a street closed off from traffic. He passed under a neon sign—Welcome to Patong Beach—arching over the promenade packed with people wearing tank tops and shorts. He saw a police box with two Thai police officers watching the crowd. He wasn't afraid of the police. They were just people after all and could be disposed of if necessary, but he didn't want the hassle or the attention. The nomad sheathed his new toy and slipped it into his back pocket.

Only three blocks long, the promenade called Bangla Road felt like a circus but with liquor and sex and electronic billboards. Whatever one desired was there for a price. Ladyboys dressed in showgirl costumes posed for photos with tourists hoping for a 100-baht tip. Wranglers stopped passing tourists with laminated signs promising exotic shows with naked girls. Electronic music pulsated from the dozens of go-go bars and beer bars lining both sides of the street and down the side alleys. Bangla Road was pathetic, obnoxious and glorious all at the same time. An adult playground.

The nomad walked onto a side street and into a go-go club called Harem. Inside naked girls slowly gyrated under blue lights. Their bodies were painted with fluorescent butterflies, tigers and birds. He sat down and ordered a light beer. One of the dancers caught his attention and smiled. He motioned to the waitress and gave her the number on the dancer's wrist. The waitress walked over to the dancer and told her the customer wanted to buy her a drink when she was done with her set. The dancer nodded and smiled to the nomad. He sat emotionless waiting. When her set finished the dancer climbed down off the stage and approached the nomad. She bowed to him before offering her hand.

"What your name?" she asked.

"Kyle. Would you like a drink?"

"Yes. Thank you. I order. I need to wash paint. I be back."

The nomad nodded. She walked to the back of the club and disappeared through a doorway. The next group of girls danced on stage. Some wore skimpy belly dancer costumes and others danced topless or totally naked. The waitress walked over with the painted girl's drink and set it down on the nomad's table. The nomad paid her without a tip. The painted dancer returned wearing one of the belly dancing costumes. Her side had a dark scar from a childhood wound. The paint had hidden the scar. She sat down next him and again bowed thank you for the drink. He looked down at the scar.

"You're a liar" said the nomad. He rose and walked out leaving the young girl crushed and confused.

The nomad entered his hotel room and inserted his keycard into the power switch and the lights came on. He closed the door and threw the deadbolt under the doorknob. He didn't like to be disturbed. He pulled out the karambit from his pocket and unsheathed it. The knife could be held in two different ways. The first was with the blade downward with the forefinger in the ring at the bottom on the handle. This was good for a front attack when facing an opponent. The blade could be used to slash or stab if necessary. The second method was to the hold the knife with the blade upward with the little finger in the ring. This was good when moving up behind a victim and drawing the blade across their throat. He tried both styles of holding the knife and twirled it around back and forth using the ring in the handle. He would need to practice drawing the knife until it became second nature. He ran his finger over the blade. It was sharp to the touch but he could feel slight imperfections on the edge. *Cheap drop-forged Indonesian steel* he thought. It would never do for precision work but was sufficient for the brute force of self-defense in a pinch. He liked the look of the knife and the feel of it in his hand. It was menacing with its inward curving design like a reaper's sickle.

The nomad surveyed the room. He picked up one of the two ceramic cups used for complimentary coffee and turned it upside down on the desk exposing the rough ring on the bottom that keeps the cup from easily sliding off the saucer. He opened his bag and pulled out his spare leather belt. The belt was a solid piece of thick leather with no stitching on the sides. Using the cup's rough ring, he slid the knife's blade ten times on each side going with the steel's grain. Any rough edges or burrs on the blade were now removed. He slid the belt through the buckle and made a loop on one end. He slid the loop over his foot then wrapped a turn of leather around his hand

and pulled to stiffen the belt. Going against the grain of the leather but with the grain of the knife's blade he stropped the knife's edge like a barber hones his razor before a shave. Again he tested the blade's edge with his finger. It was sharp and smooth. Satisfied he slipped the blade into its sheath and back into his pocket.

He slipped off his loafers and loosened the top button on his shirt and removed one of the pillows setting it aside. He lay on the bed perfectly flat with his hands clasped on his chest and stared at the ceiling. He thought about his purpose on earth as an essential cog in the machine of life. He was the harbinger of pain and chaos. The grain of sand in an oyster that spawned a beautiful pearl. Creation from agitation and destruction. His sacrifices would make the world strong again. He and his need were important. The idea calmed him. His mind stilled. He closed his eyes and slept.

Billy walked up to a ticket counter. Above the Tiger restaurant and bar was the Bangla Boxing Stadium, an open-air structure made mostly from steel tubing and concrete. Seeing the approaching farang the attendant motioned to a nearby English-speaking salesgirl with a tight fitting white dress. She headed Billy off and stuck a price list in front of him.

"How many VIP seats you want?"

"Just one and I don't want VIP seat. Ringside seat is okay."

"No ringside seats. Sold out."

"You and I both know that's not true."

"Okay okay. I make you good price. VIP seat is 2500 baht. I sell to you for 2300 baht cuz you handsome."

"That not a good deal."

"And I give you first beer free."

Billy knew the drill. She would continue to grind him until he was worn down to a nub. It was too hot to argue anyway. Billy held up his hands in surrender.

"One VIP seat."

He pulled out his money clip and paid the girl.

"Only one seat. You alone? No girlfriend?"

"No. No girlfriend."

She smiled and handed him his ticket.

"Maybe you take me for drink after fight?" she said.

"Lady, you got a weird way of seducing a man" said Billy.

Billy turned and climbed the stairs to the entrance and walked into the arena. The first fight was about to start. The VIP seats were cushioned chairs on the floor on two sides of the boxing ring. The cheaper ringside seats were on wooden risers but offered a better view. The attendant took his ticket and moved toward the VIP seats.

"No. I go here" said Billy and motioned to the

ringside seats."

"No. VIP seat" said the attendant.

"No. You take VIP. I sit ringside."

"Okay okay. But you go premium snack bar okay?" The attendant pointed to a concession stand with red drapes hung from horizontal poles giving the illusion of privacy. The prices were higher but it was luxury according to Thai standards.

Billy nodded and handed him a 20-baht tip. The attendant bowed his thanks, touched the end of his fingers to the tip of his nose and briefly closed his eyes as if in prayer. Billy gave him a courtesy bow back in the same manner.

The Thai sitting on the wooden risers gave Billy dirty looks like he was invading their space. He should have been with the other farang in the VIP seats. Ignoring them Billy sat next to two older Thai men. Billy caught the attention of a waiter taking orders in the premium seats. Billy held up three fingers then gave him a hang-loose gesture which was also the intentional sign for a drink. The waiter shrugged his shoulders—not enough information. Billy mouthed Tiger. Satisfied the waiter nodded and moved off.

The waiter returned with three ice cold bottles of Tiger beer sweating from condensation. Billy handed him a 500-baht bill then held his hand up like stop, meaning the waiter could keep the change—50 baht was a good tip. The waiter bowed thanks. Billy bowed back. Billy passed two of the beers to the Thai men that sat next to him. It was his way of acknowledging he had invaded their space and to make amends. The men bowed thanks. Billy bowed back. Everybody was happy especially Billy. He remembered watching his first Muay Thai match in Bangkok two years ago. It was different than the UFC and boxing matches he had seen in the States. Fierce yet beautiful.

A small band made up of flutes and drums struck up the Sarama—the ear-piercing music that accompanied each fight. The Muay Thai fighters entered the ring. Each wore a Mongkol headdress made of tightly wrapped cord and decorated with a string of fresh flowers. The fighters began their pre-fight dance known as Wai Kru Ram Muay. It was a mix of prayerful bowing and stretching exercises dating back centuries. A few minutes into the routine, each fighter broke into his own version of the dance—very controlled very precise. Finally the fighters bowed to the audience on all four sides of the arena and moved to their respective corners where the headdress was removed and their trainer helped them with their final stretching exercises. Another quick prayer and the fighters moved to the center of the ring where the referee waited.

Muay Thai was kickboxing, boxing and wrestling all wrapped into one. Elbow and knee blows were allowed. Muay Thai fighters started their training between 6 and 8 years old and lived in the training camp most of their lives. Thai fighters were extremely lean and incredibly flexible. In the heavyweight divisions farang fighters from the USA, Australia and the UK had dominated the sport while they abandoned many of the rituals. It was just physics. A punch or kick from a 150-pound Thai could not compete with a blow from a 300-pound farang. Billy always liked watching the matches between two Thai fighters over matches with farang.

It's one thing to visit a country and observe their culture thought Billy. It's another to fuck with their traditions.

The referee dropped his hand and the match began. For the first few minutes the fighters threw half-strength punches and kicks as they felt each other out and respected the Thai tradition. It was just plain rude to knock out your opponent in the first two minutes of a match.

For the first two rounds the two fighters seemed equally matched. The crowd cheered with each punch and kick that landed. In Muay Thai a kick by a skilled fighter did far more damage than a well-placed punch. Late in the third round, the smaller fighter got into trouble when the larger fighter grabbed him from behind and lifted him off the mat in preparation of slamming him down. With incredible agility, the smaller fighter clinched his fists together then used the strength of both arms as he swung his right elbow all the way around, slamming it into his opponent's jaw. Stunned the opponent released his hold and dropped the smaller fighter. Not giving him any time to recover, the smaller fighter leapt into the air and smashed his opponent with a well-placed kick in the face. The opponent fell backward on the mat like a sack of rice. The crowd roared. The referee counted. Elated the smaller opponent jumped up on the ring ropes and waved his arms in victory. A moment later he jumped down and knelt next to his opponent to ensure he was okay.

That's the Thai Billy thought. A loving caring people who can totally kick the shit out of you.

CHAPTER 7

The room was dark. The nomad lay on the bed staring into the stillness. It was like this most nights. He slept little, maybe one or two hours a night maybe none. No matter. It gave him time to think about important things.

His mother had taught him to pray at an early age and to believe in an all-powerful being who loved him and would protect him and forgive him no matter what he did wrong. He was a Catholic, his mother explained. In church he would often stare at Jesus crucified above the altar as the priest offered a sermon. He wondered how God the father of Jesus could let his son suffer the crown of thorns and the iron stakes piercing his hands and feet. He had a gaping wound in his side and his face was filled with anguish. Is this the way a father treats a son?

The boy was six the first time he was sodomized by his father's fist, punishment for knocking over his glass of bourbon. His mother was powerless to protect him, herself a victim of his father's drunken rage. She watched in tears. Where was God that night? Off creating other worlds or just busy with the prayers and adorations of others worthier? The boy's torn body bled for weeks.

It was not long before his father became more creative, never using the same form of punishment twice. The need for variety was an amusement to his father when bored at work or while listening to his mother drone on about the neighbor's dog always barking or that the house needed painting. It was the fear of not knowing what might happen next that created true terror in the young boy's mind. The boy learned from his father.

On his tenth birthday the boy used his new BB gun, a present from his parents, to shoot out the eyes of the neighbor's dog through a knot hole in the fence. His father didn't punish him for the offense, instead telling him to keep his mouth shut until the fuss blew over. The dog never barked again and the boy learned.

At fourteen the boy watched paralyzed by fear as his father seared his mother's face then beat her to death with an iron skillet still hot from burning the evening's pork chops. The boy screamed until he was hoarse then screamed some more unable to stop. His father had him committed to a mental institution claiming it was the boy who killed his mother. Again the boy learned from his mentor.

At seventeen the boy was transferred to a halfway house and allowed a day pass so he could attend high school and hopefully prepare for his eventual release when he turned eighteen. In the beginning he liked school. He had grown into a handsome young man and the scars from his father's beatings were mostly hidden beneath his clothes. Girls glanced at him and whispered to their friends as he opened his locker or walked down the hall. He was full of confidence when he asked the head cheerleader to the homecoming dance. He wasn't surprised when she accepted. It was a deception though. She was trying to make her football player ex-boyfriend jealous. It worked. When she told the boy that she had to renege on his invitation he accepted it with grace then burned down the school auditorium during the dance. The cheerleader suffered third-degree burns to her face and legs. The boy was recommitted to the mental institution.

When the boy was finally released he was in his late twenties, now a man, his mind healed according the doctors. His first stop was his father's house. They visited like old friends drinking bourbon together and smoking the two Cuban cigars that he brought knowing his father's fondness for them. They reminisced about the good times of his childhood. There were good times—family picnics, early morning fishing on the pier, building a wooden fort in the rafters of their house. Nobody is 100% evil. There is some good in everyone. It's just a matter of degrees and which self we choose to let out at any given moment. As the boy left, he shook his father's hand then gutted him with a bait knife from lower abdomen to chin just like a fish, just like his father had taught him. The boy had learned well. He had little desire to return to the mental hospital. There was little chance he would ever be set free again—not after this. The doctors would never understand why it was necessary. It was time for the boy to run to lands far away and lose himself in the sea of humanity. It was time to start his journey.

It was hot in his hotel room—the overworked air conditioner recycling but not cooling. He rose, the bedsheets sticking to his back. He slipped on his clothes then grabbed his money clip and room card before exiting.

He walked. It wasn't much cooler outside than in his room but at least the air was somewhat fresh. The warm breeze dried his sweat leaving him sticky. He walked through the night market now closed, the vendors stacking crates, tables and chairs in tuk-tuks and pickup trucks. The concrete was greasy from spattered cooking oil and water used to keep the fish fresh. He walked over to a fruit shake vendor packing up the last of the fruit in a crate. He pulled out 60 baht from his pocket.

"Dragonfruit shake no sugar water."

"No. I close. Go to 7-11. I go home now."

The nomad put his hand on top of the crate she was loading stopping her. "Dragonfruit shake. No sugar water."

The woman tried to push his hand away but he was too strong. She cursed him drawing the attention of the other vendors around her. Still he didn't move.

"Okay okay."

She grabbed her blender already packed away, plugged it in and filled the plastic pitcher with dragonfruit and ice.

"No sugar water."

"Yes yes…no fucking sugar water."

She blended the shake. The nomad glanced around at the other vendors some still glaring at the pushy farang. He smiled back at them. Annoyed but too tired to take any action they went back to loading up for the night. The fruit shake vendor poured his shake into a plastic cup, capped it with a plastic lid then slipped it into its plastic handle so he could carry it without getting his hands cold. The final touch was the thick straw before handing it to him and taking the money. He took a quick sip then gave her an approving nod. She flipped him off. *Thailand had a lot of problems but fruit shakes were not among them* he thought as he walked away.

The nomad wondered about God as he walked—the great creator and benevolent father. Experience had shown him that the existence of the devil was actually more probable than that of God. There was by far more evidence of the devil's existence. The devil spread pain and suffering a plenty—challenges to mankind. Overcoming challenges had made the nomad strong and kept his mind sharp and his knife swift. Chaos was a good thing. And maybe just maybe the nomad was part of the plan—a cog in the devil's clock doing his part to cull the herd.

And what of good and evil? As far as he could tell there was no difference. Constructs of kings and popes to pacify their flocks and keep them in power. He was not a sheep and owed no allegiance to their judgements. It was fine that others followed. It made them predictable and easy prey. But not him. There were no sins or rules he could break.

The fruit shake had cooled him down nicely. He could feel his mind calming. Maybe now he could sleep for an hour or two. It was going to be a busy day. He needed to find a kill room—someplace remote enough that he would not be bothered. That was the hardest part about being a nomad, privacy when you needed it most.

Billy and Noi walked up a steep hillside. Noi bowed before the giant statue of Buddha sitting cross-legged on top of the hill. Billy watched as Noi lit three sticks of incense and stuck them in an empty glass in front of a small buddha statue covered in gold leaf. Noi wrote a prayer on a slip of orange-colored paper and tied it to a wire along with hundreds of other prayers. She used a round block of wood hanging from two ropes to ring the brass bell three times sending her prayer to the heavens. Noi glanced over at the brass collection box.

"How much?" said Billy.

"One hundred baht" said Noi.

Billy dug into his pocket and handed her a 100-baht bill. She took the bill in both hands and bowed to

Billy touching the bill to her nose and forehead for good luck and to say thank you. She folded the bill and pushed it into the slit on top of the collection box and offered another prayer.

Noi picked out two turtles and three snake-like fish from a vendor beside a lake. The vendor slipped the turtles and fish into separate plastic bags and blew air into each bag before twisting the tops and tying them closed with a rubber band. Billy paid the vendor. They walked down to a dock. Noi knelt and prayed touching her hands to her nose and bowing to touch her forehead to the wooden planks. She released the turtles and fish into the water.

"Ya know that lady that sold them to us is just gonna wrangle 'em up after we leave."

"Yes but they happy now. They free" said Noi.

Billy shrugged. It was hard to argue with Thai logic. Billy looked down at Noi kneeling by the water watching the turtles swim off. It was coming up on a week he'd been here in Phuket. It was time for him to go. *Maybe I'll take her with me* he thought. *We could see the world together.* But Billy knew better. She'd go if he asked, but she'd be miserable. And who could blame her. She already lived in paradise. Noi got up from the deck and walked over to Billy and gave him a hug. Billy looked off in the distance at the dark clouds that boiled over the mountains.

"Monsoon come soon" said Billy.

"Yes. Good for rice" said Noi.

"I suppose."

"When big rain come farang go. I take vacation time. Maybe we go to Chiang Mai?"

"Who would take care of Tougtong?"

"We take Tougtong with us."

"Ya can't take a cat on a plane."

"Why? I see people do. They put cat in plastic box with holes so he breathe okay."

"I mean ya can but—"

"Good. Tougtong go with us."

"Girl, arguing with you is like putting socks on a rooster."

"Tougtong go yes?"

"Yes Tougtong go."

"And maybe the little fish too?"

"Oh lord."

He would stay a little longer. She was worth the risk.

The nomad sat on the balcony and smoked a Vegas Robiana cigar and enjoyed the sounds of the city at the end of the day. He winced from a bolt of pain that shot through his temple like a red hot needle. *God not again* he thought.

He rushed inside and retrieved his toilet kit from the bathroom sink. He opened the container and pulled out the statdose pen and reached for a cartridge—the container was empty. He had used his last cartridge. *You fucking idiot!* he thought throwing the plastic container against the wall in frustration. The container bounced off the tile floor and landed behind the toilet. He reached down to retrieve it and another bolt of pain hit him driving him to his knees. It slowly subsided. He struggled to his feet. A cold sweat poured down his face soaking his silk shirt. *Move you motherfucker before another one hits* he thought.

He stumbled out of the bathroom and to his luggage bag. He unzipped and searched several pockets until he found a plastic pencil holder filled with small pieces of paper. He unzipped the pencil holder and thumbed through several pieces of paper. He pulled out a prescription, dropped everything on the floor and rushed out his hotel room like a man possessed.

The nomad exited the hotel and ran down the street, his eyes looking for a pharmacy. He saw a sign with a green cross halfway down the block on the other side of the street. He ran into the street dodging traffic just as another attack hit him. He stumbled in pain and fell in the street. A tuk-tuk skidded to a halt barely missing his head. The driver cursed him in Thai. He climbed to his feet and limped into the pharmacy. He pushed his way past a customer talking with the pharmacist and opened his hand holding the prescription.

"Fill it now."

The pharmacist saw he was in severe pain. She read the prescription. It listed Vance Dunn as the patient.

"Mr. Dunn this prescription expired in May. You need your doctor to—"

"FILL IT!"

The pharmacist saw that he was desperate. The nomad pulled out his money clip filled with thousand baht bills and shoved it into the pharmacist's hand.

"Please!"

She nodded and moved into the back where the expensive drugs were kept and searched the drug drawers and pulled out a plastic sealed pouch. She approached the nomad and showed him the drug pouch.

"We don't stock the stat-dose cartridges but we have the nasal cartridges. It should have the same effect."

The nomad ripped the package from her hand and tore it open and shot the one dose cartridge into his left nostril. His hands were shaking violently. There was nothing left to do but wait. Overwhelmed by the pain he slid to the floor with his back against the counter. The pain slowly subsided like the relief a heroin addict feels when they finally fix and the drug enters the brain. He was drenched in sweat.

"Are you okay?" asked the pharmacist.

The nomad almost in a dream state nodded.

"Do you want me to call anyone?"

He shook his head and closed his eyes. He was asleep on the floor.

CHAPTER 8

Billy walked along the sidewalk in front of Patong Beach. Vendors sold fresh coconuts with straws to suck out the sweet milk and their tops loped off with a machete. Lounge chair with umbrellas for rent and massage tables under canopies with ocean views shaded the hot sand. He glanced across Thawewong Road paralleling the beach and saw a target range wedged between a sunglass shop and a travel kiosk.

Billy stepped out into the traffic and put his hand up signaling the drivers that he was crossing whether they liked it or not. He was careful not to make eye contact with the drivers. Motorscooters and tuk-tuks braked slowing to let him pass.

Billy slapped down 100 baht on the counter. The vendor filled a pellet pistol in the shape of a .45 semi-automatic with compressed air from a bottle. Billy picked up the pistol and took aim at the paper target hanging from a clip at the end of a guide wire. He kept both eyes open and took a breath and let half of it out before slow squeezing the trigger. The first pellet hit low and to the right of the center of the target. The gun's notch and post sight was off as he expected. He adjusted and took aim at a spot up and to the left. Again he took a breath and let half of it out. He squeezed off 14 rounds in rapid succession. The pistol's slide locked back over an open ejection port. The pistol was empty.

"Were you in the military?"

Billy turned to see the nomad standing next to him.

"Ya gotta a funny way of sneaking up on folks, don't ya?"

The nomad shrugged.

"Military? No. I grew up in Wyoming. The nurses give newborn babies guns instead of pacifiers. You shoot?" Billy said.

"No. Guns are too impersonal."

"That's kinda the point. Keeps the bears and mountain lions at a distance."

"What's the fun in that? It doesn't seem very sportsman-like."

"Yeah, but it'll keep ya breathing another day."

The vendor pulled the guide wire to retrieve the target. All fourteen shots were in a tight cluster punching out most of the solid black rings in the center.

"Impressive" said the nomad. "Are you a real cowboy?"

"'Bout as real as they get nowadays 'cept I raised horses not cows."

"Which breed?"

"Appaloosa mostly."

"Appaloosa is a pattern not a breed."

"Well, like most folks, you'd be wrong. Been a breed for a while now. Pretty animals. Though they do have a tendency to break your toes."

"Break your toes?"

"Yeah when you're cleaning their hoofs of stones and shit, they like to take their other hoof and step on the end of your boot then they sort of lean into it with all their weight."

"Why would they do that?"

"I suppose they like the pop they hear when your toes break. Gives 'em a sense of satisfaction. You break them they break you sort of thing. I don't miss that too much."

"It's difficult to tell when your stories are lies and when they are real."

"That's how ya know I'm a real cowboy."

"And I thought it was the boots."

"Anybody can buy a pair of boots."

"You'll be leaving soon?"

"What makes you say that?"

"The girl at the hotel."

"Noi?"

"She seemed sad this morning."

"Yeah well…that would be between her and I."

"You promised to teach me pool."

"I don't remember it so much as a promise as a conversation. So what are ya doin' in this neck of the woods?"

"Neck of the woods. Interesting. I going to the immigration office. I am coming up on 30 days in Thailand and I need to extend my visa."

"Ya stayin' longer?"

"Until I find what I am looking for."

"And what's that? What're ya lookin' for?"

"The ultimate thrill."

"Well ya came to the right town for that."

"Yes. A modern day Sodom and Gomorra."

"Not sure I'd go that far. But the Thai are a fun lovin' bunch. They have a sayin'—A day without laughter is a day wasted."

"Are you an expert on the Thai?"

"Not an expert but I've been around 'em a bit."

"I look forward to your insight."

"I doubt that."

Billy put another 100 baht on the counter and the vendor reloaded the pistol.

"You think I have a closed mind?" said the nomad.

"I think you've already passed judgement."

"Perhaps. But one can always change their opinion."

"You don't seem the type to change his opinion."

"That doesn't mean I'm wrong."

"I question the value of foreigners judgin' a people they know little to nothin' about."

"Funny. I didn't take you for a liberal."

"I ain't. I've seen the devastation judgement can bring about on a people."

"The American Indian?"

"Government agencies shipped the tribes' children off to boarding schools so they could learn to assimilate into white Christian society. Cut their hair.

Changed their clothes. Forbade them from speaking their native tongue. When the children finally returned, their parents didn't recognize them. An entire generation lost between two worlds—one red one white. A good number committed suicide. All because one people judged another without really understanding."

"And you're afraid we foreigners are going to civilize the Thai?"

"I think the Thai can take care of themselves. But we'd do them a service just to butt out and keep our opinions to ourselves. We're guests here."

"And in the meantime what happens to the teenage girls with their babies living in the streets of Bangkok. No mercy for them?"

"They'll find their way."

"You paint an overly optimistic picture. This is not the utopia you make it out to be."

"Maybe not but whatever it is it's theirs and we best keep our noises out of it."

Billy eyed the nomad's passport in the nomad's shirt pocket. The vendor handed Billy the reloaded pistol.

"You know you're right. I did promise that I'd teach ya pool" said Billy. "Why don't you meet me at the Tiger Club on Bangla Road around 8. The pool tables are in the back on the first floor."

The nomad nodded and walked away. Billy took aim

and fired at the target.

Eve held a photo of Billy and followed a lieutenant through the Thai police station.

"I no have men available" said the lieutenant.

"Interpol has issued a red notice on this man" said Eve.

"Let Interpol send men to help you find him."

"I don't need help finding him. I will do that. I just need your men nearby when I do find him. I don't want to lose him again."

"You lose before?"

"Aye. While I was waiting for police. That's why I need your help. I need two officers."

"How long?"

"One week."

"That long time."

"This man will cause you problems."

"He kill someone?"

"No. He stole money. Lots of money."

"From rich Americans. Not Thai. This not our problem."

"But it could be. He could cause problems with tourists. Steal money from them. If tourists are unhappy that's not good for you."

"Tourists always unhappy."

"Maybe but they say Phuket is not safe because police don't help."

"I no like you."

"I don't want to be a problem for you. I want to take this man away so he is not a problem for you."

"Men cost money."

"I realize that. I would be happy to make a donation to whatever charity or organization you wish."

"You not understand Thai way."

"No but I am happy to learn" Eve said pulling out a wad of Thai baht. The lieutenant nodded. They would do business.

It was night. Dark clouds rolled over the mountains extinguishing the stars. Billy walked down Bangla Road with the case holding his pool cue slung over his shoulder. He entered the Tiger Club and walked to the back. Music pounded. Girls in bikinis danced on platforms. The back of the club was quieter. The nomad sat waiting by one of the pool tables.

"I thought you might not show" said the nomad.

"Thought never crossed my mind. Did ya get your passport stamped?"

"Yes."

"Immigration office is kind of a mad house ain't it?"

"Organized chaos."

"It's surprising they ever get anything done but they do."

"Eventually."

Billy assembled his cue by screwing the two halves together.

"First thing you wanna do is pick out a good cue."

The nomad selected a cue stick from a rack.

"Roll it on the felt to see if it's true."

The nomad rolled the cue on the table top. The stick wobbled.

"It may take a few tries. All this rain and heat tends to warp the wood."

The nomad put the cue back and tried out another and another until he found one that was not warped.

"They should discard the bad cues" said the nomad.

"Doubt that's gonna happen. Thai don't throw out nothing 'less it's broke and even then they'll try to glue it or tape it back together until all hope is lost."

"These people will never learn if they continue to settle for mediocrity."

"Still I've never met a happier people."

"Maybe they're happy because they don't know any better."

"Or maybe they know better and they just choose to keep doing things their way."

The waitress came over with a tray of balls and placed it on the table.

"What are ya havin'?" said Billy.

"Bourbon straight" said the nomad.

"Two Jim Bean. One no ice" Billy said to the waitress.

The waitress walked off to get their order.

"The ice has bacteria in it" said the nomad. "Doesn't that concern you?"

"This is Southeast Asia. Everything has bacteria in it" said Billy.

"It doesn't make you sick?"

"Sure but I ignore it and eat lots of rice. Okay. Time to pick your poison. There's straight pool also called 14.1, there's 8-ball which is the game most people play and then there's my favorite 9-ball."

"Why do you prefer 9-ball?"

"Games are shorter and the play is fast."

"Then 9-ball."

"9-ball it is."

Billy pulled out the balls 1 through 9 plus the white cue ball and placed them on the table. He set the tray with the remaining balls on the floor beneath the table and racked the nine colored balls into a diamond shape at one end of the table.

"The 1-ball is in front and the 9 is in the center" said Billy and pointed to the different positions. "The position of the other balls in the rack is random. The 1-ball must be above the foot mark and the cue ball on the break must be behind the head string. Got it?"

"You can assume I understand until I tell you otherwise" said the nomad.

"Okay. Moving right along. You only keep score when you win a game not during the game and you don't need to call your shots. The object of the game is to pocket the 9-ball. You must hit the lowest numbered ball first and you must pocket any numbered ball to continue otherwise you lose your turn. So I could shoot all eight balls in and miss the 9 and if you pocket the 9 you win. Those are the basics. Any additional rules I'll tell you about as we play. We lag the cue ball for who breaks on the first game then loser breaks thereafter. You can lag first."

"Lag?"

"You hit the cue ball to bounce it off the front cushion and try to get as close to the back cushion as possible. Closest to the back cushion wins the lag and breaks."

The nomad set the cue ball down behind the head string line and lined up his cue on the ball. He studied the shot taking several false starts.

"It's just the lag. No need to fast and pray about it" said Billy.

The nomad, annoyed at being interrupted, took his shot. The ball bounced off the front cushion and settled two inches from the back cushion. A good shot be any measure. Billy placed the chalk cube on the table's side rail to mark the nomad's ball position. Billy took his turn and lagged the ball closer to the back cushion.

"I break" said Billy.

Billy set the cue ball behind the head string line to the far end near the right rail cushion. He hit the cue ball hard. It slammed into the 1-ball at an angle and scattered the balls around the table. Several balls went into pockets including the 9-ball.

"Hmmm. I win. One to zero. Your break" said Billy.

The nomad racked the colored balls into a diamond shape and took his shot. The 5-ball went in.

"Still your turn" said Billy.

The nomad took another shot and pocketed the 1-ball. On his next turn he pocketed the 2-ball but the cue ball settled behind the 6-ball with no clear shot at the 3-ball. He would need to bank the shot to avoid a foul. The nomad carefully studied the shot taking his time.

"Not getting any younger here" said Billy.

"Your commentary is annoying."

"Not the first time I've been told that."

"And yet you persist."

"Kinda stubborn that way."

The nomad took his shot and missed.

"Oops" said Billy.

The waitress came back with their drinks. Both had ice.

"I asked for it straight" said the nomad.

"I got it" said Billy.

Billy reached in with his fingers and pulled out the ice cubes from the nomad's glass and put the cubes in his own glass. The nomad looked disgusted.

"It's alcohol. Kills all the bacteria" said Billy.

The game continued.

"You're from Wyoming. No much out there" said the nomad.

"If ya call the Grand Tetons nothing."

"I meant in the way of civilization."

"That's the way most folks out there prefer it. The less civilization the better. Where do you hail from?"

"Boston."

"A Yankee. What type of work ya do?"

"I manage my family's investment portfolio."

"Old money."

"Very old."

"Must be nice being born into money not havin' to work for a livin'."

"It is."

"I wouldn't know. I suppose it's difficult finding a sense of self-worth with a silver spoon in your mouth."

"Actually it's quite easy."

Billy pocketed the 9-ball.

"I win again. Gettin' to be a habit."

"Does it make you feel important…winning?"

"Better 'n losing."

"The girl at the hotel what does she cost you?"

"Ya might wanna change the subject."

"Or I might not. I was just curious. With you leaving I might want some company one night. Or does she rent by the week?"

"You like to push buttons don't ya?"

"Did I offend you cowboy?"

"From the moment your screaming bitch of a mother pushed you through her cunt" said Billy.

The nomad's face tightened. "You should be careful" said the nomad.

"Not part of my nature. 'Sides I can see a pussy like you coming a mile away."

"Really?"

The nomad slammed the tip of his cue on the edge of the table snapping the tip off leaving a long wooden shard like a spear.

"Did you see that coming cowboy?" said the nomad.

The waitress walked in with another round of drinks and saw the two men about to fight and dropped her tray and ran out.

"Ya might wanna put that down 'fore I decide to take it from ya and shove it up your ass sideways" said Billy.

"Stop talking and start doing cowboy."

Two large Thai bouncers ran into the pool room. One of the bouncers had a club made from a shortened baseball bat. The waitress followed them in.

"You no fight in club. Police come" said the largest bouncer.

Billy and the nomad exchanged a look. Neither could afford a run-in with the police. Billy tossed his cue on the table. The nomad tossed the broken cue on the table.

"You break you pay" said the bouncer.

The nomad pulled a thousand baht from his pocket and tossed it on the table.

"You pay bill" said the waitress as she handed Billy the bill. He pulled out two thousand baht and handed it to her.

"Sorry we scared you."

"Speak for yourself cowboy."

"Hesh up Yankee."

"We'll have to play again sometime."

"Boy you ain't the sharpest knife in the drawer are ya?"

The nomad slipped out a side exit. Billy picked up his cue and case and exited in the opposite direction.

A few rain drops hit the pavement with a faint pat-pat-pat. Big drops usually meant big rain. The sidewalk vendors rolled down their plastic sheets and covered their freestanding racks. The sprinkles turned to a torrent. Tourists ran for cover in nearby bars and stores. The nomad walked calm and undisturbed by the growing downpour. His gaze distant as if deep in thought.

A Thai bargirl in a short black dress called out as he passed.

"Mister you crazy."

The nomad stopped and looked over.

"You wet. Come here. I make you dry. Then you make me wet."

The nomad's eyes surveyed her body head to toe and back again. Her fingers hiked up the bottom of her dress revealing her lack of panties. His stare was cold and unmoved. He walked on.

Billy was drenched. He walked into the hotel bar his eyes searching. No nomad. Billy crossed to the bar and sat with his back to the wall giving a good view of both openings leading to the street. Noi approached with a clean bar towel and wiped his face and hair dry.

"Thanks darlin'."

"San Miguel Light Mr. Billy?"

"No. Double Jim Beam."

"You want rocks?"

Billy tensed as a man appeared from around the corner and jogged toward the bar in the rain. The man's face was covered by a piece of cardboard he was using as an umbrella. He entered the bar and dropped the cardboard revealing his face. It was not the nomad.

"Mr. Billy?"

"I'm sorry. What?"

"You want ice?"

"Yeah. Ice."

Noi poured two jiggers of bourbon into a tumbler then filled it to the rim with big cubes from the blue igloo cooler used as the bar's clean ice bucket. She set the tumbler in front of Billy. He took a swallow. His eyes still searched for signs of the nomad.

"Noi. The guy that checked in a few days ago. The penthouse."

"Mr. Kyle?"

"Yeah. Have you seen him tonight?"

"No."

Noi spoke in Thai to the two other girls tending bar with her. They each shook their heads.

"Okay. Thanks."

Billy took a big pull of bourbon.

"Are you okay Mr. Billy?"

"I'm fine. Just a little tired."

"You need good sleep. Maybe get massage."

"Yeah you're right. I should."

Across the street in the darkness of a half-finished hotel, a brown rat scampered through the building materials stacked in the lobby. Tougtong lowered into a stalking crouch and watched the rat. Tougtong sprinted after the rat and past a pair of loafers. The nomad silently watched the bar through the pouring rain.

CHAPTER 9

The rain stopped. Billy was naked and stared at Noi asleep next to him. The bed sheet just covered her perfectly formed buttocks. Her brown skin was highlighted by the soft moonlight peeking through the drapes. Noi stirred and snuggled up next to him.

"You want another massage?" she asked sleepily.

"I should give you one."

"That sound nice. Maybe next time. I need find Tougtong and go home."

Noi kissed him on his chest and rose from the bed and let the sheets drop to reveal her body. She searched in the dark for her panties and bra. Billy flipped on the light to help her.

"You could stay here. It ain't like I'm chasing ya off."

"No. I go home feed Tougtong and my fish."

"I've been thinking. Maybe we should go to Chiang Mai tomorrow."

"That be nice. I thought you need to go."

"I do but we can go to Chiang Mai first."

"I need to ask boss for time off."

"I thought you were the boss."

"I manager. Manager have boss. But I think it be okay."

Noi slipped on her dress and zipped it up. She pulled a comb from her purse and combed the tangles out of her long red hair. God she's beautiful even when she's combing her hair thought Billy.

"When we get back maybe we should talk about you going with me."

Noi stopped combing her hair.

"Go with you?"

"Yeah. I've been traveling for a few years now and I get lonely and you've never been outside of Thailand. There's a whole big world out there that you haven't seen and I could show it to you."

"Mr. Billy, I Thai. I want to see my country but I no have dreams like you. No need to see world. And I have Expat. Owner need me. Customer need me. Tougtong need me. Why not you stay here with me and Tougtong?"

"I would but I can't."

"You could buy condo and get retirement visa. No problem."

"It's not the visa that's the problem."

"You no have money?"

"No. I have the money."

"I no understand."

"I need to explain so you understand. We can talk about it later."

"In Chiang Mai?"

"Yes. In Chiang Mai. It's late. Do you want me go with you?"

"No. I have Tougtong. He protect me."

"He's a cat."

"Yes. But he a mighty cat."

"How about a taxi?"

"No. I have motor scooter with basket for Tougtong. I fine Mr. Billy."

Noi finished dressing. She walked over to Billy still lying on the bed pulled back the sheets and kissed him lightly on his flaccid penis.

"You get good sleep now" said Noi.

"I will."

"And no worry so much. You in Thailand and Thailand loves you."

Noi turned off the lights and walked out. Billy lay back down and closed his eyes.

Noi exited the elevator and entered the bar now closed and mostly dark. A few of the backlit signs advertising cold beer and bottles of liquor held by buxom blonds in low-cut evening gowns still illuminated the bar tables and stools. Her eyes searched through the shadows.

"Tougtong?" she called softly not wanting to wake any of the hotel guests. No movement. She looked below the bar and in the back of the kitchen—Tougtong's usual hiding places. No Tougtong.

"Tougtong mommy need to feed fish. Come Tougtong."

Still nothing. Frustrated Noi walked outside the bar and into the rain. She looked under cars and near the hotel trash dumpster and called softly for Tougtong and clicked her tongue. She heard a shuffling across the street in the half-finished hotel. She crossed the street and climbed the concrete steps into the lobby.

"Tougtong?"

Through the darkness Noi saw a black mass and the

reflection of a pair of soulless eyes. They didn't belong to Tougtong. The nomad stepped forward silently with the karambit knife in his hand. Nothing needed to be said.

It was still dark. The door to the Expat's electronics room flew open with the wood around the door frame doorknob and deadbolt splintered and cracked. The nomad entered with his empty backpack and a flashlight. He studied the wires leading to the five security camera monitors. All the wires led to the same computer attached to a single external hard drive. It was a simple system using old technology. It was a direct connect with no phone lines or ethernet cables. He doubted there was an offsite backup. He pulled the power plugs and took out his karambit knife. He sliced off all the wires running to the back of the computer and hard drive. He slipped the computer and hard drive into his backpack and zipped it closed. *No fire tonight* he thought. He exited and left the door ajar.

Billy woke hungry. He glanced at his iPhone— 6:45am. He dressed and pulled on his boots. He wanted to pick up Noi from her house and leave for Chiang Mai right after breakfast and avoid another encounter with the crazy American. It was against his nature to shun a fight. He had learned to stand up against bullies like his brother Lowell, but this was a fight he didn't need. The Thai police had a bad habit of arresting both parties in any fight, especially if a farang was involved. It didn't matter who was at fault. After a few hours in a Thai jail the farang were always willing to part with 10,000 baht for their freedom. It wasn't a few hours in jail that concerned Billy. It was that the police would confiscate his passport and maybe even run a check on it. That was something he had to avoid at all costs. Better to skulk away and keep his freedom.

He exited the elevator and sat at the bar. Kahjee the morning bargirl offered him a menu. He didn't need it. He had it memorized.

"Coffee black strong and English breakfast. Eggs scrambled 70% cooked. No mushrooms. Extra beans."

She walked into the kitchen and ordered his breakfast. Billy noticed the broken door to the electronics room.

"Kahjee what happened to the door?"

"Someone break last night. Steal computer. Owner very angry. Computer expensive."

Oh shit thought Billy.

"Kahjee, are the police coming?" asked Billy.

"No. Police no do nothing if no pay. Computer man come fix tomorrow."

Billy relaxed. He watched a rugby match on one of the HDTVs. He liked rugby. It reminded him of football but without all the padding and helmets. The rugby players were tough. An ear would almost get ripped off during a rough tackle. The team doc would slap a couple of pieces of tape on it and the player would be right back in the mix before the next scrum. Billy was startled when Tougtong jumped up on the bar beside him.

"What are you doing here?" said Billy.

Kahjee returned to the bar and started making Billy's black coffee from two shots of expresso.

"Kahjee, is Noi here?"

"No. She sleep now in home."

"So what's Tougtong doing here?"

"Sometimes he hide from Noi so he can go be with lady cat."

Billy turned to Tougtong. "You get some last night? You're probably hungry."

Kahjee swatted Tougtong on the butt. "You go eat rat! That your job!"

Tougtong jumped off the bar and ran off. Khajee slid the coffee in front of Billy.

"So you and Noi boom-boom?"

"What's that mean... boom-boom?"

"You know... fuck?"

"Oh well... you'd have to ask Noi."

"She no say. She think she a lady."

"She is a lady."

"No. She same as bargirl. But she nice. You lucky

man."

"I am."

Billy's breakfast appeared in the kitchen window. Khajee grabbed it and slid it in front of Billy.

A police car with two Thai officers and Eve in the backseat turned onto the cul-de-sac of hotels and parked in the street. The Expat Hotel was at the far end. Eve stepped out and turned to the two police officers.

"You stay here while I check the hotels. If I need you I'll call you. Okay?"

They nodded and watched as Eve pulled out the photo of Billy and entered the first hotel on the cul-de-sac. One officer turned to the other and made a snide remark in Thai. They didn't like the pushy American woman.

Billy stepped out of the shower and toweled himself dry. He walked back into the bedroom and over to his bag on rollers where he kept his clothes in case he needed to leave in a hurry. It wasn't where he always kept it. He looked around and saw his clothes neatly stacked on a shelf. Now he was confused and didn't like the feeling. He again looked around the room and saw his wheeled bag sitting upright in the corner.

"What're you doin' over there?"

He approached the bag cautiously and grabbed it by the handle. It was very heavy. He laid it down horizontally and unzipped the main compartment and partially pulled back the cover until he saw a wisp of red hair.

He jumped back and pushed himself against the bed. He stared at the strands of red hair dangling out of the bag. He tried to breathe but it felt like an elephant was sitting his chest. His mind tried to comprehend what his eyes saw.

He steeled himself again, moved to the bag and flipped open the cover. Inside Noi's lifeless body was stacked like cords of wood, her joints broken where needed to make her entire body fit in the bag. There was little blood. Noi's face was shrouded by her hair. Billy had to be sure. He carefully brushed the hair away from Noi's face. Noi's eyes were missing like hollow holes scooped out with a melon-baller.

Billy convulsed and puked hard down his front and on the floor in front of him. He didn't move. His eyes focused on Noi's face. Tears streamed down his cheeks. His mind was locked with sadness. No room for other thoughts. Just overwhelming sadness.

Billy sat on the floor next to Noi for several minutes. A light knock on the door broke the silence. At first it barely registered in Billy's mind—the three girls from Myanmar that cleaned the rooms. Then another knock and the door began to open. He scrambled for the door.

"No!" he said and shoved his shoulder against the door and slammed it closed. "I'm not dressed."

"Come back later?" said one of the girls through the door.

"Yes later."

He heard the girls move off and knock on the room next door. His heart pounded. He felt sick and ran into the bathroom and turned on the shower. The cold water calmed him. I have to move now he thought. One foot in front of the other. Don't think. Just do.

He shut off the water and pulled down the towel and wiped himself down. He moved back into the bedroom and got dressed forcing himself not to look at Noi's lifeless body. He finished dressing and pulled on his boots. He moved over to the bag and knelt down beside her. He fought back the tears. He promised himself he would mourn her later.

"I'm so sorry this happened to you. I would give anything to trade places with you" he said looking at her one last time. He gently placed the wisp of red hair back inside and zipped up the bag. He opened the door and rolled the bag into the hallway. He rolled the case past the open doorway of the room now being cleaned by the Burmese girls. One of the girls walked out carrying the bed sheets.

"You go now Mr. Billy?"

"I'll be back. Just leave the room. Don't clean."

He pulled three hundred baht from his pocket and stuffed it in her hand.

"For you and the other girls. Don't clean my room okay?"

"No clean. Okay."

Billy rolled the bag to the elevator. There were two ways out of the hotel. The elevator and the stairs. Both led to the lobby bar where there would be more witnesses. It couldn't be helped. His only hope to remain free was to get her body out of the hotel and someplace where it wouldn't be discovered. It wasn't right and it wasn't fair to a beautiful human like Noi, but it was what had to be done. After that he would see that she was properly cremated according to Buddhist tradition. He pressed the button and called the elevator.Eve entered the lobby bar and crossed to the front desk. Khajee stepped from behind the bar and approached Eve.

"You check in?"

"Ah no. I'm looking for a man." Eve pulled out the photo of Billy. She saw the recognition on Khajee's face.

"You know this man?"

"Why you want him? He your boyfriend?"

"No. I work for the government. He won the lottery." Eve nodded enthusiastically.

"Mr. Billy won American lottery?! That good!" said Khajee.

"Aye very good!" said Eve.

The elevator bell rang as it reached the lobby and the doors opened and Billy stepped out with the wheeled bag in tow.

"Mr. Billy you win lottery!" said Khajee.

Billy looked over and saw Eve standing next to a smiling Khajee. Their eyes met. Eve blinked hardly believing she was standing ten feet from the man she had been chasing for the last six months. Billy looked down at the wheeled bag holding Noi's body then back at Eve.

"Oh shit" he said flatly.

Eve snapped out of her daze and speed-dialed her phone keeping her eyes locked on Billy.

"I've got him. The suspect is in the Expat hotel lobby" said Eve.

"I'm sorry" Billy said to the bag holding Noi. He bolted to the street leaving the bag. Eve ran after him.

Billy exited the bar at a full run. An Aussie laid down a motor scooter to avoid hitting him. Billy kept running. The Aussie cursed him. The motor scooter blocked Eve's path. She jumped over the Aussie and the scooter without slowing down and landed on the other side. She stumbled and hit the pavement hard and rolled.

Billy ran past a water truck performing a three-point U-turn. He realized he was running the wrong way and there was a dead end at the end of the cul-de-sac. He stopped. His eyes searched for a way out. There was none. He had trapped himself.

Eve climbed to her feet and saw Billy disappear behind the water truck at the end of the cul-de-sac.

She slowed knowing he could get past her by going around the other side of the truck if she followed him behind it. She moved forward cautiously. She turned back to see the two Thai officers rounding the corner 100 feet away. She motioned for them to watch the opposite side of the truck. She moved around the side of the truck where Billy disappeared. No Billy. The truck completed its U-turn headed back down the street past the two officers. No sign of Billy anywhere.

Eve looked at the truck turning the corner around the Expat and heading toward the main street. The lid on the water tank bounced and water spilled out as the truck hit a pot hole. Eve ran after the water truck and ran past the officers.

"He's in the water truck" she said without breaking stride. The officers ran after her. Eve rounded the corner and caught up with the water truck. She grabbed onto the ladder on the back of the tank and pulled herself up and climbed onto the top of the tank. She pulled open the heavy lid to the tank and looked inside at the sloshing water. She saw into the bottom of the tank. Nothing. She lowered her head into the opening and looked farther in toward the front of the tank. Nothing but sloshing water.

"Fuck me" she said.

She pulled her head out of the tank and stood up on the tank and looked around for any sign of Billy. The officers caught up to the truck. Eve climbed down and hopped off.

"Let's go back to the cul-de-sac. He's gotta be there" she said. Out of breath from running, the officers followed her back into the cul-de-sac.

Inside the water truck tank near the front Billy laid horizontally under the water with his feet and hands wedged up against the walls of the tank keeping him submerged but out of the sunlight coming through the hatchway. Out of breath he buckled and swam to the top and gasped for air. The water sloshed up and down like a stormy ocean. He swam to the hatchway, pulled himself up and out to the roof of the tank and laid flat and looked back down the street. No sign of the American woman. He climbed down the ladder and dropped off the truck as it slowed for a stoplight. He jogged down a side street. He was still free for the moment.

Billy sat down at a restaurant and ordered a coke. He pulled out his iPhone and water dripped out the bottom. He pulled off his boots and poured out the water and set them on the seat next to him. What now? he thought. Make a run for the airport before the police set up a perimeter? That's a sure way to get caught. And what about Noi? You left her you fucking coward. No. There was nothing you could do for her. She already was gone. Don't think about that now. Survive. Maybe a bus or ferry to one of the islands. Lay low until things calm down. Find a way across the border. Get out of Thailand. If you make it across the border you'll be safe. But what about Noi's killer? He'll get away for sure. No. He's already gone. He's not stupid. The big question for Billy was how he was going to find him.

Eve reentered the bar lobby at the Expat Hotel and saw Billy's wheeled bag still by the elevator. She grabbed it to wheel it back to the police car but was surprised by the weight. She laid it on its side and knelt down beside it and opened the zipper. Nori's lifeless arm fell out with her hand palm up as if expecting something. Eve stumbled backward. The two officers entered the bar lobby.

"You need to call your boss now" she said.

CHAPTER 10

It was late at night and raining. The Expat lobby bar was filled with police interviewing customers and staff. The bargirls and housekeepers were in tears. Eve finished her statement to the Thai police detectives. She was tired and sweaty from the heat and humidity. Noi's naked and broken body had been removed from the bag and laid out on the bar floor. Thai police held up a plastic tarp as a privacy curtain. A forensic investigator took photos. Nori's neck was badly bruised. Eve hoped the girl had been strangled to death before her joints were broken.

My God. Slow death by asphyxiation is the best the universe can offer this poor girl? Eve thought. She felt nauseated. She pushed her way past the police and witnesses. The perimeter of the lobby bar was roped off by orange police tape written in both Thai and English. Eve pushed past the crowd of gawkers and press photographers snapping photos with their telescopic lenses and high-powered flash bars. Eve made it to the street and bent down to catch her breath. She wanted to vomit but thought better of it.

"I hope you burn for this, Billy Gamble" she said.

The rain soaked her blouse and cooled her down. It felt good. She stood up and hailed the closest taxi and climbed in. The taxi drove down the cul-de-sac and turned onto the main road.

Across the street Billy sat on a rented motor scooter and watched. His face was concealed in the shadow of a wet hoodie. He started the two-cycle engine and pulled out into traffic and followed the taxi.

The taxi pulled up to Eve's hotel and let her out. She entered the lobby and crossed to the elevator and entered. She was exhausted. She exited the elevator and walked down the hallway to her room, opened the door, walked into her room and inserted her keycard into the wall slot by the door. The room lights came on automatically once the keycard tripped the power switch.

Outside in the rain Billy parked his motor scooter in front of Eve's hotel and watched the windows scaling the eight-story tower. A light came on in one of the rooms. *Sixth floor, three from the west corner* Billy thought.

Inside Eve shut the door and locked the deadbolt. It was a good habit for anyone but especially after a day like today. She tossed her purse on the desk. She squatted down to open the refrigerator and raid the minibar. She grabbed two bottles of Johnnie Walker Red and a Snickers bar. She opened the freezer shelf and pulled out an empty ice tray. *Shit. No ice and I bet they still charge me ten bucks a bottle* she thought. *Nice fucking customer service.* She tossed the empty tray back inside the freezer shelf and closed the refrigerator rattling the remaining bottles inside. She moved to the bed and fell backward with the bottles of scotch and the Snickers bar still in her hands. She really wanted a shower but exhaustion took its toll. Her eyes blinked twice then closed. She was out.

Outside, Billy continued to watch and wait.

It was a short flight from Phuket to Penang. The nomad stood in line with the other foreigners waiting for his turn. The nomad was relaxed and confident as he approached the immigration officer. She was wearing a dark blue hijab, the traditional Muslim head scarf worn by most women in Malaysia. With a gentle smile he handed her his passport. Expressionless the officer flipped the passport open to the data page and scanned the machine readable code into her computer and pulled up the passport holder's personal information. She glanced back and forth checking the data on her screen and the passport to ensure they matched. Next she glanced at his photo then at the nomad's face to ensure a match. She motioned to the camera and the nomad looked at the red light on top of the camera. She took the nomad's photo for her records. She pointed to the fingerprint scanner under the camera. The nomad allowed the machine to scan his fingerprints. She flipped through the visa pages until she found an empty page and stamped his passport. No words were necessary. He now had 30 days to visit Malaysia as a tourist. She handed the passport back to the nomad who again smiled cordially and moved through the automated gateway with a sign that read Welcome to Malaysia in English.

The nomad walked out of the airport and crossed over to the taxi stand. A driver loaded his bag into the trunk. The nomad climbed into the backseat and the taxi left the airport.

Eve, 17, entered a classroom. A man stood at the opposite end staring out the window.

"Eve Donoghue?"

"Aye sir."

He turned and studied her. She felt uneasy.

"Am I in trouble?"

"I don't know. Are ya?"

"No sir. Not that I know."

He crossed to a desk where a file lay open and studied the file. His questions were slow and deliberate.

"You're an orphan?"

"Aye sir. My parents were killed in a bombing when I was twelve."

"Why weren't you adopted?"

"The couples that visit the orphanage want babies not teenagers."

"Your school marks are impressive. You've done well for yourself."

"It's all I have."

"School?"

"Aye sir."

"And when you graduate?"

"A university if I can get a scholarship."

"You have the marks for it. What will you study?"

"I don't know. Law maybe."

"You're uncommonly pretty."

"Thank you sir. My mother was pretty."

"You belong to several societies and clubs."

"Aye sir. A few."

"More than a few."

"Aye sir."

"Why?"

"I don't know. I like them."

"Trying to fit in? Trying to belong?"

"I suppose. Aye sir."

"You're Catholic?"

"Aye sir. My parents were catholic."

"That must be difficult being Catholic in Northern Ireland."

"No sir. Not if you have faith."

"And do you have faith?"

"Some yes. Enough."

"You've heard of Sinn Fein?"

"It's Ireland sir. Everyone has heard of Sinn Fein."

"Have you ever been approached?"

"Approached sir?"

"By a member of Sinn Fein. A recruiter perhaps."

Eve thought before responding. "And if I had?"

"What did you say?"

"I don't want to kill."

"Of course not. You're still young."

"What does youth have to do with it? There are plenty my age out there killing. On both sides."

"Aye there are."

"Who are you?"

"Would you like to put an end to the killing?"

"Of course. I want a million zonk too. But I don't see either happening anytime soon."

"No. Neither do I. Still we must try."

"I suppose."

The man closed the folder and again studied her. "Ms. Donoghue."

"Aye sir?"

"Your country needs you."The man watched. Eve was dressed in a cadet's uniform. She crossed a stage and received her certificate of graduation from the RUC Academy.The man introduced Eve now wearing a constable uniform to a deputy chief constable.

"Do you attend church regularly?" said the deputy chief constable.

"Not regularly but I—"

"Start."Eve made passionate love to a young man. The bedroom door exploded. She rolled off her lover and grabbed the sheet and covered herself. Five heavily armored men with their faces hidden by riot helmets entered. One of the intruders shot her lover in the chest and head with a tactical machine gun. He turned his gun's barrel to Eve, a red laser dot marking her forehead.

"No" said the unit commander. "She's one of ours."

"Is she now?" said the shooter keeping her in his sight. Her life hung by the twitch of his finger.

"I said she is one of us" the unit commander said pushing the shooter's barrel to the ceiling.

"Little Catholic bitch. Can't trust 'em. Not a one" said the shooter.

"Fuck off" said the commander slapping a body bag into the chest of the shooter. "Put your mess in a body bag and check your brass."

The commander crossed to Eve curled up in the corner. Eve's eyes stared at her dead lover.

"You okay?"

Eve thought for a moment then nodded.

"He was a terrorist. Bombed a pub. Killed three. You did good. You saved lives."

Eve nodded. The commander moved off.

Eve awoke. The bedspread was wrapped around her. She felt something sticking her in the side. She pulled out the Snickers bar from under the bedspread. It was a melted clump of chocolate peanuts and nougat still sealed in its plastic wrapper. It reminded her she was hungry. She jumped up and searched through the papers on the desk and found the hotel's policies that all guests were given on check-in. Item three on the list read complementary buffet breakfast 7-10 am. She pulled her iPhone from her purse and looked at the time—9:45am. She sniffed her blouse near the armpits and shrugged—an acceptable level of stink. She slipped on her shoes, grabbed the room key and exited her room.

In the hotel cafe Eve scooped up a bowl of Thai congee from a metal chaffing container. She added few green onions and some dried pork and cracked a raw egg and let it slide from the shell on to the top of the hot rice porridge. The steam from the porridge cooked the egg. She balanced the bowl in one hand and made herself a cafe latte from the automatic expresso machine. She grabbed a slice of toast that slid out the bottom of the chain-belt toaster, stuck it in her mouth, grabbed her latte from the machine and headed for the closest empty table.

She sat alone and dipped her toast in the latte and sucked off the excess foam. She picked up the yellow bottle already sitting on the table and shook out ten drops of a dark liquid on her porridge. It was a Thai version of soy sauce but with more spices. She stirred the half-cooked egg and dried pork and green onions into the congee and dug in. After a few bites the image of Noi's broken body flashed in her mind. Eve quickly lost her appetite. She sat trying to make sense of what had happened. *He killed her but why?* she thought. This didn't seem like the actions of the guy she had studied and chased for the last six months. *Yeah sure he was a thief but a murderer?* It didn't fit his profile. But she knew that profiles were an imperfect picture of a suspect. She must have missed something. It didn't matter now. Her job was finished. There wasn't going to be any extradition back to the States and no finder's fee for her. Billy Gamble was a white fugitive in a land of brown faces. His face would be on the television news 24-7 until he was found. All the airports, bus stations and cruise line terminals would be covered. *It was only a matter of time. Once the Thai police catch him he'll be lucky if he's not killed during the arrest* she thought. The Thai welcomed western tourists but they had no tolerance for murderers and rapists. If he made it to trial Thai justice would put him away for life.

Eve drained her latte cup and got up and headed for the elevator. She pulled out her phone and started searching for flights back to the US. She entered the elevator with several other hotel guests. She didn't notice the man wearing a hoodie who stepped in behind her and stood with his back to her in front of the elevator buttons. She glanced at his height and surmised that he probably wasn't Thai which meant he probably understood English.

"Six please" she said.

The man pressed the button for six. Several guests got off on each floor until only Eve and the man in the hoodie remained in the elevator. As the elevator started up to Eve's floor the man reached out and pulled the emergency stop button. The elevator lunged to a halt and the alarm bell rang. Eve looked up from her phone and saw that she was alone with the man. Instinct kicked in. She reached into her purse and fumbled for a can of pepper spray. The man turned and pulled off his hoodie. It was Billy.

"Get the fuck away from me" Eve said.

She backed up against the elevator wall and crossed to the opposite corner putting as much distance as possible between them.

"Relax. I just want to talk" he said and held up his

hands to show he was unarmed. "I'm not here to hurt you. I wouldn't do that."

"Yeah is that what you told that girl?"

"Her name was Noi."

Eve yelled for help.

"Settle down. I just want to talk."

Eve pulled out her can of pepper spray attached to her keychain and twisted the safety with her thumb and pointed it toward Billy's face. Billy rushed forward and grabbed the keychain and ripped it out of her hand. Eve kneed him in the groin. He dropped the keychain and stumbled backward and clutched his crotch.

"Christ O'mighty. You're a mean one" said Billy.

Eve picked up the keychain and aimed the can and squirted the pepper juice at Billy's face. Billy pitched to the side and avoided the spray. He ran forward and grabbed her around the waist and slammed her back against the elevator wall with his full weight. She gasped for breath and dropped the keychain and crumbled to the floor. Billy kicked the keychain to the opposite side of the elevator.

"I meant what I said. I just want to talk. Now are you gonna settle down?"

"Fuck you."

"Okay. If that makes ya feel better catch your breath and bring it."

"I think you broke my ribs."

"I doubt it. Ya just got the wind knocked out of ya."

"How do you know?"

"Cuz I've had my ribs broken. 'Sides I didn't hit ya hard enough to break anything."

Eve righted herself and leaned against the elevator wall. "You know that hotel security is probably watching us on that camera right now." She pointed to the security camera in the upper corner of the elevator. "They'll get the maintenance crew to override the elevator."

"It'll take 'em a few minutes. That's all I need."

"What do you want?"

"I didn't kill Noi."

"Okay. I understand. I'm sure you didn't."

"Don't patronize me."

"Okay. Then save it for the judge you sick fuck."

"Look I've done a lot of things wrong in my life but I wouldn't do that to another human being, especially someone I loved. I'm not a killer."

"I'm not the one you have to convince."

"No. You're exactly who I have to convince."

"Why would that be?"

"I need your help."

"My help? I think you need a good lawyer who speaks Thai."

"The police, the judge, the jury…oh hell I don't even know if they have juries here. But it doesn't matter. They're never going to listen. Not after what I have done."

"What did you do?"

"I didn't kill her. If that's what you mean."

"Look. I get it. You're in trouble. Your best shot is to turn yourself in and cooperate with the police."

"Yeah. Is that what you would do?"
"What do you want me to say?"

"Just be straight with me."

"Okay. You're fucked."

"That we can agree upon."

"I can't help you."

"Yes you can. You can find him."

"Find who?"

"The guy who killed Noi. Kyle. Kyle Tanner."

"You know the guy who did it?"

"I don't know him. I mean…I met him. We played pool together."

"You played pool?"

"I pissed him off and we got into a fight."

"So he killed a girl to—"

"Her name was Noi. Stop calling her a girl like she's just some thing."

"Sorry. So he killed Noi to set you up?"

"I know it sounds lame but this guy was seriously disturbed."

"You need to be telling this to the police."

"They are not going to listen and you know it. They'll never find him. They'll never even look once they catch me."

"You don't know that."

"Stop patronizing me damn it! My life's on the line here!" Billy took a moment to calm himself. "I'm really fucked aren't I?"

Eve studied him before responding. "Even if what you say is true. Yeah. You're really fucked."

"Yeah. That's the truth of it. So whatever time I have left I'm gonna spend it finding Noi's killer."

"Good plan. Go get him."

"And you're gonna help me."

"Uh no thank you. I was hired to find you. There you are. Mission accomplished. I'm done."

"To get paid you've got to bring me back and get me to return the money I stole, don't you?"

"I have to have you extradited. But that's not going to happen now. Once the Thai police get their hands on you…"

"They'll throw away the key."

"I don't know a lot about Thai law, but yeah probably."

"But even if they catch me, what if I still return the money?"

"Why would you do that?"

"Call it a bounty. You help me find Noi's killer and I'll return the money."

"Even if you're caught?"

"Even if I'm caught."

"What makes you think I can find him?"

"You found me."

"How much of the money is left?"

"All of it."

"You didn't spend any of it?"

"That's right."

"What have you been using to travel?"

"I had my own money."

"You felt guilty?"

"It wasn't mine to spend."

"How do I know you still have it?"

"I'll show you the bank accounts where I keep it."

"Cayman Islands?"

"Some of it."

"And the rest of it?"

"Spread around."

"And you'll show me the accounts?"

"Yes. But you don't get a dollar until Noi's killer is caught."

"And then you'll just turn it over?"

"Yes."

"And extradition back to the US?"

"What do you care? You'll have the money and you'll get paid."

"Not unless I extradite you."

"They want their pound of flesh?"

"They do."

"Okay. We catch him I go back."

"You'd give up your freedom to avenge her?"

"Yes."

"Well then there is only one problem standing in our way."

"I'm a thief and you don't trust me."

"Aye."

"Best laid plans of mice and men huh?"

"I don't suppose you would consider turning yourself in and giving back the money then let me find this guy Kyle on my own?"

"No."

"Then we are at an impasse."

"Seems so. But thanks for hearing me out."

"Not like I had much of a choice."

"I suppose not."

"Now what?"

Billy pushed the emergency button back in and the alarm stopped and the elevator rose. He pressed the button for the floor below her floor.

"Might wanna put some ice on 'em. Your ribs" Billy said.

"I'll do that."

The doors opened and Billy stepped out.

"You really didn't kill her did you?"

"No. I loved her."

The doors closed and the elevator rose and carried Eve to her floor.

A Burmese housekeeper knocked on room 801's door at the Expat Hotel. No answer. She used her pass card to open the door. The room was empty. No bags. The nomad was gone. She moved out onto the patio. The ashtray was already empty. She wiped down the furniture and swept the balcony. She found the remains of Kyle's cigar on the floor. Most of the cigar had burned down to the wrapper band. She threw the remains into the trash. She pulled the sheets from the bed. She mopped the bathroom floor and spotted the empty statdose container behind the toilet. She threw the statdose container in the same trashcan containing the cigar remains. She tied the trashcan liner into a knot and tossed it on her cart with the other full trashcan liners.

Billy rode his scooter up a winding mountain road. The jungle on both sides of the road was thick. He rounded a hairpin turn and saw a roadblock. Three Thai police officers stopped cars and checked IDs. One officer was armed with a tactical machine gun. Billy pulled over and watched. *If I could take out the guy with the machine gun I might stand a chance at running* he thought. He revved the scooter's engine. Another Thai officer emerged from the forest and zipped up the fly on his trousers. He picked up the machine gun he had left leaning against a tree.

"Shit" said Billy. He turned his scooter around and headed back to Patong Beach.

Billy rode his scooter down off the mountain that separated Patong Beach from Kamala Beach, careful to stay under the speed limit. He drove down Thawewong Road and rode along the beach. He glanced at the tourists walking on the sidewalk and crossing the street. Some stared back. A farang cowboy in Thailand. He never really fit in but he never cared. But now things were different and fitting in was about survival.

Billy turned off the beach street and weaved his way through the back alleys of several hotels and turned on to Soi Sansabai, a street lined with clothing and souvenir vendors. He pulled his scooter to a stop and hopped off. He paid the parking attendant 20 baht to park his scooter and walked along the vendor stalls. He bought shorts and sandals and a knock-off pair of Oakley wrap-around sunglasses and a baseball hat and a "No I Don't Want a Fucking Tuk-Tuk" t-shirt. He walked into the Wicked Bar and ordered a Singha on tap. He asked the woman bartender for the toilet. She pointed to the back of the bar.

Billy entered the toilet and changed out of his old clothes and into his new. He picked up his right boot and unzipped a long secret compartment on the inside. He pulled 30 one hundred US dollar bills neatly folded to the size of the compartment and tucked half of the bills into the front pocket of his shorts and the other half of the bills back into his boot. He placed his boots and clothes into a plastic bag and tied the opening in a knot. He thought it more likely that someone rummaging through the bag would take the belt with its silver rodeo buckle over his old boots. His backup stash was safer in his boot. He exited the toilet and walked back to the bar where his beer was waiting on the counter. He looked like all the other tourists in Patong Beach. The bartender watched the news on the television.

Billy's original passport photo was on the screen. The news anchor spoke in Thai but Billy caught the gist of what he was saying. The screen changed to an ID photo of Noi smiling with her red hair. *Not yet, Billy* he thought. *I can't let them catch me yet.* He continued to the bar and sat down. The bartender looked over at him. He could see the recognition in her eyes. Billy pulled five thousand baht—more than double what the bartender made in a week.

"Can you do me a favor?"

"Favor?" said the bartender.

He held up the plastic bag tied in a knot. "Will you keep this for me?"

"What in it?"

"My boots and clothes."

"How long?"

"A few days."

"Okay."

Billy handed her the bag and the five thousand baht. She tucked the bag under the counter.

"And I will give you another five thousand baht when I pick up the bag."

"Five thousand baht when pick up?"

"Yes. When I pick up. Okay?"

She nodded. Billy knew it was a risk that even with the hope of another 5 thousand baht the bartender might still contact the police and report him. There was nothing more he could do. He took a sip of his beer and reached for his billfold.

"Bill please."

"No bill. On house."

"Much obliged."

He pulled on his baseball hat and slipped on his sunglasses and exited the bar.

Eve lay on a lounge chair by the hotel pool. On her phone the Expedia app showed the booking for a flight to London with her personal information and credit card already entered. She simply needed to press book to finish the transaction. But she didn't press it.

Billy sat on the beach in a lounge chair under an umbrella. His hat was pulled down and shaded his face. His wrap-around sunglasses hid his eyes. He appeared to be just another tourist working on his tan. He fit in. But his mind was far from relaxed. He thought about the nomad and where he might have gone. It was a futile effort but he persisted.

What would I have done? he thought. Leave Thailand for starters. Why take the risk? With the police chasing me, he had time. Probably took a flight out of Phuket International. I don't think he would go far. Too cool for that. He came to Southeast Asia for a reason. He wouldn't want to just run away. Not him. Maybe just across the border. Malaysia, Myanmar, Laos or Cambodia. Maybe a little farther like Singapore, Vietnam, Indonesia or the Philippines. I suppose India and China are two more possibilities. He could easily get lost in India or China. But China and India require visas. Myanmar and Vietnam require visas too. He didn't have a visa. There wasn't enough time. Cambodia, Laos and Indonesia give visa-on-arrival to Americans. The Philippines, Malaysia, Singapore and Indonesia are visa free for Americans. So that's seven countries he could have entered without breaking a sweat. Gotta start somewhere. I'll start with those.

He heard the roar of a jet engine in the distance. A jetliner took off from Phuket International and banked north over the beach. Billy watched it fly overhead envious of its passengers. When he lowered his eyes from the sky above he saw three policemen. They patrolled the beach and checked the faces of the farang. One was armed with a tactical machine gun. He called over a beach vendor selling souvenir wristbands and picked one out and asked for the vendor to stand in front of him to block the sun so he could examine the wristband more closely. He set the wristband in his lap and tilted his head down to examine it. His face was totally hidden by the brim of his hat. The policemen passed without spotting him and moved farther down the beach. Billy paid the vendor 100 baht for the wristband. The danger was gone for now. He lay back in the lounger and closed his eyes. He hadn't slept in three days. His hand opened and the wristband slipped from his fingers and fell on the sand. He was asleep.

He dreamt of Wyoming. *Six appaloosas ran in a mountain meadow. The grass knee-high and brown from the summer sun. The big blue sky over the rocky peaks of Tetons were still patched with white glaciers. A younger Billy sat in his saddle and watched. If God ever lay claim to his greatest creation, without a doubt he would choose Wyoming.*

One of the appaloosas fell hard. Billy could see it struggling to get up thrashing the grass around it. He kicked his horse into a run toward the fallen horse. His hat flew off and rolled across the top of the grass. He reined his horse to a stop and jumped off. He saw the fallen horse was a sorrel mare with three socks and a white powdering on her buttocks. It was Snowdrop. Her leg was broken below the knee and the shattered cannon bone poked out thru the skin. The horse whinnied in pain. He looked around for help. There was none in sight. He was alone.

He heard a growl and turned to see a mountain lion waiting in the long grass. He walked to his saddle and drew his rifle, a Winchester Model 94. He loaded a bullet with a swing of the lever-action. He took aim and fired into the ground in front of the mountain lion. The mountain lion ran off. Billy walked back to the fallen horse and stood guard over it. The sun swung swiftly across the sky and set behind the Tetons. It was twilight. Another growl from the long grass. Billy turned to see a wolf waiting.

"Where are the others?" he said.

Two more growls from two more wolves.

"I thought as much."

The horse tried to get up. Her thrashing only brought more pain. She whinnied again. The wolves growled and drool dripped from their mouths. They were hungry.

"Won't be long now Snowdrop."

Billy fired another round in front of one of the wolves. It startled the wolf but he didn't move off. Hunger conquered fear. It was getting dark. The wolves' eyes shone yellow like distant campfires. Billy checked his rifle. Only one more bullet. He again scanned the horizon for help. Nothing. The wolves growled and inched forward.

"I'm sorry this happened to you."

He lowered his rifle barrel and fired into Snowdrop's head.

Billy woke to see the silhouette of a woman standing over him her back to the sun.

"Mr. Billy?"

He smiled. "Noi?"

"Noi dead. You kill Mr. Billy."

His irises slowly closed and the face came into focus.

It was Khajee from the Expat.

"Khajee no. I didn't—"

It was too late. Khajee shouted for help in Thai. Billy turned to see the three policemen patrolling the beach running toward him. One of the policeman spoke into his radio handset. Billy rolled out of the lounger and onto the sand. He climbed to his feet and ran back toward the beach road.

He reached the street and saw a police car swerve to a stop and two more policemen got out and gave chase. Billy cut back and ran along the sidewalk in front of the beach. The three police patrolling the beach paralleled him. A row of tourists on loungers blocked their way. He ran in front of the massage vendors on the beach. Another police car skidded to a stop in the street in front of him and two more policeman jumped out and ran toward him. He was trapped.

He jumped onto a massage table and ran across the tables and dodged the Thai masseurs and stepped over the farang customers lying on the tables. He passed the two policemen from the street in front of him and jumped off the tables. He crossed the street and entered an alley between a hotel and a large seafood restaurant. Two of the policemen jumped back in their patrol car and sped away hoping to cut him off on the other side of the alley. Five policemen entered the alley and chased after Billy on foot.

Billy didn't recognize the alley but he knew he was paralleling Bangla Road. At the end of the alley he could see Jung Ceylon Mall. There were lots of farang in the mall. He could mix with the crowds and maybe lose the police. But the mall had few exits and there were security guards that would help in the chase. He could get cornered. He couldn't risk it. He would have to find another way to lose them.

He exited the alley. A police car skidded to a stop directly in front of him. He turned and saw another police car speeding toward him from the opposite side of the street. A farang on a motor scooter skidded and laid down his scooter and rolled off to avoid the oncoming police car. The police car skidded to a stop just missing the scooter and rider. Billy ran to the scooter and picked it up and climbed on. He gunned the engine and jumped the street curb and drove toward the entrance of the mall. The police jumped out of their car and joined the other police from the alley chasing Billy. Billy skidded to a stop and waited until the mall's sliding glass doors opened. He gunned the engine and sped into the mall. The confused security guard at the entrance saluted him as he drove past. Moments later the policemen entered and continued the chase. One of the policemen yelled at the security guard in Thai and the security guard radioed the other security guards in the mall.

Billy raced past the storefronts and dodged shoppers jumping out of his way. He exited one section of the mall and entered the outdoor dancing fountain area. Security guards and policemen were running toward him from all sides. He crossed the open area and entered the opposite indoor section of the mall. He again dodged shoppers and sped through the mall until he reached the Big C superstore. He entered the store and sped down one of the aisles to the back of the store. He turned up a sloping ramp for shoppers with carts and rode up to the second floor. The policemen slowed and fanned out, some following Billy up the ramp and others moving to cover all the exits from the second floor to the first floor.

Billy exited Big C and slowed his scooter to a stop at the edge of the second floor balcony in the main part of the mall. He had a good view of the first floor and watched the police block the exits. An announcement over the mall sound system warned shoppers in Thai and English to stay out of the way of the police. Billy turned to see the policemen approaching him from behind. He revved his engine. The policemen slowed and moved to encircle him. One of the policemen below on the first floor moved up an escalator and walked backward to stay in a central position as the stairs continued to move upward. Billy gunned his engine and let the clutch open. The back tires on the scooter spun leaving a thick black mark on the tile floor. The scooter's tire caught hold and Billy took off toward the escalator. He rode down the opposite side of the escalator. The policeman on the escalator jumped across and grabbed Billy as he rode down the stairs and was dragged for a few moments on the rubber rail, let go and fell on the stairs behind the scooter. Billy rode off the escalator and out an exit.

Outside the mall Billy jumped the scooter off the sidewalk and back onto the street and looked around. No police in sight. He turned down a side street as the policemen from the mall exited. Billy was gone.

The nomad sat at the rooftop bar in his hotel. The boutique hotel was located in the center of

Georgetown, Malaysia, with panoramic views of Chinatown and the surrounding neighborhoods. The sun was low and the buildings below cast long shadows. Behind the hotel sat a Chinese temple with an orange tile roof and giant iron cauldrons filled with sand and burning candle-sized sticks of incense in its courtyard. There were plenty of vacant buildings in need of restoration in the Chinatown area. They were easy to spot—their walls covered with dark mold and roofs partially collapsed and doors tied closed with chain and lock. He needed one with thick walls and windows intact to dampen the sound of screaming. He wasn't in a hurry. There was plenty of time. His hunger was quenched for the moment by Noi's death.

He wondered about the cowboy Billy Gamble and made a mental note to check the internet for news of his arrest. The cowboy had been out-matched from the beginning. He just didn't know it. He should have been more cautious. The Thai were going to lock him away where he would sleep on concrete and drink the local water filled with bacteria making him shit until his ass bled. Then if he was lucky he would get shived by the member of a prison gang and die in a pool of blood and piss. He thought he should feel sympathy for the cowboy but he didn't. He hadn't felt anything for anyone since he was a child and even then it was mostly hate or fear.

He watched an American couple soak in one of two Jacuzzis on the side of the bar. The woman's fake breasts almost fell out of her American flag bikini top. They were not something the conservative Malay would appreciate. By their accent the nomad guessed the couple was from Dallas. He didn't run into many Americans in Southeast Asia especially Texans. Americans preferred London and Paris over Bangkok and Jakarta which was fine with him. Southeast Asia was more the turf of Australians and Europeans. The Europeans were tolerable but God how he loathed Australians —drunkards and ruffians without manners bred from thieves, murderers and society's outcasts. *Fucking Aussies* he thought. *Nuke 'em all*.

A young Malaysian waiter carried a tray with a cocktail and crossed the deck to the nomad.

"Your Mexican martini sir" said the waiter and set the cocktail on the table next to the nomad's lounger. The nomad billed it to his room and the waiter moved off. He sipped his drink. He liked Mexico. The girls were cheap and gullible much like the Thai. He remembered a young girl from Veracruz he met at Adelitas Bar in Zona Central in Tijuana. She couldn't have been more than sixteen and was inexperienced and a bit shy. He took her to a short-time room on the second floor of the hotel next door and raped her and gave her fifty dollars plus another five for the panties he had torn off her. She seemed happy with the money. He didn't want to kill her. It was too easy and wouldn't have fulfilled his need.

The woman in the Jacuzzi laughed a little too loudly at something her husband said. The nomad was annoyed. They were ruining his happy hour.

He considered them both for his next victims. He had never done two at the same time. He thought how he might bind and gag the husband and let him watch as he raped and tortured his wife to death. Or maybe it would be better the other way around. That would be more interesting. He wasn't homosexual but the idea of the wife watching her husband get raped by another man before he died pleased the nomad. Fear meant power. He loved to feel his victim's fear, especially when they begged.

But they were so obviously American. And Texan at that. Why come all this way to taste a thing readily available at home? He might as well eat at McDonalds. He would need to shop elsewhere but still he despised rude people almost as much as Australians. The nomad glanced over at the bar staff busy gossiping with each other on the opposite side of the rooftop. The nomad set his drink down and rose from the lounger and walked over to the Jacuzzi. The couple looked up at him and smiled.

"Good evening" said the wife.

"Nice night" said the husband.

"It will be" said the nomad. He unzipped his slacks and urinated into the Jacuzzi.

"Hey! Are you out of your fucking mind?" said the husband.

"To a degree I suppose. But aren't we all?" said the nomad and continued to arch his stream playfully. The couple climbed out of the Jacuzzi and grabbed their towels, entered the elevator and disappeared when the doors closed. *Point made* thought the nomad. He tapped twice, zipped up his slacks, sat back down on his lounger and finished his drink in peace.

CHAPTER 11

It rained hard. The streets were empty. A lone tuk-tuk driver waited and hoped for a fare. Down a side street Billy sat in the corner of a small bar well past its prime. He nursed a bottle of beer. The bar owner, a woman in her 50s, cleaned up for the night. Closing time. Billy had no place to go. He couldn't think straight and his ninth beer wasn't helping.

"Buy a girl a drink?"

Billy turned to see Eve holding an umbrella standing outside the bar in the rain.

"Sure."

Eve stepped into the bar and shook the rain off the umbrella and sat next to Billy.

"What're ya havin'?"

"Jameson."

"We closed mister" said the owner.

Billy pulled out three thousand baht. "We'll take the bottle with two glasses and some ice."

The owner nodded and went in back to get a new bottle.

"How'd ya find me?"

"It wasn't hard. More about where not to look."

The owner returned with the bottle and two glasses with ice and set them on the bar.

"You can turn out the lights. We'll just sit and talk. No trouble."

The owner nodded and turned off the lights and left.

Billy unscrewed the bottle top. Eve emptied the ice from one of the glasses into the sink. "No need to water it down."

Billy poured the whiskey and they drank.

"What are you gonna do if you find him?" Eve said.

Billy didn't respond.

"He's not just gonna confess ya know."

"I reckon he won't."

"And without a confession you're still up shit creek without a paddle."

"Looks that way."

"So why not just run like you've been doing?"

"And he walks?"

"Catchin' him ain't gonna bring her back."

"No. It won't."

"So don't be a muppet. Run."

"I can't."

"Yeah. I thought not."

They sat in silence and drank.

"So here's the deal" she said.

"There's a deal?"

"Aye and it's non-negotiable. You take it as is or I'm on the next plane back to London."

Billy nodded.

"I will help you find him. We will collect whatever evidence we can that he committed the murder."

"What if there is no evidence?"

"There is always some evidence. You just need to

know where to look."

"I'll have to trust you on that one."

"When we find him we turn him over to the police and let them sort it out."

Billy squirmed.

"You thought you'd kill 'im did ya?"

"The thought had crossed my mind."

"I won't be part of an assassination. I'm done with that."

"And if he refuses to cooperate?"

"Then you can beat the shit out of him until he does. But you can't kill him. That's a deal breaker for me. I won't be part of it unless I have your word on it."

"You'd take my word?"

"I'm not completely sure why but aye. I'll take you at your word. Should I keep going?"

Billy nodded.

"Once he is in police custody you will turn over the money you stole."

"All right."

"There's more. Before we start you're going to give me the bank accounts where you have stashed the money. All of them. And you are going to give me online access to the accounts so I can place transaction and security alerts that go to my phone. If you move the money I'll know. If you cancel the alerts I'll know. You fuck with me in any way shape or form I'll know and the deal is off. I will help the Thai police hunt you down and put you away for life. No second chances. It's one and done. Are we clear on that?"

"How do I know you won't take the money for yourself and leave me hanging?"

"You don't. But as I see it you don't have many options left."

"No I don't."

"And you're not gonna find him without me."

"Probably not."

"Last condition. If the Thai police let you off the hook for Noi's murder you go back with me and plead guilty for the charges against you in the United States."

"How long you figure I'll be in prison?"

"Five to ten years. But it'll be an American prison and if you keep out of trouble you'll probably only do half the time before they let you out on parole. You'll still be a young man."

They again sat in silence and drank.

"You really think we can find him?" said Billy.

"Aye."

"Then you got yourself a deal."

"And I have your word that you won't kill him?"

"You have my word."

It was early. Billy woke in Eve's hotel room. His back was stiff from sleeping on the tile floor with only Eve's extra pillow for his head. Eve was still asleep. He rose quietly to his feet and walked to the window. Mornings were his favorite time of day. He opened the sliding glass door and walked out onto the balcony. He could smell the wood burning stoves that the Thai used to cook their food and tea. The air was damp and hot. His shirt already stuck to his skin. He heard the whine of passing motor scooters and tuk-tuks. Nothing was open yet. Most Thai stores stayed open late but then stayed closed until 10 am. It would be several hours before he could even get a decent breakfast beyond the hotel's buffet. He looked out at the hills and the gray morning sky. Images of Noi slipped through his mind. Her naked body in the morning light. Her cute yawn as she woke. Her smile on seeing him still beside her. His sadness was deep.

He walked back into the room and opened a fresh bottle of water and poured it into the electric kettle and plugged it in. The water boiled in less than a minute, one of the great advantages of 220 volt appliances. He tore open a packet of Nescafe instant and poured it and the hot water into one of the ceramic coffee cups. Eve stirred from the smell.

"Mmmm…that smells heavenly."

"Sorry. Didn't mean to wake ya. Coffee?"

"Tea with a bit of cream please. There should be some milk in the minibar."

Billy made her tea.

"I didn't know my room came with a butler."

"24/7 service. I aim to please."

"How was the floor?"

"I've slept on worse but not by much."

"I'll get you a roll away bed for tonight."

"No. I'll get used to it after a night or two. 'Sides I don't want to raise any suspensions that ya got someone else sleeping in your room. My face is still all over the news."

"Good point. Let's keep the 'Do Not Disturb' sign on the door handle. That should keep housekeeping away. If we need any supplies, I'll get them. I can get you some extra blankets without raising any questions. I'll just tell them the air conditioning is making me cold at night."

"Much obliged."

He brought over her tea.

"You were going to give me those account numbers?"

"I'm gonna need my boots."

"Your boots?"

"I left them in the care of a bartender. The account

numbers are hidden inside my boots."

"Well then I guess I better retrieve them."

"I'd appreciate it. I feel naked without 'em."

"We can't have that."

"The bartender gets 5000 baht for holding them for me and keeping her mouth shut."

"Okay. I'll see to it. Do you think she'll keep quiet?"

"Hard to say. She won't want to get in trouble and she won't want the police to confiscate the money I gave her. That might be enough. We're gonna have to risk it if we want those account numbers."

"Then we risk it. Anything else?"

"I wouldn't mind something to eat."

"Of course. Do you think you can make do with the minibar for a few hours? I need to go to your hotel as soon as possible."

"Why is that?"

"We need a photo of the suspect. Your hotel will have a copy of his passport with a photo."

"I'll be fine. Take whatever time you need."

"Did he or any of the staff ever mention where his room was located in the hotel?"

"Yeah. The penthouse. Eight floor next to the pool. I think it's the only room on the floor."

"Good. That helps. While I'm gone I'd like you to call all the airlines serving Phuket. Google the list of airlines on my laptop. Password is gofuckyourself all lowercase no hyphens or spaces. Tell the airline agent you're Kyle and that your wallet was stolen along with your itinerary. Find out if Kyle has or had a reservation. We need to figure out where and when he's going or where he's gone."

"What if they ask me questions like where I am flying?"

"Start stuttering like you're trying to get the answer out but can't. Do that for a minute or so and they'll give you the information. If that doesn't work hang up and call back until you reach another agent then fake Tourette's syndrome. A few fuck-your-mother and go-shit-yourself and they'll give you anything to get you off the phone."

"Lady you're gonna burn in hell."

"Probably. Once you're finished with the airlines I want you to make a list of everything you remember about the suspect. Things he said. Things he did. Habits. Hobbies. Sports he watched. Family he might have mentioned. Did he drink or smoke?"

"Burbon and cigars. Cubans."

"Good. Cubans are good. Did he mention or did you see what brand?"

"Vegas Robiana I think. It had a gold R on the wrapper band."

"I've never heard of them. That's good. That means they're exotic. Exotic is easier to track. Make note of it. Don't leave anything out no matter how insignificant you might think it is. It's the details that usually make the difference."

"I can do that."

"Do you still have your phone?"

"Yeah but it's shot to shit. It got soaked when I was bouncing around in the water tank."

"Okay. I'll get you a prepaid mobile when I—wait. You were in the water truck? I looked in the tank."

"Yeah. I was under the water. I saw you looking for me."

"How long did you stay under?"

"Two minutes give or take. Growing up my brother and I had contests to see who could stay under the longest in a horse trough. It was the only thing I ever remember beating him at."

"You fuckin' cute whore, I had you cornered."

"Yeah I thought I was caught for sure. Mind if I hit the head before you take a shower?"

"I'll take a shower when I get back."

"Can ya do me a little favor?"

"I thought I was doing you a big favor?"

"You are and I appreciate it."

"So what's the little favor?"

"My boots got wet and the leather's gonna crack if I don't oil 'em soon."

"You want me to pick up oil for your boots? You realize we're tracking a killer."

"Yeah. I know it sound stupid but it's important to me."

"Well I live to make you happy Billy Gamble."

"Then you'll do it?"

"Aye for Christ's sake."

Eve put the 'Do Not Disturb' hanger on the doorknob and walked out and closed the door. Billy crossed into the bathroom.

Eve held a cup of coffee and entered the lobby bar at the Expat. A lone policeman sat behind the reception counter protecting the murder scene. Eve set her coffee on the reception counter.

"Hi. I was here last night. I found the body of the girl who was murdered. Your police captain said I should contact him if I remembered anything else about what happened. Last night I remembered a couple of things that I thought might help in your investigation so this morning I looked for the card that he had given me with his mobile phone number and I couldn't find it."

"You go police station" said policeman.

"Actually I was hoping I could just find the card. I was standing right over there when he gave it to me. And I thought if I just looked." Eve knocked over her coffee cup with her elbow spilling hot coffee in the police officer's lap.

"I'm so sorry. I'm just all thumbs today."

The young policeman cursed her in Thai and walked off toward the bathroom. Eve grabbed some napkins from the bar counter and mopped up some of the coffee. She moved behind the reception desk and went to work. She found an accordion file holding copies of the guests' passports along with the admittance forms. She pulled the paperwork for every customer. No Kyle Tanner.

"You're a smart one aren't ya? You took the only copy before the police showed up."

She looked over at the cut wires and the dusty footprint of the missing computer.

"You were very thorough. I bet you took the security camera footage too."

Eve searched through the keycard box until she found the penthouse keycard. Eve slipped over to the stairway and quickly moved up the stairs.

Eve entered the hallway on the eighth floor and moved to the door marked 801. Using the keycard she opened the door and entered and flipped on the lights. The bed was already made and the trash had been emptied. She was too late. The housekeepers had cleaned the room. A housekeeper walked in with an armful of towels.

"Where do you put the trash?"

"Trash?"

"From the trashcans in the rooms."

"You lose?"

"Aye. My birth control pills. Very important."

"Trash in bin behind hotel."

"What day do they pick up bin?"

"Today" said the housekeeper. Eve handed the housekeeper 200 baht and ran down the stairs.

Eve ran into the alley behind the hotel. A trash truck was already parked in the alley and two trash men were wheeling the hotel's dumpster onto the truck's loading forks.

"Wait" said Eve. "I want to buy the trash."

"Buy trash? said one of the trash men."

"Aye. How much for trash?" Eve pulled out 600 baht. "Three hundred baht each okay?"

"And driver?" said one of the trash men pointing to the front of the truck.

"Fine. Another 300 for driver." She handed him 900 baht. She picked out a trash liner from the bin.

"I just want these okay?"

The two men nodded and unloaded all the trashcan liners and stacked them in a pile next to the dumpster. They loaded the rest of the trash in the truck and moved off. Eve put on rubber gloves and opened each one of the trashcan liners and examined the contents. Halfway through the pile she opened a trash liner with only two items—a stat-dose container and a cigar stub with a wrapper band and a golden R on the label and the words Vegas Robiana Famoso printed in small type.

"Gotcha."

She examined the statdose container but did not recognize it. She put the cigar stub and the statdose container in two separate evidence bags and put the sealed bags in her pocket.

Down the street the iceman sat on his side-cargo tuk-tuk and watched Eve exit the alley behind the hotel and climb into a taxi. The taxi pulled away and down the street. The iceman followed.

Eve walked down the street and approached the Wicked Bar where Billy had left his clothes and boots. She stopped short and crossed over to a vender selling t-shirts and backpacks just down from the bar. She browsed through several t-shirts and asked the price for one. She glanced around the area and saw a man standing across the street in front of a 7-11. He was reading a Thai newspaper and looking up every thirty to forty seconds and studying anyone new in the area.

Could be nothing could be something she thought. She looked around the area and saw several children playing a game similar to tag in front of a pharmacy. Eve glanced around the vendor's booth and pointed to a backpack hanging overhead and asked the price.

A young girl wearing a purple backpack entered the Wicked Bar and walked up to the bartender. The young girl said something in Thai and removed an envelope from her backpack. The bartender pulled Billy's bag from underneath the bar and set it on the counter. The young girl handed the bartender the envelope and she opened it. Inside the envelope was 5000 baht. The bartender nodded and the young girl grabbed the bag from the counter, stuffed the bag into her backpack, zipped it up, slipped the backpack onto her shoulder and walked out of the bar. The bartender moved from behind the bar and signaled the man with the newspaper that the young girl with the backpack had the bag. The man with the newspaper followed the young girl down the street. Halfway down the street the young girl ducked into a pharmacy. The man stopped and watched. A few moments later a young boy wearing a purple backpack exited the pharmacy and slipped down a side street.

Inside the pharmacy Eve watched through the window as the man with the newspaper followed the young boy down the side street and disappeared. Beside Eve stood the young girl. The young girl handed Eve the purple backpack. Eve removed the bag from the backpack and slipped it into an oversized purse and handed the empty purple backpack to the young girl along with 400 baht. The young girl bowed thanks and Eve bowed back. They both exited the pharmacy. The young girl walked one way and Eve walked in the opposite direction with the oversized purse over her shoulder.

Billy sat on the balcony making the list Eve had requested. It was early afternoon and still sunny. In the distance dark clouds that would carry the afternoon rain drifted over the mountains. He thought about each time he saw the nomad and what he said and did. It was hard to stay objective. He wondered if he had ever hated any person like he truly hated this man. No not a man…a rabid animal that needed to be put down before he did any more harm. He wondered about his promise to Eve to not kill the nomad. He didn't really know what he would do when and if the time came. What was his word still worth after all he had done? Surely one more sin wouldn't matter. Billy heard the door open. He turned to see Eve walk into the room.

"How'd it go?"

Eve pulled out the evidence bag holding the cigar stub. "Was that his brand?"

Billy examined it. "That's it."

Eve pulled out the second evidence bag with the empty statdose container and handed it to Billy. "Any idea what that is? I found it in the same trashcan liner as the cigar stub."

"No idea. Some kinda container for something the size and shape of a rifle bullet."

"A rifle bullet?"

"A 30-30 casing is about that size. But I ain't never seen any kind of ammo box like that especially not one that only held two bullets."

"When you have time see if you can come up with a photo match on Google."

"Will do."

She pulled out two tin foil-wrapped shawarmas. "Room service."

"Much obliged."

"They're shawarmas. I didn't know if you ate lamb so I got you chicken."

"That'll be fine. I'd eat barbecued snake at this point."

Billy tore off the foil from one and ate half in one bite. Eve pulled out a new cellphone and handed it to him. "It's prepaid."

"You're kinda like Santa Claus."

"San Nioclás. I'm Irish."

She pulled out the bag holding his clothing and boots. "There's also a bottle of shoe conditioner in there. Thai aren't big on boots."

"It'll do fine. Did you have any trouble picking it up?"

"There was man watching the bar. Nothing I couldn't handle."

Billy dropped the shawarma on a side table and pulled his boots from the bag. He reached inside the left boot and unzipped a hidden pocket sewn into the side of the boot and pulled out a laminated strip of paper with writing on it and handed it to Eve.

"Those are the banks and account numbers. I'll give you the online codes whenever you're ready for 'em."

"Thanks. So how did you do with the airlines?"

"Not good. I checked with every airline in Phuket and Krabi. None of them have any information on a Kyle Tanner. Do you think he could still be here?"

"Doubtful. Why take the risk? He set you up to give himself time to escape. Staying in Thailand would defeat that purpose. He's probably using a second passport under another name. That's gonna make our job a lot tougher. How is the list of details coming along?"

"I'm working on it."

"You said you got in a fight with him."

"Yeah. We were playing pool at the Tiger Club on Bangla Road."

"Were there any witnesses?"

"A waitress and two bouncers."

"Did you happen to notice if there were any security cameras?"

"No but it's a pretty big place. I bet they have 'em."

"What day was it?"

"It was the day before I found Noi's body."

"And the time?"

"It was early. The club had just opened. Probably a little after eight."

"Okay. I'm gonna check it out. While I'm gone I want you to search Thai news websites. Let's see if there are any other similar murders."

"You think he's done this before?"

"It's possible. Start with Phuket then work your way through the top ten cities in Thailand according to population."

Eve exited. Billy pulled the money out of his boot and stripped down to his underwear and slipped on his jeans and pulled on his boots.

"I missed ya."

He sat back down at the laptop and searched for Thai news websites.

CHAPTER 12

The nomad rode a motor scooter along Pengkalan Weld—a street that ran along the water separating the island of Penang from mainland Malaysia. He pulled over and studied a map of the area. He focused on a collection of several piers called the Clan Jetties. The jetties were neighborhoods constructed on pier pilings to house Chinese immigrants in the 19th and early 20th centuries. Each jetty was named after a clan from the seven providences in China. Immigrants fleeing the oppressive Chinese mandarins and overwhelming poverty arrived in Malaysia and immediately moved into their clan's respective jetty for protection and support. Nowadays the clan jetties were a tourist attraction filled with restaurants and souvenir shops.

Normally the nomad had no interest in tourist sites but the idea of multiple piers with hundreds of buildings and warehouses intrigued him. Some would likely be abandoned or waiting to be repaired. He pulled the motor scooter back out into traffic and rode along the water until he found the pier he was seeking.

The nomad walked out onto the pier. The old boards creaked and wobbled as he stepped. At the end of the pier he looked back at the seven clan jetties. The buildings and houses on the piers were too close together. Even late at night someone might hear a scream. No need to take that kind of risk. He would keep looking. He again pulled out his map and studied the area. He found something of interest. He looked up from the map and searched the area. In the distance off by itself the nomad spotted another pier and a rusting cargo ship long since abandoned listing to one side in the thick mud left by the outgoing tide. There was little around it in the way of buildings or houses. He liked the look of it and walked back to his motor scooter.

He drove along the street until he came to an area of abandoned warehouses and the pier holding the ship. He pulled over and parked his motor scooter. He walked past the abandoned warehouses and came to the edge of the pier. Some of the boards were missing and others were loose. He would need to be careful but he also saw the advantage. The disrepair of the pier would keep others away and give him the privacy that he desired. He walked out onto the pier and toward the abandoned ship laying alongside. As he walked he looked down through the hole from a missing board and saw several crabs scurrying across the black mud below. The smell of sewage mixed with rotting fish was pungent. There were boards bleached grey and warped stacked in a pile next to a large hole in the pier like someone had tried to repair the pier but then gave up long ago.

The ship was an old American freighter—probably a leftover from the Vietnam War that found its way to Malaysia. The ship listed to the port side and was deep in the mud so the hull no longer rose or lowered with the tide. The weight of the ship leaning against the pier had uprooted several of the pilings making the pier unstable. He saw the gangway hanging over the edge of the main deck ten feet above the pier and there was no other way on or off the ship. *Good* he thought. *No squatters living aboard.* There was an old frayed rope tied to a pier cleat that once held the ship in place before it snapped from a storm. Another piece of the rope hung from the aft deck. He examined the rope on the pier in hopes that it might provide a way onto the ship. The rope crumbled in his hand as he unwound it from the cleat. He immediately ruled out the rope as useful.

He looked around on the pier for some way to get on the ship and saw another cleat on the opposite side of the pier with a rope attached and leading over the side. He walked over and pulled the rope up. It was attached to an old tire used as a boat bumper. The rope was fairly new and in good condition. He untied the rope and let the tire fall into the mud below. He again looked around and saw the top of a broken piling with a rusted carriage bolt hanging loose. He pried the bolt from the rotten wood and tied one end of the rope around the bolt to give it some weight and act as a makeshift grappling hook.

He crossed back over the pier to the freighter and tossed the end of the rope with the carriage bolt up to the gangway until it wrapped around the railing. He pulled on the rope. The gangway inched over the side until the balance of its weight was over the edge and it tipped. One end of the gangway came down hard on the pier and broke several boards. The other end of the gangway remained on the edge of the main deck on the ship. He gathered several old boards from the pile of repair boards next to the hole in the pier and used the boards to cover the hole that the gangplank had made in the pier. The gangplank was secure. He climbed aboard the ship.

The nomad checked the ship's deck for stability before putting his full weight on it. It was old and rusted but it held. The ship's deck was tilted to the port side but level enough to walk on. The forward cargo hold was sealed shut. He climbed a ladder to the bridge tower. He looked through several portholes but it was too dark to see anything. He walked over to a partially open door hatch. He pulled and yanked until the rusted hinges gave way. He opened the door enough for him to fit through.

He entered a hallway and walked to another open hatchway. He looked inside. It was the crew quarters. The air was stale and smelled musty. Most of the bunk mattresses had been stolen long ago. Those that remained were torn beyond repair. He moved down the hallway and entered another hatchway. It was the galley and had been stripped clean of food, pots, pans, plates and utensils. A dented coffee maker lay on its side. The lock on the standing freezer had been broken off and the door was partially open. He looked inside. Although faint it still smelled of rotten food and mold. Two more hatchways brought him into the head and the wheelhouse with broken window glass and navigational charts strewn across the floor. The nomad exited the hallway, walked toward the stern and overlooked the stern cargo hold. It was open. He climbed down a ladder to the rear deck.

The nomad looked into the open hatch of the stern cargo hold. It was empty and dark. The boom on the mizzenmast was rusted in place directly over the open cargo hatch. The cable from the cargo winch hung down from the boom with a hook on the end. He looked around and found a piece of broken cargo net. He threw one end of the net onto the hook and tugged hard. It held. The cable and boom were solid and could still take a considerable amount of weight. He climbed down the rusted stairs leading into the hold. At the bottom of the hold he looked up at the opening and at the cable with its hook hanging overhead.

Yes he thought. *This will do nicely.*

Eve walked down Bangla Road. It was like a boom town that had changed into a ghost town when the sun rose. A few street vendors selling sunglasses milled around hoping to catch a farang or two passing through from the beach to their hotel. Their sales pitch was always the same. They would compliment a passerby on his sunglasses and ask to see them. Once they had the sunglasses they wouldn't give them back until the passerby tried on the vendor's sunglasses and heard the entire sales pitch on why the vendor's sunglasses were superior. It was annoying as hell but it worked and they sold a lot of sunglasses.

Eve crossed the empty street and entered the Tiger Club. The cleaning crew swept the floors and wiped down the sticky bar counters. Beer distributors restocked each of the bars and carried out thousands of empty beer bottles tucked away in their original boxes. She studied the ceiling and saw several security cameras and approached a man checking off the cases of beer brought in by each distributor and asked for the head of security. He pointed her to the room in the back of the club.

She walked to the room and heard a man yelling in Thai. She knocked. She heard something in Thai that sounded like it could be "come in" and she entered the room. The head of security sat behind a desk and was on the phone. He was angry with whomever was on the other end. He saw Eve and motioned for her to sit. She sat. He hung up the phone. Eve introduced herself.

"How I help you?" said the head of security.

"There was a fight here a few nights ago."

"There fight every night. Farang drink too much."

"This was in the pool room around 8 pm. One of the farang broke a cue stick."

"Yes yes. I remember."

"I would like to talk with the waitress and the two bouncers who stopped the fight. I would also like to look at the security camera footage of the fight."

"Security camera footage property of club."

"I don't want to take the footage. I just want to see it."

"You lawyer? You sue club?"

"I am not a lawyer and I don't want to sue your club."

"I very busy. No time."

"Of course. I should pay you for your time."

Eve pulled out 1000 baht. The man gave her an incredulous look.

"I head of security not bartender."

"I'm sorry. I didn't mean to offend you."

She pulled out another 2000 baht.

"It will only take a few minutes. I promise."

He nodded and took the money. He picked up the phone and called his assistant. "Girl and two bouncers come at 6" he said. "You talk then."

The assistant appeared at the door. The two men conversed in Thai.

"You go with this man and he show you video."

Eve got up and followed the assistant to the security monitoring room. She sat down at a console with several monitors. The assistant showed her how to use the system. She found the correct file by time and date and reviewed the footage from the pool room. After a few minutes she found the footage of the fight. It was a bad angle and didn't show the nomad's face clearly.

"Do you have more angles?"

The assistant looked confused.

"More security cameras of this?"

The assistant nodded and pulled up several more files. Eve reviewed the new footage until she found a fairly clear shot of the nomad.

"Is this connected to the internet?"

Again the assistant looked confused.

"Wifi. This have wifi?" she asked.

He nodded.

"Can you bring up Google?"

He nodded and brought up Google on one of the screens. Eve opened her Google drive account and transferred a copy of the file footage to her cloud drive.

The afternoon rain rolled in right on schedule. Eve returned to her hotel by tuk-tuk. She paid the driver 300 baht and ran inside the lobby to keep from getting wet. Motorbike taxis were the fastest and cheapest way around Phuket because the drivers could weave through streets crowded with pedestrians coming or going to the beach. But motorbike taxis were also very dangerous and would often get in accidents usually because the passenger on the back didn't understand when to lean into a curve or wasn't hanging on when the driver goosed the throttle and they flipped off the back. Taxi cars and minivans were the safest but were often stuck in traffic jams and weren't able to take advantage of back alleys and shortcuts. Tuk-tuks were a good compromise between safety and speed. The drivers were still crazy and wove in and around pedestrians and cars at high speeds but at least the passengers had a steel-tube cage to protect them.

Billy sat on the balcony and rubbed his boots with the conditioner and watched the rain come down in sheets pounding on the tin roofs of the buildings and houses below like a snare drum. Eve entered the room and walked out the open sliding door to the balcony.

"Are your boots gonna survive?"

"They're cowboy boots. They'll survive."

"Good to know. You finished with your homework?"

"Yeah. Turns out there's a lot of murders in Thailand. Drunken husband beats on his wife and his wife hits him in the head with a frying pan. I did find two new stories that could be him. Both victims were bargirls. One in Chang Mai four months ago and one in Bangkok three weeks ago. Both bodies were found in suitcases."

"That sounds like our guy."

"So he's a serial killer?"

"Seems like it. It's also possible he hasn't limited his killing to Thailand. He could have been killing and traveling from country to country for years and nobody would know as long as he kept moving."

"A nomad" said Billy.

"Yeah. A nomad" said Eve. "This certainly changes things."

"In what way?"

"We can pretty much bet he's gonna kill again…and soon."

"Why?"

"Four months then three weeks and then three days ago. His cycle is shortening. Serial killers don't just kill randomly. They do it to satisfy a growing feeling or need like an itch that has to be scratched. They more they try to fight it the more the feeling grows until they are overwhelmed. Once they kill the feeling subsides sometimes for months or even years until the feeling grows again. It's an endless cycle. But with this guy the cycle is shortening which means he probably doesn't feel fully satisfied even after he kills and his need continues to grow stronger so he needs to kill more often. Kinda like a heroin addict. There is never enough."

"I knew he was batshit crazy when I met him."

"And yet you played pool with him. Why is that?"

Billy hesitated. "He was an American. I wanted his passport."

"But you look nothing like each other."

"Actually we do where it counts. Biometrics. The distance between facial features. They're hard to fake and US immigration computers can pick 'em up. He and I are a very close match."

"How did you know that your biometrics matched?"

"I can just see that kinda thing in my mind. Weird. I know."

"You're a super matcher?"

"If that's what you call it."

"That's what the intelligence community calls them" she said. "Super matchers can pick out a suspect in a crowd faster than a computer and with more accuracy. I've heard about guys like you but I've never met one."

"Well congrats now you have. So how did you do at Tiger Club?"

"Good. I talked to the waitress and the two bouncers. They'll collaborate your story about your fight with the suspect. Plus we have footage of the actual fight from the security cameras. I'm sending a few frames to a friend of mine. He'll enhance the images and send 'em back. We should end up with a pretty good photo of the suspect."

"You keep calling him the suspect. He's not a suspect.

He's Noi's killer."

"Sorry. It's just police talk. Old habits die hard."

"I didn't mean to snap at you like that. I'm not used to being caged up like this. It makes ornery. I know you're doing your best and I appreciate it."

"You're probably just hungry."

"I could eat."

"I'll order room service. What'll ya have?"

"Steak medium rare."

"Ya know they have a lovely chicken pad Thai."

"Steak medium rare and a baked potato with sour cream and butter if they got it."

"Well then—it's your heart."

Eve walked inside to place the order for room service.

"Damn right it is" said Billy.

Billy and Eve sat on the floor with their backs up against the bed eating their dinner. Eve had a Thai chicken salad and Billy ate his steak and potato.

"You said old habits die hard." said Billy.

"I did." said Eve.

"You were a cop?"

"Of sorts. I was a constable in the RUC during the

Troubles."

"The Troubles?"

"The war in Northern Ireland between Unionists and Nationalists. Over 3600 died and 50000 were maimed mostly from bombings. We shot them. They bombed us. My unit in the RUC was tasked with hunting down the members of Sinn Fein. They were smart fellows and believed in what they were doing but so did we."

"And when you found 'em?"

"We killed 'em. We had convinced ourselves it was a matter of survival and we had the law on our side. But it was murder plain and simple. And I'll never be part of it again."

Billy decided not to push her anymore. They sat in silence eating.

"Why did you take the money?" said Eve.

"You don't beat around the bush much do ya?"

"What's the point? Were ya trying to save the family farm or something?"

"No. It was too late for that. We lost our ranch a few years back after my father passed."

"So what was it? Were ya poor?"

"No not at that point. I went to work for a gas lease broker. Turned out I was pretty good at it. Analyzing land values and oil deposits."

"You were good with numbers?"

"Yeah. It was during the shale boom. Folks needed someone that could tell 'em what their land was really worth when they found oil on it. I kinda got a reputation for fair dealing so the families would hire our firm to represent 'em when dealing with the big oil companies that wanted to lease their oil rights. I was doing pretty good until I found out our broker was tampering with the oil surveys. He was using a shill to buy the leases based on the fake surveys then re-selling them to the oil companies based on the real data. He was making millions."

"So you decided to play Robin Hood?"

"Somethin' like that. I don't know what I was thinkin'. I was just mad."

"But you didn't return the money to the families."

"I tried. But any funds I transferred to the families were confiscated by the FBI and returned to the broker. I was stuck in limbo. I didn't feel right about giving the money back to the bastard who stole it and I couldn't give it to the families who deserved it."

"You understand that my client paid the insurance claim made by your broker?"

"I do. And I also understand that as long as that money is not returned to your client, my broker will not be able to get insurance or cheat anyone else."

"So, my client is collateral damage in your little war?"

"I suppose. Anyway it wasn't long before things sort of spun out of control. So I left."

"To Thailand?"

"Not at first. Like most desperados I went south down to Mexico then Central and South America. Spent a year just traveling around. Saw some pretty good stuff. Lots of Aztec and Mayan ruins. Beautiful beaches. Went to Carnival in Rio. Hiked through Patagonia. Spent a couple of days with some Gauchos riding herd. Now they know how to make a steak. Took a boat up the Amazon. The people were really nice. Food was good."

"Then where?"

"Africa. Did one of them photo safaris. Didn't have a camera but it was still pretty good. Saw a pack of lions take down a giraffe while she was giving birth. That was kinda sad but beautiful in its own right. South Africa was nice along the coast. Went up to Zululand and saw a reed dance with over a thousand Zulu maidens. Beautiful people. Very proud. I made my way up to Zambezi and saw Victoria Falls then Egypt and saw the pyramids. It's funny. I thought they'd be out in the middle of the desert but they were just right there on the edge of Cairo. I walked to 'em from my hotel."

"How many countries have you visited?"

"Don't know. Lost count. I suppose I could figure it out if I sat down with a map."

"Guess."

"60 maybe 70."

"You've seen one-third of the world."

"Something like that. Still a lot more to see. But I won't be getting the chance will I?"

"Not for a while. But you're still young."

"I don't feel young anymore. Traveling's interesting and even fun sometimes but it wears ya down. Some days ya just wanna stop and catch your breath. But ya can't cuz there's always some train ya gotta catch or some temple ya just gotta see at sunrise."

"Most people would give their right eye to see a fraction of what you've already seen."

"Maybe. But what wouldn't I give for a couple of days fishing on the Wind River. Just standing in the current in my waders watching the water go by without worrying about where it's going or what time it's gonna get there."

"A cowboy without a range?"

"I suppose."

"It was your choice to take the money and run."

"Yeah. They say ya pick your own hell. Well I sure as shit picked mine."

"We all do."

Again they ate in silence.

"So how did you find me in Tokyo and then again here in Phuket?" Billy said.

"Trade secret. Like a magician. I can't tell ya."

"Bullshit. What's it matter now? Ya got me. I'm not going anywhere."

"Okay. You made money transfers to your ex-wife at the same time each month. Alimony I'm guessing. Although there was no court order. That was a bit strange."

"She never would have told you that."

"No she didn't."

Billy thought for a moment. "You got to someone at her bank."

"I did. A teller with a gambling problem. A state lottery addict. Three hundred dollars would get me an emailed copy of any transfer you made into your ex-wife's account. The transfer showed the originating Western Union office. I figured that's where you were at."

"That was pretty sneaky."

"Thank you."

"It wasn't alimony" said Billy.

"Child support? But there was no court order. I checked that too."

"I didn't need a court order."

"So let me get this straight. You steal $4.2 million dollars and yet you feel guilty enough about having a kid that you send your ex-wife child support each and every month?"

"Just because my child has a thief for a father doesn't mean she should suffer."

"A daughter?"

"Yes."

"She got a name?"

"Hazel."

"Oh that's a bit cruel isn't it?"

"Fuck you."

"I'm just saying."

"It was my grandmother's name. Okay?"

"Men should never be allowed to name their children. They're way too emotional."

"I'm gonna be glad when we catch him and this is over."

"Stop your sulking Billy. Hazel's a fine name. Besides it's not just about catching him. To get you off the hook we have to prove that he did it. Even after we find him we're gonna need to follow him until he makes a mistake."

"You mean until he kills someone else."

"God willing we'll stop him before he does it again but we can't have him arrested without evidence. The police don't like arresting foreigners. It's bad for tourism."

"Chiang Mai, Bangkok, Phuket. He's heading south" said Billy.

"So what are you thinking?"

"He didn't have time to get a visa. Malaysia, Singapore and Indonesia don't require visas for Americans. They're where I would go."

"Maybe. But you're somewhat sane. This guy has a major personality defect. We shouldn't assume he will act rationally or that his motivations are logical. Still I like the pattern. Any idea on cities?"

"Singapore's easy. The entire country is basically one big city. Malaysia has Kuala Lumpur, Penang, Langkawi, Kuching and maybe four or five other possibilities. Indonesia is bigger and has more people and more to see but still there's only so many places a foreigner would probably go. Ubad on Bali, Jakarta, Yogyakarta, and Lombok plus another four or five."

"Twenty cities. That's a lot of ground."

"Yeah but he likes bargirls so he's gonna be staying in or around the red light districts in each of those cities."

"True. That helps once we find the actual city he is in."

"So how do we narrow it down?" said Billy.

"We need to create a profile."

"How do we do that?"

"Creating a profile is like building a box and then filling it with information. The walls of the box are his personality. You start with his major personality traits then fill in the details of his day-to-day life, his hobbies, his preferences, his habits—any information we can find that paints an accurate picture of who he is. We'll use the list you made of your conversations to start building the box. Once the box is complete, we go after his information trail. His real name would be a good start plus any aliases he might be using. Then email addresses, phone numbers, social security number, bank accounts, credit cards. Once the box is full we'll know everything about him and how to track him. Plus we'll have a good chance at predicting what he'll do next."

"How are we gonna find any information when we don't even know his real name?"

"There's always a way. We'll find it. We don't have the resources or the advantages that the police have but we don't have to play by their rules either. We need a break so let's make one."

CHAPTER 13

Billy lay awake on the floor. He looked over at Eve asleep on the bed. He pulled his boots on and rose to his feet. He walked to the door and pulled the hotel room key card from the power switch, opened the door and looked out in the hallway. Nobody in sight. He exited the room and slowly closed the door until it clicked shut. Inside the room the air conditioner switched off.

Billy took the stairs down to the lobby and slipped out a side door without anyone noticing him. It was raining hard. He walked into an alley leading to the next street and kept out of the light and away from passing motor scooters.

Billy walked into a small bar, sat down in the corner and ordered a beer. He squeezed the rain out of his hair and off his face. He drank his beer in silence and ordered another and drank it. He finished the second beer and signaled the bartender for the bill. He paid the bill and left the bar and headed back the way he came again keeping out of sight as much as possible. He walked back into the alley near the hotel. Something hit him in the back of the head and he collapsed unconscious.

Billy woke a few minutes later to see the iceman standing over him with the neck of a broken beer bottle in his hand. The iceman knelt down and placed the broken shards of the bottle against Billy's neck.

"What the fuck?" said Billy.

"You kill Noi" said the iceman.

Billy tried to focus. His head was still spinning from the blow.

"I know you. You deliver ice to Expat bar" said Billy.

The iceman pressed the shards into Billy's neck drawing blood.

"Boy you're pissing me off" said Billy.

Billy grabbed the iceman's hand and twisted the broken bottle away from his neck, rolled into the iceman's arm and pulled the iceman down. The iceman was no match for a man Billy's size and strength. Billy was now on top of the iceman. He slammed the iceman's hand onto the ground and forced him to release the broken bottle.

"You kill Noi" said the iceman. "Now you kill me."

"I'm not gonna kill you." Billy climbed off and let

him up. The iceman crawled to the opposite side of the alley and leaned against the wall and held his bruised wrist.

"I didn't kill her. I loved her" said Billy.

"She no love you. She love me" said the iceman.

"What are you talking about?"

"We married."

"Noi was married?"

"Yes. Me marry her. She meet you and leave me. Now she dead. You kill."

"Stop saying that. I didn't kill her."

"We have son together. I take care him. She pay money every month."

"Noi had a son? She never said anything."

"Farang no like women with baby. She no say she have."

"I didn't know. I wouldn't care if she had told me she had a son. I have a daughter."

"She pay rent and food for me and boy."

"Is that what this is? A shakedown?"

"Noi dead. I no have money pay rent."

"Yeah yeah. I get it. You could've just asked. You didn't need to hit me with a bottle."

"Farang give money to Thai woman not Thai man."

"Okay. How much is rent?"

"Nine thousand baht."

Billy pulled out his billfold and peeled off nine thousand baht and handed it to the iceman. "What's your name?"

"You tell police I hit you with bottle?"

"No. I send you money each month. I need your name so Western Union knows who to give it to. If boy gets sick or needs clothes or needs money for school, you email me. I'll send more money."

"You do that?"

"Yes. I will do that. For Noi."

Eve awoke in a sweat. The room was hot.

"Billy did you turn off the air conditioner?"

No response.

"Billy?"

She flipped the light switch. Nothing happened. She jumped up and ran to the power switch. The keycard was gone.

"Oh shit."

She grabbed her pants and pulled them on. She heard the door lock click. The door opened and Billy bare waist up walked in holding his shirt to the back of his head and put the keycard back in the power switch. The air conditioner and lights came on.

"Where in the hell have you been?"

"I went for a couple of beers."

"You're an idiot. If someone had recognized you."

"Yeah I know. I just had to get out for a few minutes. I was going stir crazy. I figured it was raining and no moon. No one was going to see me."

Billy pulled the shirt from the back of his head. It was soaked with blood.

"Jesus. What the hell happened to you?"

"A guy hit me with a beer bottle."

She walked over to take a look. "Why?"

"Long story."

"You're gonna need stitches."

"I've had worse. I'll be fine."

"No you won't be fine. It's gonna keep bleeding."

Eve crossed to the bathroom and pulled out a sewing kit and a pair of toe nail clippers from her toilet kit and grabbed a towel.

"What are you planning on doing with that?"

"We can't take ya to the hospital."

"So you're gonna do it?"

Eve pulled out a needle and thread and threaded the needle. "We have no choice."

"Have you ever stitched up someone before?"

"No. But I made my own dresses in high school. Besides I figure I'm not gonna learn any younger."

"I don't like this."

"Neither do I. I suggest you make a quick trip to the minibar before we get started."

Billy opened the minibar and pulled out several bottles of liquor and drank the first one.

"Don't drink too many. It'll thin your blood and you'll just bleed more." Eve motioned to a chair. "Sit."

Billy sat and drank another bottle.

"That needle and thread don't look very sterile."

"Oh they're not. I assure you."

"And that doesn't worry ya?"

"Me? No. It's not my head they are going in."

"You're a real character aren't ya? My uncle John was a character. Man could lie like the devil and look ya straight in the eye the whole time. He'd start a story with something small then work his way up to being the King of Moravia. He always said the key to a lie was to always start with the truth."

"You're stalling."

"Hell yes I'm stalling. Can you blame me? Ah shit. Get on with it."

"Hand me the vodka."

Billy handed her the mini bottle of vodka. Eve poured some vodka on the wound and used the towel to soak up the run-off. She poured more vodka on the needle and thread and went to work and stitched his wound.

"Just so we're clear, if you leave again the deal is off and I'm gonna turn you over to the Thai police myself. Do ya understand?"

"I understand."

"So this long story?"

"I met Noi's husband."

"Noi had a husband?"

"And a son."

"And you didn't know?"

"No. I didn't."

"Poor child. Growing up without his mother."

"I can't help but feel like this is all my fault."

"That's because it is. Ya can't expect to have no consequences for your actions. Even if the consequences are unrelated, Karma will always catch up. It's how the world stays in balance."

"Great. That makes me feel better."

"It's not my job to make you feel better."

"You can be a real bitch sometimes ya know."

"Maybe but you might not want to be calling the woman sewing the back of your head together a bitch. If you know what I mean."

"Sorry."

Eve finished the last stitch, tied it off and used the toenail clippers to cut the remaining thread.

"Good as new. I'll get you some proper stringent and some antibiotics tomorrow when the stores open."

"Much obliged."

"So does this change things for you?"

"You mean catching 'er killer?"

"Yeah."

"No."

"Good. I'd hate to be wasting my time."

The nomad stood looking up at the Sri Mahamariamman Temple in the middle of Georgetown. The tower was covered with overly colorful sculptures of Hindu gods and goddesses. He didn't see what all the fuss was about. It looked like something an unsupervised child would make out of Play Dough. He walked back to the entrance and retrieved his loafers from the old lady who watched shoes. She held out her hand for a tip. *Another scam* he thought. He walked off.

The nomad stood in a crowded cable car as it climbed Penang Hill. It was hot. The people around him smelled of sweat and strange spices. A fat Chinese woman taking a video with her phone backed up toward him. He never cared much for the Chinese because they had little regard for personal space and he loathed the overweight. He pulled his kamabit from his pocket and unsheathed the blade. He held the knife in a reverse grip and hid the blade against his wrist with the point sticking outward. The woman moved backward into him and into the point of the blade. It stuck her and she let out a yelp and turned around. He looked down at her expressionless. She put her hand over the puncture wound. He had drawn blood. Not much but enough to express his opinion. She moved away.

The cable car reached the top of the hill. The nomad stepped out of the cable car and walked up the hillside and on to an observation platform with an impressive view of the entire area. The city below was covered in light smog giving it a dreamy look. In the distance over a hundred cargo ships crowded the bay in front of the port. Young couples and families took selfies with the city as the background. He could see Georgetown and what he thought was his hotel. He bought an ice cream from a vendor and walked farther up the hill. There was another ornate Hindu temple on top of the hill. *More Play Dough* he thought.

The nomad stepped off the hop-on-hop-off bus and walked up another hill to Kek Lok Si, the largest Buddhist temple in Malaysia. The path to the temple was lined with souvenir shops and food vendors, none of which interested the nomad and blocked any chance of a breeze to cool him down. He reached the turtle pond and looked down at hundreds of turtles stepping on each other and looking up as if begging for food. He spat into the water and several turtles went after it. He climbed farther up the path and entered an inclined elevator that carried him up the rest of the hill. He stepped off the lift and saw the Kuan Yin statue and stone-carved pavilion towering above him. The statue looked out over Penang and the sea beyond. The goddess of mercy—a poor excuse for veneration. Mercy was for the weak.

CHAPTER 14

The nomad entered a modern shopping mall. Like most Asian buildings the mall was tall with 7-stories and the public spaces were filled with elaborate decorations and kiosks made use of every meter of floor space. The nomad wore a wide brimmed hat and tilted it slightly to hide his face as he passed security cameras. He strolled past several store windows displaying the latest western fashions on Asian-style mannequins. He settled in front of a cutlery shop window that displayed hundreds of knifes and swords. Some knives were cheap fashion blades and others were made of fine German steal. The nomad entered the cutlery shop and an older British man approached.

"How may I be of service?"

"I'm looking for a boning knife."

"Steel or ceramic?"

"Steel. Full tang and partial bolster. Curved butt. Double taper with an Eastern edge."

The British man pulled several knifes from a case and laid them on a felt cloth on top of a glass display case and pointed to each knife as he described it.

"The Henckels Pro-S. The Shun Classic. The Global G-21. And my personal favorite the Wusthof Classic 6-inch."

The nomad picked up each knife and examined its construction and finish. He felt the balance and the weight. He started with the Henckel Pro-S knife.

"Henckels Professional S knife comes in a 5.5-inch blade. It's a little shorter than the others but well within reason. The blade is made of Friodurf high carbon stainless steel and is hand honed. The handle is black Novodur. It's perfect for separating the delicate meat such as the breast from the bone."

Unimpressed, the nomad set the knife down and picked up the next knife.

"The Shun Classic has a 6-inch blade and is made from 32 layers of stainless damask steel. It is extremely hard and its blade's sharpness is second to none. The Shun knife gets its unique character by refining the natural beauty of the damask steel grain. Each knife is a piece of art. If I need to carve through a lot of ligament or muscle this is the knife I'd choose."

The nomad set the knife down and picked up the next knife.

"The Global G-21 boning knife features a slightly longer 6 1/4-inch blade and unlike the other knives is constructed entirely from one piece of vanadium stainless steel making it extremely durable. The dimples crafted into the handle provide exceptional traction. I find it to be slightly stiffer than the other knifes but is still classified as flexible. The knife can easily cut through even the toughest material like collagen, membrane, tendon or even small bone."

"It doesn't feel natural."

"It does take some getting used to but customers rave about it. Once they have owned one they become extremely loyal and won't even consider any other brand."

The nomad set the knife down and picked up the final knife.

"I prefer the Wusthof because it is extremely sharp and will hold its edge through an entire session of carving. It's also very flexible which will allow you to remove any skin with ease. There is a slight curvature in the handle that allows for an overall better grip and more control when carving difficult areas around a joint or spine. It's more expensive than the others but it will last a lifetime and then some."

"It has a good feel to it" said the nomad.

"Yes. Always an important factor when boning. Much more enjoyable."

The nomad tossed the knife from hand to hand and flipped the knife upside down switching back and forth between different styles of grips. "Yes. This one is good. I'll take it."

"I am sure you will be pleased with your purchase. I love mine."

"I'll need a honing steel and a whetstone."

The British man set his recommendations on the counter.

"Wusthof makes a nice twelve-inch steel with a slip-resistant handle and an oversized guard. As far as the whetstone I prefer Naniwa. They have a set of three with a grid 600, 2000 and 5000. I have witnessed the factory representative slice a human hair in mid-air after sharpening a Santoku knife with the 5000 grid. It was quite impressive I assure you."

"Okay. I'll take them."

"Excellent. I will include a small bottle of purified water for the whetstones at no additional cost. The stones are natural so you do not need to soak the stones. Just add a few drops of water to each stone right before use."

The British man set a small plastic bottle of water with a red cap covering the dropper with the other items on the counter and rang up the purchases. The nomad paid with Malay ringgit. The British man placed the knife in a fitted cardboard box and sealed the box shut with some ribbon so that it couldn't accidentally open. He wrapped the honing steel in heavy paper and folded the end covering the point closed and sealed it with some tape. He opened the box of whetstones to ensure that all three stones were present along with the sharpening block. He sealed the box shut with tape. He placed the knife box, the wrapped honing steel, the small bottle of water and the whetstone box in a stiff paper bag with string handles and handed it to the nomad.

"You know your blades. Are you a professional chef?"

"No. It's more a hobby but I like a good filet" said the nomad. He turned and walked out.Billy lay flat on the floor, his head propped up with a rolled-up towel. Eve sat at the desk checking her email. She glanced over at Billy staring at the ceiling.

"How's your head?"

"Feels like someone hit me over the head with a bottle."

"Did ya take the antibiotics I brought ya?"

"Nope. I decided to let it get infected and commit suicide."

"That's a lousy way to kill yourself."

"Probably but I don't take drugs and I don't have a gun."

"You could choke yourself to death."

"I'll consider it."

Eve opened an email attachment. An enhanced still from the Tiger Club security video came up on her laptop's screen. The photo was a good likeness of the nomad. She picked up the laptop and showed it to Billy so he didn't have to get up.

"May I assume that's our man?"

"Assume nothing. That's him."

She set the laptop back down on the desk, rose from the chair and crossed to the door.

"Where you heading?"

"I am going to make some copies on the hotel's printer. Sit tight. I'll just be a few minutes."

"You don't need your laptop?"

"The cloud, love. The cloud."

She left. Billy rose from the floor and opened the minibar. Slim pickings. He grabbed a beer and held it to the swollen wound on his head to stop the throbbing. He glanced over at the plastic statdose container in the evidence bag and picked it up and turned it around to study it.

"What the hell are ya?"

He looked closer at the inside of the lid. There was a patent warning label with a patent number. He sat down at the laptop and opened a Google search window and typed in the word patent. A website for patent searches appeared in the list of search results. He clicked on the website. On the main page was a search box asking for a patent number. He entered the patent number into the website search box. After a moment the patent page appeared including the name of the company that was awarded the patent— Roxbury Laboratories Inc. Billy entered the company name in a new search window and selected the product catalog on the main page. The plastic container appeared on an online brochure for the injection version of Sumatriptan—a medication for migraine headaches. He read through the brochure.

He pulled up Google Maps and typed Patong Beach Pharmacy in the search box. A list of pharmacies with addresses popped up. He selected and copied the list, opened Gmail, pasted the list into a blank email page, typed in Eve's email address and sent it. Eve reentered the room with a handful of photo copies.

"I think I got something" said Billy. "I found a patent marking on the plastic container that was in his trashcan liner. It belongs to a pharmaceutical company that makes Sumatriptan—a medication for—"

"— migraines."

"Yeah how did you know?"

"My sister suffered from migraines. She had a prescription for Sumatriptan but it was in pill form."

"Yeah well this little guy is for the injectable version. It's primarily used for patients suffering from cluster migraines. It's a portable container for a statdose pen and two medication cartridges. Anyway I was thinking—the container is empty. What if he ran out of medication cartridges? He would need to—"

"—refill his prescription" she said. "I'll need a list of all the pharmacies around the hotel where he was staying."

"I just emailed it to your iPhone."

"Really?"

He nodded. Eve looked at her iPhone and opened the email.

"Good work Billy."Eve walked out of a small pharmacy and checked off the address on her iPhone. She looked at the next pharmacy on the list. The pharmacy's address was on the same street. She looked down the street and saw a green cross on a sign. She walked down the street and into the pharmacy that the nomad had visited and approached the pharmacist.

"Hi. Do you speak English?" said Eve.

"Yes. How may I serve you?" said the pharmacist.

"I'm looking for my brother." Eve showed the pharmacist the photo of the nomad. "He might have come here."

"Five days ago."

"You saw him?"

"Yes. He needed a prescription filled."

"Sumatriptan?"

"Yes. He was in very much pain."

"Aye. I bet he was. Did he show you his prescription?"

"Yes. It was expired. He needs to go to doctor and get new prescription."

"That's why I am trying to find him. I want to help him. Take him to the doctor. Did you make a copy of the prescription?"

"Yes."

"May I see the copy?"

"No. It's private."

"I understand."

"I cannot give even to his family unless police say it okay. It Thai law."

Eve pulled out 5000 baht from her wallet.

"Would this help make it more public?"

The pharmacist considered the money—5000 baht was more than she made in a week. The pharmacist nodded in agreement and began searching through her paperwork. Eve looked around the small pharmacy.

"Did my brother use a credit card to pay for his medicine?"

"No. He pay in baht."

Eve noticed a security camera up in the corner.

"Your security camera—where do you keep the footage?"

"It's on the computer."

"Can you find the footage of my brother?"

"Yes."

Eve pulled out another 3000 baht. "I'll need a copy of that too."

The Pharmacist nodded. "You brother very sick man."

"Aye. He is that. More than you know."

The pharmacist pulled out the copy of the prescription and handed it to Eve. She examined the copy. "You're sure this is the prescription my brother gave you?"

"Yes. Very sure."

"Can you email me a link to the security video?"

"Yes I can do."

"Thank you for your help."

Eve wrote her email address on a slip of paper and handed it to the pharmacist along with the money and left.

Eve entered the hotel room. Billy was asleep on the floor.

"Wake up."

Billy blinked and sat up. The rolled-up towel stuck to the back of his head.

"I'm up. I'm up." He carefully pulled the towel off the back of his head. There was a patch of dried blood on the towel.

"Why didn't you sleep on the bed?"

"Didn't want to get blood on it."

"Well aren't you sweet. We've got the name of the doctor who originally prescribed the medication and more importantly we've got a new name for Noi's killer."

"His name isn't Kyle? "

"No it's not. At least it wasn't Kyle when he was originally prescribed the medication. It was Vance Dunn."

"He's using an alias."

"Or was using an alias when he got the original prescription. Look it doesn't matter. We follow each name using the same methodology until the trail runs out or we find the nomad. Hopefully the latter."

"What's next?"

"I'm going to contact his doctor and see what I can find out. You work the internet. We got a name and a photo. We need to check every social media website and database we can access. Start with Facebook, LinkedIn and Google Plus. If that doesn't work try dating sites and classmates.com. We'll get thousands of hits but we can cross check with the photo and make sure it's actually the nomad and not just someone with the same name."

"You're by far better at this computer stuff" he said. "Why don't you let me call the doctor?"

"Billy, my man, a call like this requires the gift of tongue and a unique skill set that can only be developed with years of experience."

"You're gonna lie."

"Like a gypsy. Oh and I almost forgot." Eve opened the email folder on her iPhone and opened an email from the pharmacist and clicked on a link to the security video. A video of the nomad entering the pharmacy appeared on her iPhone screen. "We've got more video of the nomad."

The video showed the nomad in the pharmacy suffering from pain and yelling at the pharmacist and taking his medicine and collapsing.

"Poor bastard" said Eve.

"That's nothing compared to what he did to Noi" said Billy.

"And here I thought you were going soft on me."

"Not hardly."

"Then let's get to it."

Billy went to work on the laptop. Eve dialed the number for the nomad's doctor. The receptionist answered. Eve gave her the name of the doctor and was put on hold. The doctor's nurse came on the line.

"Dr. Spencer's office."

"Hi this Pamela Holmes from Becker Pharmacy in Birmingham Alabama. I have a Mr. Vance Dunn trying to refill an expired prescription for Sumatriptan. He says Dr. Spencer will verbally renew the prescription. Oh and I'm going to need to confirm your records on Mr. Dunn's phone and address for identity purposes."

"Vance Dunn?"

"Yes."

"Will you hold please?"

"Of course."

"That's crafty" said Billy.

Eve shushed him. A man came on the line.

"This is Dr. Spencer. Who did you say is in your pharmacy?"

"Mr. Vance Dunn."

"That's not possible."

"Why is that Dr. Spencer?"

"Mr. Dunn is a long-term patient under my care. He hasn't left the hospital for eleven years."

"The hospital?"

"Marshall-Fields Psychiatric Hospital. The facility you are calling."

"Well there seems to be some confusion."

"There is no confusion. Whomever you have in your pharmacy is an imposter attempting to fill a stolen prescription with my name on it. I suggest you call the police and let them straighten it out."

"Of course doctor. I appreciate your help. By the way do you have a Kyle Tanner under your care?"

There was a long pause on the phone.

"How do you know Kyle Tanner?"

"Mr. Dunn mentioned his name. So, Mr. Tanner is also your patient."

"I didn't say that. Where did you say you were from?"

"Becker Pharmacy in Birmingham Alabama. Were there any other patients that may have known Mr. Dunn or Mr. Tanner?"

"You're not a pharmacist. Who are you?"

"Thank you for your time doctor." Eve hung up.

"What was that all about?" asked Billy.

"You can stop your search. His name's not Vance Dunn either."

"Another alias?"

"Yeah. Vance Dunn is a long-term patient at the

231

hospital and so was Kyle Tanner."

"He's stealing the identities of mental patients?"

"Ya know it's actually bloody brilliant when you think about it. A patient enters long-term care at a young age before getting any kind of photo identification like a driver's license so there is no official record of what they look like. He steals their Social Security number from the hospital records and petitions the county for a copy of their birth certificate. With a social security number and a birth certificate he can get any kind of official document he wants—a driver's license, passport, whatever—and it will have his photo not the real person's photo."

"What about the fingerprints on the birth certificate? They won't match his adult fingerprints when he applies for a passport."

"Birth certificates in the U.S. don't have fingerprints. They have footprints. It wouldn't matter anyway. A baby's fingerprints aren't fully formed when they are born. They could never be used to compare accurately. This bastard may be mad as a box of frogs, but he's smart too."

Eve searched her contact list and dialed another number on her phone.

"Daesh it's Eve. I need full work ups on a Vance Dunn and a Kyle Tanner both somewhere in the Boston area and both patients at Marshall-Fields Psychiatric Hospital. I need criminal records, credit reports, past and pending legal proceedings, the works. And I need them pronto. Yeah I'll pay the rush fee. Email your results as soon as you get them. Piece meal 'em if you need to. Thanks." Eve hung up.

"Who's Daesh?" said Billy.

"He's a data miner."

"You mean a hacker?"

"Six o' one, half a dozen of the other. If there is something out there on any of them he'll find it."

Eve searched the contact list on her phone and dialed another number. "Walter it's Eve. Yeah it has been a long time. Are you up for a little freelance work? Good. I'd like you to go up to Marshall-Fields Psychiatric Hospital in Boston and discretely interview a few of the staff. I'm looking for information on a Kyle Tanner and a Vance Dunn both patients. And keep an eye out for a Dr. Spencer. He may be on to us. There may be a third player that is connected to Vance and Tanner but I don't have a name. He's our target. I'll pay you a day rate plus expenses but keep it under control. This one's out of my wallet. Thanks." She hung up.

"Walter?" said Billy.

"He was a constable with the RUC now retired. He went to live with his son in Boston. He's as good as it gets with investigative work and he has no problem bending the rules when necessary."

"So what do we do now?"

"Nothing. We wait and see what they dig up."

CHAPTER 15

Eve sat the bed playing solitaire with a deck of cards. Billy sat in a chair pitching 5 baht coins against the wall trying to get as close to possible to the baseboard.

"Do you believe in God?" Eve said.

"Sure" said Billy.

"Why?" asked Eve.

"You got something against God?"

"No. I'm just curious."

"I suppose 'cuz my mama believed in him."

"Are you sure it's a he?"

"You like to stir the pot don't ya?"

"I do. It makes conversations more interesting."

"Bible says God is a guy. End of discussion."

"Have you ever read it?"

"What—the Bible?"

"That's what we're talking about isn't it?"

"I don't know what we're talking about but yeah, when I was younger I picked it up a few times."

"That's not really reading it, picking it up, now is it?"

"You mean like cover to cover? No I haven't read it. Have you read it?"

"I have. A few times."

"And?"

"It was interesting but I can't say I believe much of it was true."

"You an atheist?"

"Just because I don't believe in the Bible doesn't mean I don't believe in God. I could believe in Krishna or Allah or Buddha for that matter."

"So which is it?"

"None of them. Religion is a load of crap."

"So you are an atheist."

"More of an agnostic. I'm willing to concede I might be wrong."

"Sounds like fence-sitting to me. You're hedging your bet just in case you wake up dead."

Eve's phone chimed. She picked it up and studied the screen. It was an email from Daesh. "We've got something" she said.

Eve opened the attachment to the email and studied a credit report. "Okay we've got an active credit card on Dunn's credit report."

"That's good right?"

"Maybe. We'll know after we look at the purchases that have been made and where."

Eve accessed the website for the card issuer on her laptop and found the contact phone number. "You're gonna call the issuer and pretend you're Dunn. The goal is to get an active email address where he's having the statements sent for the card."

"What about phone and address?"

"They're a bonus if you can get 'em but focus on the email address. We can get whatever we want once we have an active email address. You don't want to throw up any red flags that might have the issuer send a text alert to our target's phone. So don't actually change any information on the account. If you get stuck just keep spinning the story."

"Okay."

Eve showed Billy the credit card issuer's phone number on her iPhone. Billy dialed. "Hi. This is Vance Dunn. I have a Visa with you. Account number?"

Eve pointed to the Visa account number on her iPhone.

"4809 0983 8901 2392 Expiration Date?"

Eve pointed to the expiration date.

"June 2021. Security Number on back of card?"

Eve shook her head.

"I don't actually have the card with me. Is there something else I could give you? Last four digits of my Social Security Number?"

Eve nodded and frantically scrolled through her iPhone.

"Ah…it's…it's? What happened to my high school grammar? I meant they."

Eve found the Social Security Number on the credit report and showed it to Billy.

"They are 8167. You're welcome. I'd like to confirm you have my most current email. It's VDunn9523 at gmail. Oh really. What email address do you show? ParadiseLost1975 at yahoo?"

Billy wrote it down.

"Actually that's one of my alternative emails. It still

forwards to my current Gmail so let's just keep that one on file. Now what are you showing for my mailing address and phone?" Billy wrote them down. "Yep those are correct. Okay I think I am good. Thank you for your help."

Billy hung up.

"So how are we going to get his email password?" said Billy.

"You're going to call his phone company, tell them that you dropped your phone in the toilet and you need your calls forwarded to a new number until your phone is repaired."

Eve held up a new prepaid phone in a plastic package.

"Why don't I just use my phone number?"

"We use this phone once then throw it away. That way he can't track us or use it against us."

"Smart."

"We have his Social Security Number so it shouldn't be too difficult getting past the phone company customer service rep. Next we go online to his email account. Since we can't access the account without the password, we reset his email password. His email provider will send a confirmation number to his phone which in turn will forward it to the forwarding phone number and we can use the confirmation code to change his email password."

"Wait a minute. Won't he see copies of the text and

email messages on his phone even if they are forwarded?"

"That's the tricky part. It depends how he setup his phone originally. Some people delete messages and emails once viewed and others keep copies of them on their phones even if they are deleted from the server. There is no way for us to know how he setup his phone without actually having it in our hands. So we have to assume he will see a copy of any email or text message even if we delete it."

"He'll change his passcodes if he finds out and we'll be locked out."

"Aye. It's a one-shot deal. So we'll wait until early morning when he is asleep. With any luck he won't read his email or text messages until the next morning. That'll give us time to raid his emails and hack any other accounts we can get access to. We should have three or four hours to get everything we can before he figures everything out and changes his passcodes and forwarding number. It's going to be a busy night so let's get some sleep now."

"He's gonna know someone is after him" said Billy.

"Aye and he's gonna be pissed" said Eve.

The nomad sat at the hotel dining room drinking an Italian chianti and eating a medium-rare ribeye steak from Australia sliced into thin strips. The chef exited the kitchen and walked from table to table checking on his customers. He crossed over to the nomad. The nomad did not acknowledge him.

"Is everything to your liking?" said the chef.

"It was until you disturbed my meal" said the nomad without looking up.

"I am so sorry."

The chef retreated back into the kitchen. The nomad set his wine glass down and looked at the wooden cutting board that served as his plate. The steak was in the center with mash potatoes in a cup to one side. Blood ran from the center of the cutting board into a channel around the edge. He used a piece of bread to sop up the blood and ate it.

The nomad sipped brandy in a proper glass which was a sign of a well-stocked bar. He sat on a leather couch by a fireplace in the hotel lobby which was unusual for a country where the temperature rarely dipped below 25 degrees Celsius. He watched as a young Italian couple checked in and crossed the lobby following the bellhop to the elevator. The woman's full lips were tight as if angry and pouting. Her lover—a tall man dressed in a t-shirt and black jacket—tried to cheer her up joking in Italian and smiling. She wasn't amused. He was probably caught stealing a look at a Malaysian beauty. No sex tonight.

The nomad entered his hotel room and closed the door. He threw the deadbolt below the doorknob and slid his room card into the power switch. The lights came on. It was a small room with a king-sized bed leaving only enough room for a leather chair and side table. The nomad set his phone on the nightstand next to the bed and plugged it in to recharge. He sat in the leather chair and picked up the remote and turned on the television. He watched a Malaysian soap opera set in the 15th century during the first mass immigration from China. The cast fought each other with swords, lances and magic. Heroes died and their lovers committed suicide to join them in the afterlife. *Boring* thought the nomad. He changed the channel several times until he settled on a true crime documentary on the Manson family murders in English with Malay subtitles. He had mixed emotions about Charles Manson the leader of the cult. Manson was brilliant in the way he recruited members into his family but careless in the way he covered his tracks after the Sharon Tate murders. The nomad knew better than to make a rookie mistake like Manson.

The drapes were drawn and the lights were out. It was pitch dark in the room. The nomad was asleep. On the nightstand his cell phone sat silent. The phone's screen lit up and chimed an alert. The room was illuminated. He stirred. After a moment the phone screen again went dark. The nomad fell back into a deeper sleep.

Eve and Billy sat at the small table in the corner of the room. Several empty cans of RedBull sat beside the laptop they watched intently. On the screen was a list of email messages from Vance Dunn's account.

"That one! Air Asia four days ago" said Billy.

Eve opened the email and the attached boarding pass and zoomed in on the departure and arrival information.

"You were right. He's in Penang, Malaysia" Eve said.

"Gotcha ya son of a bitch" said Billy.

"We don't got 'im...yet. But we are getting closer."

"He's probably staying in Georgetown. It's on an island where all the westerners hang out. I was there last year. I know the area pretty good" Billy said.

Eve scrolled down the email list and selected an email from Expedia and opened it. It was a reservation for a boutique hotel in Georgetown.

"Do you know this place?"

"No. I don't think so. Can you select directions to the hotel so I can look at the map?"

She selected directions and brought up a map. He studied it.

"Yeah. I know this area. It's in Chinatown near the mall. There's a good number of hotels in the area but it won't be hard to find."

"Okay we leave tomorrow."

"Have you given any thought to how I'm going to get out of Thailand? Even if I get another passport the police have my photo plastered all over the airports and bus stations."

"I've got one or two ideas. You know anything about fishing?"

"Fly or spin?"

"Net." said Eve.

It was early when the nomad woke. He reached for his phone and checked the time. He saw the text messages notifying him that during the night his phone number had been forwarded to another number that he did not recognize and another message that his email password had been changed. He was angry, but quickly calmed and considered the possibilities. The forwarding number was from Thailand.

"Is that you cowboy?"

He dialed the forwarding number and it rang.Billy sat alone and stared at the ringing prepaid phone that sat on the table. He knew who was calling. He was tempted to answer it, but knew better. Hunting required patience he reminded himself. He picked up the phone as it continued to ring and walked out onto the balcony and threw the phone with all his strength. It landed on the street below and was immediately run over by a passing truck.

He moved back inside the room and sat down at the laptop and studied a map of Georgetown and familiarized himself with the lay of the land around the nomad's hotel. Eve entered carrying a plastic shopping bag.

"Okay. Good news. I've got a fisherman willing to smuggle you across to Malaysia. His name is Thaqif. He lives in Malaysia but has a Thai wife and kids so he comes here on weekends to visit his family. Jump up will ya?" said Eve.

Billy rose from the table and Eve sat down at the laptop. She pulled a map up of Southern Thailand and Northern Malaysia and pointed out the travel path as she explained.

"So here is the plan. You'll take a bus and meet Thaqif in Tammalang. It's a fishing village in Satun province just 10 kilometers on this side of the Thai-Malay border. After sunset you'll take his boat out to sea in international waters then travel south for a couple of hours. At sunrise you'll come back in on the Malaysia side and mix with the other fishing boats from Kuala Perlis—a Malaysian fishing village just on the other side of the Thai-Malay border. Once you get into port you'll take a bus to Penang and meet me at a hotel in Georgetown."

"You trust this guy Thaqif?" asked Billy.

"He really didn't say much. You should watch yourself to be on the safe side. But I think he's the best shot at getting you across undetected. The Malaysian Coast Guard rarely searches the fishing boats especially if they have Malaysian crews."

"If they do search the boat and I get caught?"

"Don't get caught."

Eve opened the bag and fished out a small can of brown shoe polish and a contact lens container.

"Brown shoe polish and brown contacts like you asked. There's also a beard trimmer and some batteries. I bought some clothes that I thought might make you fit in a little better. Biggest size they had was XL so they'll have to do."

She dropped the contacts and shoe polish back in the bag and handed it him.

"Once you cross over into Malaysia the police are not going to be hunting for you. You'll be free to move around again. There's not a lot of rebel activity in the area so the odds are slim that you'll hit a roadblock checking papers once you're on main road. If you ever get stopped and the police ask for your passport tell them it was stolen and you are on your way to the US Embassy in Kuala Lumpur to get a replacement. They usually will not bother to check any further. After all you are tall, white and sound like an American. They have no reason to doubt you so don't give them one. Just play clueless American and you should be fine."

"I can do that."

Billy moved into the bathroom and closed the door. He looked in the mirror and slipped the batteries into the beard trimmer and shaved his head to a slight stubble. He stripped down naked. He opened the can of brown shoe polish and rubbed the ends of fingers in it and rubbed it over his face, hair and body. His skin tone changed dramatically to dark brown. He wiped the excess shoe polished from his fingertips. He opened the contact lens case and inserted the contact lens. His eyes changed to dark brown. He put on the new clothes and studied his new look in the mirror. He didn't look Malaysian or Thai because of his height and broad shoulders but he didn't look like a farang either. Maybe Indian or even Tongan. He walked out of the bathroom. Eve laughed on seeing him.

"You're a real confidence builder lady."

"I'm sorry. It was hard enough when you were a cowboy. Now you're a...honestly I don't know what you are."

"I'm fucked. That's what I am."

"No no. You'll be fine. Really. You just need to keep out of sight as much as possible. Don't make eye contact and maybe...I don't know...stay hunched over a bit and tuck in your shoulders.

Billy tried to look smaller and Eve laughed even louder.

"It's not funny Eve."

"No it is. It really is."

"I'm going to Thai jail."

"Probably."

"Will you watch my boots?"

"Your boots? You're wanted for murder and you're about to be smuggled across an international border and who knows what will happen if you're caught and you're worried about your boots?"

"Yes. It took over a year to break them in the way I like 'em."

"Christ. Ya sound like a girl."

"Will you watch my damn boots?"

"Aye. I'll guard them with my life."

"It's not like I'm asking for a kidney. Just don't let 'em get wet and keep 'em out of the sun. And if you could carry them on the plane instead of checking 'em I'd appreciate it."

"Oh my Mary Mother of Jesus" she said.

CHAPTER 16

The afternoon rain had come and gone. Only the clouds on the horizon remained. The nomad sat on a motor scooter overlooking the sea watching the sunset. The need inside him was growing again. He knew the signs. Soon it would be unstoppable. He had to be ready. The sun disappeared. It was twilight and beautiful and time to start the hunt. He put on his helmet and turned the key, started the scooter and drove off.

It was night and hot and humid. The nomad pulled the scooter into a small parking spot, turned off the motor and the headlamp and set the kickstand. He pulled off his helmet and dismounted. He opened the seat cover revealing a compartment and put his helmet inside, closed the seat cover and locked the compartment.

The nomad walked to the Chulia Reggae Night Club

and requested a seat on the patio from the receptionist at the front gate of the walled compound. It was early and patio seats were still available. He sat at a table under an umbrella near a small stage with a bar stool, a music stand and a microphone. A mixer and amplifier were off to the side in back and two large speakers lined the front of the stage. It was a typical setup for a single performer. The nomad ordered a Jim Beam on the rocks. He liked drinking bourbon when listening to music. It was quick and strong. He scanned his surroundings like a general studies a field the night before a big battle.

In the shady areas of the massive stone slabs that formed the patio floor were puddles of water from the afternoon rain. In its glory days the mansion that now housed the club was the home of a wealthy opium merchant and host to the social elite of Georgetown. Painted all white with patches of black mold the mansion was slowly falling apart from lack of care. The plaster chipped away on its imposing columns and the wooden baseboards rotted from standing rain water. Several of the upper floor windows were cracked. Unwilling to invest more than a few liters of whitewash each year, the owner promoted club as rustic Caribbean.

The nomad surveyed the club's patrons sitting on the patio. They sat in groups of twos and threes smoking and drinking. He despised smoking. Nasty habit. No purpose but to fuel addiction and offend those nearby. Drinking was acceptable as long as it didn't get out of hand. Drunks were unpredictable and out of control. He would never sink to that level. Ever.

The nomad watched with interest as a tall Malaysian woman wearing a red dress and carrying an acoustic guitar walked out onto the stage. Her black leather pumps gave her slender legs an extra four inches. Her long black hair was perfectly combed into loose braids that hung over her shoulder. She placed her iPhone on the music stand and brought up the words to the first song on the screen. In addition to being a reminder of the words to each song the screen acted as a mini spotlight and illuminated her face. She picked up the guitar and quickly tuned it. She motioned to the sound engineer off to the side that she was ready and he turned down the house music. With no introduction she played a mix of Southern Classic Rock. She preferred more modern music but she knew the farang liked the classics and would tip better. He voice was solid. She knew her range and didn't push it.

The nomad was enthralled. She was a beauty and he liked her confidence. His need would be fulfilled when he broke her. He imagined her face as she hung by the arms from the rusty cargo crane and watched him filet her soft skin off those long beautiful legs. He knew that she would die of shock long before she bled out especially if he was careful not to cut any of her arteries during her struggles. She was worthy.

The nomad entered his hotel room and put his keycard in the power switch and the lights came on. He closed the door, locked the deadbolt, sat on the edge of the bed and carefully removed his loafers and placed them at the base of the bed so he could easily find them in the morning. He crossed the room to the credenza and picked up the bag from the knife shop.

He pulled out the box holding the knife, removed the ribbon and opened the box. He stared at the knife sitting in the box. It was beautiful like the singer at the club. Both had a purpose and would serve his need in their own way. He removed the knife from its box and held it in his hand to get the feel of it. It was well balanced and the handle fit his hand perfectly. He crossed to the side of the bed, opened a drawer in the nightstand and removed a sheet of hotel stationary. He gave the knife's blade a sharpness test by slicing the sheet of stationary. The knife's blade stuttered several times as if hitting a slight snag or bump. He was disappointed with the results.

He crossed back to the credenza and reached inside the bag. He pulled out the wrapped honing steel, the plastic bottle of purified water and the box of whetstones. He sat in a chair and used the credenza as his workstation and opened the box of whetstones. The instructions were in Japanese, English, French and Spanish. He read the English version carefully not wanting to damage his new knife. He placed the smallest grid stone on the sharpening block and opened the purified water bottle and squirted several drops on the stone. He studied the edge of the blade to ensure the direction of the grain and the angle of the blade's edge. He slowly rubbed the blade against the stone careful to keep it at the proper angle. He felt up and down the rod for any snags or burrs that might damage the edge of the knife. He rose and walked to the nightstand and removed another sheet of stationary and walked back to the credenza and sat down. He picked up the knife like a conductor picking up his wand and sliced downward into the stationary. The stroke was smooth and continuous with not even the slightest snag or stutter like a hot knife through butter. He was pleased and saw no need to hone the edge further. It would serve his need well.

Billy rode a local bus up a mountain road pitted with potholes. The bus lacked air conditioning and the windows were up to keep out the afternoon rain storm. It was painfully hot and humid and smelled of spices and human sweat. The bus stopped at every town to drop off and pick up passengers. Anything was allowed on board—chickens in cages, bags of rice baskets of vegetables and fruit going to market, even long PVC pipes for plumbing were laid along the aisle floor. The passengers stared at strange looking traveler. Billy stared out the window and avoided eye contact. The trees and shrubs lined both sides of the road and were dark and thick and impenetrable.

The bus lurched to a stop. A tree had fallen from the hillside above and lay across the roadway blocking traffic. The tree's roots had been unable to hold the weight of the tree during the afternoon rain and now lay unearthed like medusa's head of snakes. The driver yelled back in Thai to the passengers. Several men followed him off the bus. The driver opened a compartment in the belly of the bus and handed each of the men a machete or ax. Billy wondered if he should get out and help but thought it better to stay seated where nobody would notice his height. The men went to work chopping through the tree on both sides of the roadway. The driver supervised and smoked a cigarette and drank from a plastic bottle filled with a brownish liquid. The wood was still soft from the rains and the cutting went quickly. When both sides of the tree were severed, the men rolled the log off the roadway and down the side of the mountain. The driver and the men boarded the bus and they were again on their way.

It was late afternoon by the time the bus pulled into the industrial port of Tammalang and rolled past the iron crab sculpture in the main round-a-bout. There was no bus station in the town. The bus stopped in front of the open air market. Each vendor stall was covered with a plastic tarp to fend off the sun and rain. Billy asked the driver the direction of the pier and exited the bus.

On the pier, Billy studied the fishing boats stacked five to six deep with their bows and sterns tied to the next boat closest to the pier. Most of the boats were empty—their owners and crew eating and drinking away their morning catch in the local bars before returning home to sleep. One boat at the end of the pier still had a man working on it. Billy studied the man as he approached. The man had a beard, something few Thai men could grow, and a grease-stained Songkok—a hat similar to the Turkish fez. Billy decided he was Malay and probably the man he was to meet. The Malay stood in his twenty-foot sailboat sorting his fishing nets and gear.

"Are you Thaqif?" said Billy.

Thaqif did not immediately look up from his work. Billy wondered if he had heard the question and considered repeating it but decided it was better to wait. Thaqif took his time and finished his net before he turned to Billy and gave him the once over and nodded. Billy crossed five boats all tied together to reach Thaqif's boat.

"I'm Billy."

Billy leaned across the last boat and offered his hand. Thaqif nodded again but didn't shake his hand. To Thaqif, this was a business transaction and didn't require social grace. Thaqif untied the bow line and moved to the stern line. Billy realized that he was actually leaving now with or without his passenger.

"I guess we're going" said Billy more to himself than Thaqif.

Billy stepped into Thaqif's boat just as Thaqif untied the stern line and pushed his boat away from the gaggle of boats. The boat had several places where the wood had rotted away and was patched with another piece of wood. The sail was in no better shape with several cloth patches over the canvas. Billy wondered about the vessel's seaworthiness. Thaqif turned to Billy and held out his hand for payment.

"Half now and half when we reach Malaysia" said Billy.

Thaqif nodded. Billy gave him 30,000 baht with a rubber band wrapped around the wad of bills. Thaqif stuffed the money under his Songkok. Thaqif handed Billy a pile of dirty clothes. Billy changed out of his Thai street clothes and slipped into the rags of a poor Malaysian fisherman. His transformation was now complete.

Thaqif hoisted the triangle-shaped sail on the one and only main mast and sat at the stern and used his foot to steer the boat's rudder. The boat was silhouetted by the setting sun on the western horizon. The sail caught the wind and the boat glided toward the open waters of the Andaman Sea.

Eve placed Billy's boots along with her purse on the X-ray conveyor belt at Phuket International Airport. The X-ray technician watched the boots roll by on her computer monitor and stopped the conveyor to take a closer look at the hidden compartment inside the boots. She said something in Thai to one of the security guards and the guard pulled the boots aside for further inspection and called Eve over to witness.

"Oh shit" said Eve. "Billy what have you done to me?"

"These your shoes?" said the guard.

"No. They are a friend's. He forgot them when he went to Malaysia. I am bringing them to him."

The guard reached inside each of the boots and unzipped the two hidden compartment and pulled out the contents—Billy's original passport sealed in a plastic bag, $8500 in US cash, two condoms and a laminated photo of his daughter. The guard called over her supervisor, a middle-aged woman, and talked to her in Thai.

"Why your friend hide so much money?" said the supervisor.

"I don't know. He is a man…and not very smart."

The supervisor nodded. "How much money you have?"

"I don't know. Maybe $1000 US."

"Show me."

Eve opened her purse and her wallet and pulled out all her US cash and handed it to the supervisor.

"This all your money?" said the supervisor.

"I have some Thai baht."

"Show me."

Eve reached into her pockets, purse and wallet and handed the supervisor her Thai baht. The supervisor counted all the money and used a calculator to value the baht to US dollars and added everything up. It occurred to Eve what was happening. If she was carrying over $10000 US in all currencies, which was the legal limit, she could be accused of smuggling money out of Thailand and immediately taken to jail to await trial. Eve glanced down at the total on the calculator. It was just under the limit at $9872. The supervisor handed her back the cash and the guard handed her the boots and the contents.

"Have a nice vacation" said the supervisor.

Eve gathered her purse and the boots and walked farther into the terminal. "Fucking cowboy boots." Eve's plane landed at Penang International Airport. She picked up her luggage from baggage claim and queued up in the taxi line. She rode the short distance into Georgetown and to her hotel and checked into a suite with two bedrooms.

A bellhop opened the door to the suite and carried her luggage and Billy's boots inside. He set the luggage down and placed the boots in the closet. Eve tipped the bellhop and he closed the door behind him on his way out. Eve opened the closet, picked up the boots, walked into the bathroom, opened the shower door and placed the boots inside the shower. She turned on the shower and watched the boots fill with water. She turned off the shower, closed the shower door, walked out of the bathroom and sat on the bed feeling very satisfied.

After a few moments her conscious got the better of her and she jumped up and ran into the bathroom. She opened the shower and emptied the water from the boots and used two towels to soak up the water in and on the boots.

"Damn all cowboys."

CHAPTER 17

It was pitch dark. The small boat sailed further out to sea well past any sight of land. The only light was a small oil lamp that sat on the wooden bench by Thaqif as he steered. Billy sat on the opposite end of the small boat. His feet were wet from the oily water gathered at the bottom of the boat. Thaqif pulled down the sail. The boat drifted to a stop and rocked back and forth from the deep waves of the open ocean. Thaqif opened a dirty rag holding several dry fish and took a bite out of one crunching down on the head. He offered one to Billy. This was dinner. Billy took one the crusty fish and bit down in the middle. He lasted almost thirty seconds before puking over the side. Thaqif frowned at the wasted fish.

Dinner was over. Thaqif handed Billy a frayed blanket and blew out the oil lamp. It was a waning moon that offered little in the way of natural light. Thaqif curled up. His small body barely fit on the wooden bench he used as a seat when steering the boat. For Billy, almost twice the size, it was hopeless. He gathered the blanket and used it as a pillow against the boat gunwale. Billy looked over at Thaqif already asleep. The man still had not spoken a word. He wondered if Thaqif would awake during the night and slit Billy's throat with his razor sharp fish knife and take the money that he knew Billy was carrying and throw his corpse over the side for fish food. A pleasant thought before closing his eyes. It was going to be a long night.

Billy's prepaid phone still in the pocket of his street pants chirped. Surprised that it worked this far out to sea Billy reached over and dug it out of the pants pocket. Are you okay? read the text on the phone screen.

Eve lay on her bed waiting for a response. Her phone chirped as Billy's text message appeared. Yes but I'll give you a thousand dollars for a Big Mac and a toothbrush. Eve smiled and looked over at the cowboy boots now sitting on the table and closed her eyes and slept.

It was just after sunrise. The ocean waves had subsided to a gentle roll and there was a light wind. Thaqif guided his boat under sail back toward land. With dark rings under his eyes from lack of sleep, Billy sat on the bow. In the distance he saw a group of boats. He looked back and Thaqif nodded. It was the Malaysian fishing fleet from Kuala Perlis. The fleet was a mishmash of boats and ships of varying sizes—some big commercial trawlers and others traditional vessels like Thaqif's boat. The small boats followed the trawlers equipped with powerful radar that tracked large schools of fish. They all fished together but gave each other enough space so their nets didn't tangle.

Thaqif steered clear of the trawlers and pulled his boat up next to the smaller boats and struck the sail. Thaqif grunted and reached for the net in the bottom the boat. Billy followed his lead, unfolded the net and dropped it over the side of the boat.

Thaqif sailed toward shore with the other boats in the fishing fleet. Billy sat on the bow. Billy's hands were blistered and bloody and he was disappointed in himself for feeling tired. He had grown soft from years of traveling. Twelve fish and a sea turtle flopped around at Billy's feet in the bottom of the boat. Although it was hard to tell from his stern face, Thaqif was happy. It was a lucky morning of fishing and the catch would bring good money at market. Billy glanced at a large vessel in the distance and sat up.

A Malaysian Coast Guard vessel approached the fleet. Billy looked back at Thaqif for assurance. Thaqif was emotionless and continued to sail toward shore. Billy swallowed hard and turned back around. The Coast Guard weaved its way through the fleet ignoring the fishermen as it passed. The vessel passed directly in front of Thaqif's boat. Billy and Thaqif didn't flinch and just stared straight ahead like it was just another day of fishing. Thaqif's boat rocked as it hit the wake left by the larger vessel. The danger was gone.

The fleet sailed past the breakwater protecting the

town's piers. Thaqif struck his sail and steered up to the fishing pier already thick with boats tied one to another. Billy grabbed the nearest boat and threw a line around its bow. Thaqif tossed a rope around the stern and pulled up his boat.

Billy helped unload the catch and threw the fish to Thaqif standing on the pier. Billy glanced over to where Thaqif had been sitting at the stern of the boat. Thaqif's fish knife lay on the wooden bench. He picked up the knife and examined it. The knife was rusty and the handle was well worn but Thaqif kept the blade razor sharp to gut the fish he caught.

Billy handed Thaqif the rest of the money he owed. Thaqif counted it and nodded approval as he slipped the wad of bills under his Songkok. Billy opened an oily rag from the boat. Thaqif's fishing knife was inside. Billy held up 2000 baht and nodded to the knife. Thaqif shook his head and leaned over and recovered the knife with the rag and pushed it toward Billy. They had fished together. It was a gift. Billy nodded thanks and Thaqif motioned for Billy to take off. Billy nodded and tucked the knife in the rag under his arm and left.

The man just saved my life and never said a word Billy thought.

It was early afternoon and the clouds were already rolling in over Georgetown. It was hot and getting hotter. Most restaurants in Malaysia had no air conditioning and relied on fans to keep their customers cool. Eve sat in a coffee shop directly below a ceiling fan. She wore a traditional hijab over her hair and around her face and looked surprisingly Malaysian. She watched the boutique hotel across the street. The nomad exited the front door of the hotel and crossed to his motor scooter parked along the sidewalk, unlocked the seat compartment, removed his helmet and closed the compartment.

Eve signaled the driver of a waiting taxi parked nearby. He started his engine and pulled his taxi up in front of the coffee shop. Eve put 20 ringgit on the table and walked to the taxi and got in the back seat. The nomad put on his helmet and mounted the motor scooter. He started the engine, pulled into traffic and headed down the street. Eve told the taxi driver to follow the motor scooter but to stay at a minimum distance of seven car lengths so the nomad would not notice he was being followed. The taxi followed the nomad.

The nomad parked his scooter in front of a mall and put his helmet away and went inside. Eve stepped out of the taxi and followed him into the mall. The nomad entered a sporting goods store and Eve followed. She had learned at the academy to use her peripheral vision to watch suspects so there was no need to look in their direction. She kept her distance and only looked in the nomad's direction when he moved in the opposite direction and she could be sure he would not see her. She made good use of the security mirrors mounted on the end of each aisle to watch the nomad.

The nomad browsed the mountain climbing section and surveyed the store's selection of climbing ropes. He settled on a 100-foot dynamic rope of kernmantle construction. Designed to absorb the energy of a falling climber the belaying rope would stretch as his victim struggled offering the false hope of escape like a fly caught in a spider's web wearing down the victim until exhausted. Next he moved to the carabiners. He studied the various configurations and selected a Petzl Pirana rappelling tool, nine medium-sized locking carabiners and four 10mm aluminum rapid links. He also picked out a selection of expansion bolts bolt hangers, a piton hammer and a battery-powered rock-hammer drill with a hex head attachment. He picked up a fast-setting resin to secure bolts in questionable rock faces. He was unsure how much rust had penetrated the cargo hull of the ship and didn't want to take a chance that his victim's thrashings would pull loose the bolts that secured her restraints. It would be embarrassing if he had to stop mid-filet to re-secure his victim. He also selected a large backpack to carry his tools and supplies.

He moved to the weightlifting section of the store and picked out a pair of leather ankle straps and a pair of wrist straps each lined with man-made wool padding. It was important that the victim not be chaffed or cut by the restraints during her struggle. He wanted her to only feel pain where he directed it and when he wanted it. He also selected a large steel ring used to suspend a heavy punching bag from a ceiling mount. He moved into the fishing section of the store. He loaded twenty round lead fishing weights into a double paper bag and walked to the front of the store and paid for his purchases.

The nomad exited the sporting goods store and Eve followed. He stopped to browse at a mobile phone kiosk. Eve ducked behind a kiosk selling handbags. She switched her hijab and pulled off her blouse to reveal a different blouse underneath giving her a different look. The nomad picked up a prepaid phone using the passport that he always used for communication and transportation. Sales people rarely paid much attention to the passports they were required to copy so he used one of the passports he liked the least for these types of purchases and rentals. The nomad moved on and Eve followed.

The nomad entered an electronic store and moved to the back of the store. Halfway down an aisle he abruptly stopped and looked back. Eve picked up the closest item—a small rice cooker—and pretended to read the label. She could feel his eyes studying her and kept her back to him as much as possible without causing suspicion. The nomad did not recognize the woman but something seemed strangely off about her. She sat the rice cooker down and walked in the opposite direction out the store. Seemingly satisfied the nomad continued to the parts counter at the back of the store. The nomad examined a parts catalog and showed the salesman what he wanted—a GSM-based cell phone remote control switch circuit. The salesman disappeared down an aisle of stacked drawers holding various switches and devices. He returned with a small box holding the device the nomad requested. The nomad opened the prepaid cell phone he purchased and plugged in the switch circuit. He used his other mobile phone to dial the prepaid phone. The switch light turned from yellow to green showing that the circuit had been connected. The nomad purchased the switch along with a portable

CD player with built-in speakers and a battery-powered sound-activated laser and strobe projector.

Eve waited outside the electronic store and bought a vanilla ice cream cone dipped in chocolate from a Dairy Queen and watched the nomad exit. She kept her distance and did not follow him into the next store but instead stayed outside and ate her cone.

The nomad entered a hardware store and purchased a pair of heavy leather workman gloves, sheetmetal shears, a hacksaw, an awl, a spool of heavy duty waxed string, a leatherman's needle and a six-inch steel spring.

The nomad entered a sex shop and purchased a ball-gag. He would need to muffle his victim's screams to prevent any passerby from investigating or calling the police. He thought about purchasing several canvas tarps to cover the ship's cargo hold opening before he started the filleting procedure but then realized how the ship's location was very remote and that he was just being paranoid and overly cautious. The ball-gag would be enough.

The nomad was loaded down with bags when he exited the mall—too many to safely carry on his motor scooter. He could return later and pick up the motor scooter. He gestured to call the closest taxi, which was the tax and driver that Eve had been using. The driver ignored the nomad. The nomad walked over and tapped on the window to get the driver's attention and motioned for him to roll down the window. The driver rolled down the window. "Dream Hotel" said the nomad and handed the driver an address card from the hotel.

The driver glanced over at Eve at the doors of the mall. Eve motioned for him to take the nomad. The driver nodded to the nomad and got out of the taxi. He opened the trunk and loaded the nomad's shopping bags, closed the trunk and got back in behind the wheel. The nomad climbed into the backseat. The taxi pulled away. The nomad looked out the window at Eve standing at the mall doors waving for the next taxi. *A woman leaving a mall without any purchases* he thought. *Interesting.*

The taxi pulled in front of the hotel and the nomad and the driver got out. The driver unloaded the shopping bags on the curb. The nomad walked over to a street vendor and purchased a coconut and walked back and put the coconut in one of the bags and paid the driver and picked up his shopping bags. It started to rain with heavy drops—the first signs of a cloud burst. He hurried inside the hotel with his bags.

The nomad stopped just inside the hotel and looked back out the window to the street and watched the taxi he had arrived in pull away from the hotel and move down the street. The rain turned into a downpour. He watched another taxi pull up in front of the hotel. There was a passenger in the back but he couldn't make out the face through the steamy windows of the taxi. The taxi pulled away without the passenger getting out. Could be nothing. Could be something. He reached into his pocket and fingered the karambit in its sheath. He picked up his shopping bags and crossed the lobby to the elevator and went up to his room.

CHAPTER 18

It was dark and raining. Eve stepped out of a taxi and entered her hotel lobby and crossed to the elevator. She entered the elevator, stepped in and pressed the button for her floor. The doors started to close and a man stepped inside at the last moment. It was Billy still dressed in his fishing clothes. He was even more dirty than when he had left the pier. The elevator rose.

"Oh now that's a sight" said Eve.

"I don't want to hear it" said Billy.

The smell hit her and she covered her nose. "Oh my christ. Is that all from you?"

"The driver made me ride in the back of the bus with some chickens and a goat."

"I can't say I blame him."

"Did ya find him—the nomad?

"I did. I've been following him all day. He's up to something."

"Where is he now?"

"At his hotel. Tucked in for the night I think. I've got a taxi driver watching the place. He'll call if he moves."

The elevator stopped and the doors opened. A Malay couple stood outside and stepped in. The doors began to close, and they stopped the door, stepped out and said something rude in Malay. The doors closed and the elevator continued to Eve's floor.

"I've been gettin' a lot of that" said Billy.

"Understandable."

"How are my boots?"

"Peachy. It would have been nice if you had warned me that you had $8500 in them."

"Yeah. I should have mentioned that."

The elevator stopped and they stepped off. Billy followed Eve down the hall and into the suite.

"Nice digs" said Billy.

"A suite was cheaper than two separate rooms and besides I thought it would be easier to work together in the living room."

"Makes sense."

"Would you mind taking a shower before you touch or sit on anything?"

"Sure."

"I bought you a bottle of shampoo and body scrub. Feel free to use it. All of it."

Billy stepped into the bathroom, closed the door and pulled the rag with the knife from the waistband of the pants under his shirt. He looked around the bathroom for a place to hide it. He knelt down in front of the sink and looked underneath the cabinet. He set the rag with the knife on top of the two knobs that controlled the flow of water into the sink. He rose from the floor and stripped out of his clothes. He opened the bathroom door and threw the clothes back into the living room by the door and leaned out the bathroom doorway.

"Have housekeeping burn those will ya?" said Billy.

"Right away."

Billy closed the bathroom door. Eve pulled a small bottle of perfume from her purse and shot a spritz into the air. It didn't help much. She knocked on the bathroom door.

"Are ya hungry?"

"Is the pope Catholic?" he said through the door.

Eve called room service and ordered a medium rare steak with a potato, a cobb salad and a bottle of

Spanish wine. Billy stepped out of the bathroom with a towel around his waist and used a washcloth to scrape the last of the shoe polish out of his ear. He was clean again and back to his original skin tone and he had removed the contacts from his eyes.

"Lord that feels good" said Billy.

Eve glanced over and noticed his well-defined torso and arms.

"My clothes?" he said.

"In the bag on your bed. I had them washed."

"Much obliged."

She pointed to one of the bedrooms and Billy crossed the living room and entered. Billy dressed and pulled on his boots and noticed that they were a little tighter than usual. He walked back out into the living room. There was a knock at the door.

"I got it" said Eve.

She opened the door and let the waiter from room service bring in their order. The waiter sat the tray of food and the wine with two glasses on the table. Eve signed the bill and asked the waiter to remove the clothes on the floor by the bathroom. The waiter scooped up the dirty clothes and closed the door behind him. Billy and Eve sat down and ate. Billy opened the wine.

"There's beer in the minibar refrigerator if you would prefer it" Eve said.

"I'll try the wine" said Billy and poured two glasses.

"I got a call from Walter and another email from Daesh while you were gone. Here is what we have been able to piece together. Kyle Tanner and Vance Dunn were both long-term patients at Marshal-Field Psychiatric Hospital and both were committed at an early age before they would have applied for any government documents beyond their birth certificates. At some point each of them met the nomad."

"Was the nomad a patient?"

"We don't know but considering his current behavior, it's probably safe to assume he was. Anyway both Vance and Tanner were issued driver's licenses and passports at roughly the same time but neither had left the hospital. There were also three other male patients in long-term care that were issued licenses and passports about the same time. So we pulled them up on the DMV database and they all used a photo of the nomad. We think the fingerprints and signatures are probably from the nomad too."

"You think he has five authentic passports?"

"Maybe more. That was just from one hospital that we know about."

"If he ever gets into trouble with the law he just burns his current passport and travels on one of the others."

"Yeah it looks that way. And there's something else. Kyle Tanner's mother was a prominent social lite and philanthropist in the Boston area. She made a couple big donations and hosted an annual charity event for the hospital. She was murdered in her home during a burglary about three years ago about the same time Kyle was issued his passport. Kyle inherited his mother's fortune which was placed in a trust by court order. Daesh checked around and found what he thinks is the trust account at a local bank managed by a law firm that represented the Tanner family during the trust hearing. He also found another account at a different bank under Kyle Tanner's name opened around the same time. Each month two fund transfers are issued from the trust account. One goes to the hospital to pay for Kyle's care and the other is deposited in the second account in Kyle Tanner's name."

"Why would the trustee do that?"

"Good question. My guess is that the nomad struck a deal with someone at the law firm—maybe gives them part of the money each month. In the meantime the real Kyle Tanner sits in a mental institution blowing spit bubbles none the wiser that the nomad is robbing him blind."

"Do you think the nomad killed Kyle's mother?"

"Probably. He had the most to gain from her death."

"Can we prove any of this?"

"Not without a court order. Everything we've got was collected illegally and therefore inadmissible in court. But two things we know for sure—the nomad is smart and the only way we are going to stop him is to catch him in the act. If we miss, he'll disappear and we may never find him again."

The nomad placed the shopping bag from the hardware store on the credenza in his hotel room and sat down. He took the contents out of the bag and placed them on the credenza. The nomad pulled his karambit from his pocket and unsheathed it. He used the sharp tip of the curved knife to cut the stitching on the workman's leather gloves and opened the gloves up so four pieces of leather lay flat on the top of the credenza. He studied the leather and used a pen to mark a pattern on one of the leather pieces. He cut the pattern out with the sheet metal shears. He took the cutout pattern and placed it over another leather piece and traced the outer edge of the cutout onto the piece of leather and used the shears to cut out the second cutout of leather. He placed the two mirrored leather cutouts together and was pleased with the match and size. He set the cutouts down on top of each other and slid one of the unused leather pieces underneath to create a cushion between the cutouts and the top of the credenza. He used the awl with the piton hammer to punch small holes around the edge of the mirrored cutouts. He removed the unused leather piece and set it aside. Next, he opened up the two mirrored cutouts and set them flat next to each other. He placed the steal spring down the center of one of the cutouts and arranged the 20 round lead weights on one end of the cutout. He placed the mirrored cutout on top of the cutout with the spring and weights and lined up the holes around the edges. He threaded the wax string into the eye of the weatherman's needle and carefully sewed the two cutouts together with the lead weights and steal spring inside.

The nomad was pleased with the end result—a spring-loaded sap. The spring gave the weapon an extra kick when whipped with the wrist. He hit the sap against the palm of his hand and was surprised by its power.

He rose from the credenza and crossed into the bathroom. He took one of the towels off the rack and returned to the credenza, rolled the towel into a tube and made a circle with the tube on the top of the credenza. He placed the coconut he had purchased on top of the circle to keep the coconut from rolling away. He picked up the sap and felt the weight and tried to gage how much a swing it would require. He gave the coconut a good whack with the weighted end of the sap. The shell cracked and milk flowed out through the crack and was absorbed by the towel. He studied the coconut's shell closely. The shell was cracked but did not shatter. A little less acceleration should be about right. He was upset with himself for not buying more coconuts. He would need to practice before he was ready. He didn't want to injure his victim beyond rendering her unconscious for the appropriate amount of time.

It was still a few hours before sunrise. Outside the nomad's hotel the driver sat behind the wheel of his parked taxi and smoked a cigarette and watched from a safe distance. It was hot. The windows were down to let in the breeze. He removed a bottle of Malay whiskey from a paper bag, unscrewed the top, took a quick drink and placed the bottle on the seat beside

. him.

An arm reached in through the window and across the driver's face and quickly withdrew. The driver's throat was cut and blood flowed down his dirty shirt. The nomad opened the door with his gloved hands and pushed the driver's body still twitching into the passenger seat. He closed the door and cleaned the blood off the edge of his karambit on the driver's shirt and put the sheath on the knife's blade and slid it back into his pocket. He started the engine, turned on the headlights and drove off.

The nomad parked the taxi in an alley between two buildings and turned off the headlights and the engine. He removed a cigarette pack and a lighter from the driver's shirt pocket now soaked in blood. He pulled out a cigarette from the pack and dropped it on the floor unlit along with the rest of the pack. He poured the Malay whiskey over the driver's body and used the empty bottle to break the bulb in the dome light above him so the light would not come on when he opened the door. He broke the lighter on the steering wheel and let the fluid and broken pieces of the lighter fall to the floor. He opened the door and stepped out of the taxi. He pulled a small can of lighter fluid and another lighter from his pocket and squirted more lighter fluid into the taxi through the window. He lit the fluid with the lighter and walked down the alley.

The interior of the taxi glowed orange as it was consumed with flames. He hoped the police would conclude the drunken driver lit himself on fire while lighting a cigarette with a broken lighter and not examine the burned body too closely. Even if they found the knife wound on the driver's throat, the chances were thin they could trace anything back to him. He had learned how to cover his tracks. He knew which evidence was important to destroy and what didn't really matter. He didn't know who the taxi was working for or why the driver was following him but it didn't really matter at this point. He only needed one more night before it would be time to leave Georgetown. He rounded the corner of one of the buildings and the taxi's leaky gas tank exploded.It was still dark when the nomad stepped from a taxi in front of the mall and paid the driver. The taxi drove off and the nomad walked over to his motor scooter where he had parked yesterday afternoon after shopping. He removed his helmet from the seat compartment and climbed on the scooter, put on his helmet, started the engine and drove off.

CHAPTER 19

Billy lay awake staring into the darkness waiting. He rose from his bed and walked out of his bedroom. The door to Eve's bedroom was shut and he could see under the door that the lights were out. She was asleep. He walked across the living room into the bathroom and knelt down by the sink and retrieved the rag with Thaqif's knife. He walked back to his bedroom and shut the door. He set the rag and the knife inside one of his boots. He climbed into bed and fell asleep.

Eve and Billy stepped from a taxi down the street from the nomad's hotel and Billy paid the driver and the taxi pulled away. Eve looked down the street.

"The taxi driver was supposed to be here all night" said Eve.

"Maybe he went to breakfast?"

"Maybe. We'd better get you out of sight. There's a cafe across the hotel."

They walked to the cafe. Billy kept his face turned away from the hotel and sat with his back to the cafe's open entrance. Eve kept looking for the taxi driver she had hired to watch the hotel.

"If he doesn't show soon we should get another driver and taxi to standby" said Eve.

They ordered breakfast with coffee for Billy and tea for Eve. Eve went in search of another taxi driver and Billy kept watch on the hotel.

The nomad stepped outside the hotel's front doors and walked to his motor scooter. He was wearing the backpack filled with tools and supplies. His preparations were more complex than usual and would require much of the day. He wanted to get an early start to ensure there would be enough time.

Billy saw the nomad and did not want to reveal himself. He was unsure of what to do. He walked along the wall to the corner of the cafe's entrance and took a quick peek around the corner in search of Eve. Eve was down the block talking to a taxi driver and did not see the nomad or Billy. Billy texted Eve on his phone. Eve's phone chirped and she looked at the screen and looked over at the nomad in front of the hotel getting on his motor scooter. She climbed in back of the taxi and waited. Billy put 60 ringgit on the table to cover the bill for the breakfast that still hadn't arrived.

The nomad started his scooter's engine and drove

down the street away from the hotel, past Eve's taxi and around the corner. The taxi pulled a U-turn. Billy ran for the taxi and hopped in the back.

"Go. Go. Go" said Billy.

The taxi driver drove around the corner and sped to catch up with the nomad two blocks ahead. Eve cautioned the driver to keep a safe distance. The nomad turned into an alley. The taxi followed. The alley was crowded with food carts and sidewalk vendors. The nomad easily swerved around the crowd and exited the far end of the alley. The taxi moved down the alley. A vendor rolled his cart into the middle of the alley and prevented the taxi from going any further. Billy jumped out of the taxi and ran to the end of the alley searching for the nomad. He was gone.

"Son of a bitch" said Billy.

Eve ran up beside him.

"Anything?" said Eve.

"He's gone goddamn it."

"It's my fault. I thought he was going to take a taxi. He must have picked up his scooter last night. It was a rookie mistake."

"Any idea where he went?"

"Not really. I guess he could have gone back to the mall but it's probably smarter if we wait back at the hotel until he returns."

"And if he doesn't return?"

"He wasn't carrying his luggage. He's got to go back to the hotel at some point."

Billy nodded.

The nomad pulled his scooter up the pier. He parked and placed his helmet inside the seat compartment. He walked between the abandoned buildings onto the pier and to the ship leaning in the mud. He removed the rope he had hidden behind an empty oil barrel and threw it up on the gangway sitting out of reach on the ship's top deck and pulled the gangway down and walked onto the ship. He walked up a ladder and through the outside passageway and down the ladder on the opposite end.

He set down his backpack and opened it and pulled out the large steel ring and the climbing rope. He put the ring in his pant pocket and looped one end of the rope to his belt and tied it. He climbed the rusting crane arm and shimmied out over the cargo hold and slipped the steel ring over the cargo hook. He untied the climbing rope from his belt and threaded the rope through the steel ring. He shimmied back down the crane arm. His shirt and pants were covered in rust and old grease. He didn't like to get his clothes or skin dirty but some things couldn't be helped. He would clean up and change his clothes back at the hotel before he went out for the evening's activities. He wanted to look good.

He pulled several yards of rope through the steel ring and tossed the excess rope and the remaining coil down into the cargo hold. He lifted the backpack up and carried it down the steps into the cargo hold. He unpacked the contents of the backpack and set them on the floor. He pulled out a drawing from his pocket and unfolded it. It was a hand-drawn schematic of what he hoped to create. In the center of the drawing was a naked woman suspended in mid-air with four ropes tied to her wrists and ankles. He reviewed the schematic and went to work.

He used the rock-hammer drill to punch two holes in the rusted metal floor ten feet apart. In each hole he dropped a generous amount of resin and pounded in an expandable bolt with an attached bolt holder using the piton hammer. He used the box wrench attachment on the drill to turn the bolt heads and expand the steel casings over the bolt threads. He attached an aluminum rapid link to each bolt holder and gave each bolt holder a good strong tug. The bolts held and were solid. He performed the same procedure on each side of the hold walls and secured added anchor points for the victim's wrist ropes.

He used the final four carabiners to secure each of the wrist and ankle straps and threaded the rope through the carabiners and aluminum rapid links. He threaded the rappelling tool into the rope line which would allow him to easily hoist his victim and lock the rope at the desired length. He was pleased with the end result—a series of anchor points attached by ropes and straps that allowed him to spread eagle his victim while suspended over the deck just like the schematic he had drawn.

He studied his creation and thought through the

process he would use and decided it would be best to let her struggle and grow tired before filleting her. He wanted the skin from each of her legs to peel off in one piece and to be unmarked by a careless knife stroke. He would need her to submit to achieve the desired results.

It would be nice to display the skin on a board of some sort—the hide from both legs pinned flat side by side. He didn't take souvenirs like other serial killers. His process was not ritualistic, no need to please a deity. That was the type of stupidity that could get you caught. But he liked the idea of creating a visual representation of the event, something to show his victim before the light left her eyes. He made a mental note to pick a box of roofing nails with wide heads, a rectangular piece of finished plywood—oak if it was available—and a spray can of waterproof sealant to keep the board's outer layer from soaking up the blood. He would pick up the additional supplies and bring them to the ship before returning to the hotel. He didn't like last-minute preparations that could cause problems.

He set up the portable CD player and inserted a CD. He set up the laser projector and checked to ensure the batteries had a sufficient charge. He connected both machines to the cell phone switch and connected the switch to the prepaid cell phone. He tested the setup with a quick phone call. It worked as planned and the CD player and the projector turned on. He turned off the CD player and laser projector and reset the switches.

The web was spun. Now for the fly.

CHAPTER 20

Billy and Eve sat in the coffee shop with scooter helmets on the floor by each of their chairs. They watched the nomad park his motor scooter in front of the hotel. His clothes were heavily soiled.

"His backpack is empty" said Billy.

"What happened to his clothes? It looks like he's an auto mechanic" said Eve.

The nomad walked into the hotel, crossed the lobby and rode the elevator up to his room. He opened the door, entered the room and took off his backpack and entered the bathroom. He turned on the shower and took off his soiled clothes and stepped into the shower. He washed and turned off the shower and toweled dry. Clean again. He wrapped a towel around his waist and walked out of the bathroom. It had been a long day and he wanted to be fresh for tonight. He lay down on the bed and set the alarm on his phone so he would not oversleep and would still have time to pack before he left for the evening. Even though he liked the restaurant and the rooftop bar, he had decided to burn the hotel to the ground after retrieving the security camera hard drives and the copy of his passport. There was a chance the rude couple from Texas was still here and he liked the idea of burning them alive as they slept. His mind was strangely at ease. He closed his eyes and slept.

It was dark. Eve and Billy sat in the cafe watching. A half-eaten pastry and two empty coffee cups sat on the table. The cafe staff had started the end-of-shift clean-up signaling their customers they would be closing soon. The nomad exited the hotel holding the boning knife box in one hand and a woman's helmet in the other. He was wearing a white linen jacket over his slacks and looked like he was going on a date. Billy signaled a waitress for the bill.

"Wait until he passes before putting on your helmet. Don't forget to turn on your phone earpiece. Just remember what I taught you. You take the first leg and follow him from behind. Don't crowd him. I'll follow him on a parallel street" said Eve.

The nomad walked to his scooter, opened the seat compartment, removed his helmet and placed the knife box and the woman's helmet inside and closed the compartment.

"If he turns towards me on the parallel street, you don't turn but go straight and I'll pick him up" said

Eve. "If he turns in the opposite direction, you turn with him but only once and only until we can switch places. If he pulls over, you go straight and pass him. I'll be the one who goes back to see what he's doing."

Billy nodded. The waitress brought the bill and Billy paid it. The nomad mounted the scooter and put on his helmet. He started the engine and pulled out into traffic and looked in the mirror to see if anyone had pulled out after him. It was clear. He headed down the street and past the cafe. Eve and Billy picked up their helmets off the floor and put them on. The nomad rounded the corner at the end of the block.

"Okay go" said Eve.

Eve and Billy sprinted to two motor scooters sitting in front of the cafe. They jumped on and started the engines and followed the nomad around the corner. The nomad was two blocks ahead of them. Eve took a left at the next corner and a right at the following corner. She sped up and followed the nomad on a parallel street. Billy passed several slower cars and moved up to within a block's distance of the nomad.

The nomad drove down a street with heavy traffic and glanced in his mirror and saw a large man wearing a helmet on a scooter passing a slower car several cars back. He didn't think much of it but made a note to himself of the color and style of the scooter. He glanced to his left and saw another scooter on the parallel street. The helmeted rider stared straight ahead uninterested in him. The nomad checked his mirror again and saw that the scooter behind him had moved up several cars. There was something odd about it. The nomad pulled over and stopped.

"He's pulled over" said Billy over his headset.

"He's probably checking for tails. Just go straight to the next block and turn right then left at the next street. You'll take parallel now. I'll see what he's up to."

Billy continued going straight. The nomad watched the scooter pass and could not see the rider's face because of the helmet face shield but saw that the rider was big and tall. The nomad looked down to see a cowboy boot on the scooter's foot peg.

"Is that you cowboy?" the nomad said to himself.

He watched the scooter continue down the street and take a right turn and disappear behind a building. The nomad did not move and watched. He considered turning back to the hotel and calling off his evening activities, but his need was strong and welled up inside and demanded release. He would continue with caution.

Eve turned and pulled to a stop one block up from where the nomad had pulled over and was watching. She casually looked over in the nomad's direction as if looking at the oncoming traffic and turned back to look down the other side of the street as if she was going to pull out.

The nomad looked over at the woman on a scooter who had stopped and was waiting for traffic. Her face was covered with a helmet face shield. Eve again glanced over at the nomad now staring directly at her.

She stayed calm and turned back casually to watch the traffic.

"He's on to me" said Eve in her mobile's earpiece.

A break in traffic came. Eve drove across the street and disappeared behind the same building Billy had disappeared behind. She pulled up next to Billy.

"I think he knows something's up. We'll follow him on parallel streets. Go up one street and turn left then go up two streets and turn right. We'll let him go ahead of us so he doesn't see us but if he turns, one of us will see him."

Billy nodded and followed her instructions.

The nomad waited another minute before he was satisfied nobody was following him. He pulled back out into traffic and down the street. Billy and Eve bracketed his movements on parallel streets. The nomad glanced in his rear mirror and down the side streets as he passed them and saw nothing unusual. The nomad pulled over and parked in front of the Reggae Club. Eve pulled up to the closest corner and watched from a distance. The nomad stepped off his scooter and pulled his helmet off and walked into the club.

"He's pulled over in front of a club and gone inside" said Eve into her earpiece. "Park on the Southeast corner but keep your distance."

Billy parked on the opposite corner and walked into a store and bought a Coke and watched the front of the club through the store window. Eve watched from the street corner and kneeled down as if repairing something on the scooter. It was a good angle. She saw a glimpse of the nomad through the club's open patio entrance.

The nomad sat on the patio near the front of the little stage and set his helmet on the chair beside him and ordered a drink. The singer was already performing. She recognized him from his previous visit and smiled. A fan she thought. Good for tips. Maybe he'll buy a CD.

Eve glanced down the opposite end of the street and saw a luggage store.

"Billy I've got an idea. Do you have a good enough view to keep watch for a few minutes?"

"Yeah. I'm good."

Eve walked down to the luggage store and entered. The owner was already closing up for the night.

"We closing."

"I'll only be a minute. Do you have a luggage locator and a roll of heavy-duty packing tape?"

Eve left the store with a bag and moved back to her scooter.

"Okay. I'm back" she said in her mobile earpiece.

She pulled a box from the shopping bag and opened it. She pulled out a small luggage locator device. She inserted a battery in the device and a green light blinked showing it was active. She took out her phone and entered the link for the device's app and downloaded the app on her phone. She opened the app and inputted the device's locator code on the instruction sheet. The device's location showed up on a map of the area and an arrow pointed in the direction of the device.

"Billy I am sending you a link. Install the app on your phone. It's a tracking device. It's Bluetooth so it's only good for a hundred feet but it may help if we lose him." She sent the link.

"Got it" said Billy.

Eve pulled out the roll of heavy-duty packing tape. She pulled off a small strip and folded it into a loop with the sticky side on the outside and pressed the tracking device onto one side of the tape. She walked across the street and down the sidewalk toward the club. She turned away as she walked in front of the entrance. She walked over to the nomad's scooter and pressed the tape with the tracking device under the taillight. It held. She moved off back the way she came and returned to her scooter and checked the signal. It was good.

"Billy check your app" she said.

"It works. I got 'em" he said.

The nomad sat and nursed a gin and tonic—the only sensible mixed drink for a hot and humid evening. He listened to the young singer perform. His eyes met hers for a moment and she smiled shyly at the attention. She finished the song. The nomad rose and walked over and deposited 100 ringgit in her tip jar.

"Thanks" she said.

"You're good. I want to encourage you."

"Can I play something for you?"

"No. You're doing fine without my interference. But you can join me for a drink when your set is finished."

She glanced over at a young Malaysian man sitting at a table with several male friends. The young man watched an attractive waitress in a short black dress bend over as she served drinks. The young singer was obviously miffed at his wandering eyes. *Probably her boyfriend* thought the nomad.

"Sure" said the young singer.

"Great" said the nomad with a smile.

"Just three more in the set."

"I look forward to hearing them."

The nomad sat back down at his table and she started the next song. He watched the boyfriend get up and walk toward the toilet in the back of the club. He saw the young singer watching him. The waitress also headed to the back of club where the kitchen was also located. The young singer wasn't happy. The nomad reached into his jacket pocket and pulled out a cigar. He kept the cigar out of sight beneath the table and bent the cigar until it snapped in half. He waited until the singer turned his way and pulled out the broken cigar and cursed under his breath. The singer gave him a shrug and a smile. He shrugged back and rose from the table and walked into the back of the club to buy a new cigar from the bartender.

The nomad walked past the bar and entered the bathroom at the back of the club. He could hear the boyfriend fucking the waitress in one of the two toilet stalls. The nomad moved to the urinal and unzipped. Two men who had been seated with the boyfriend came into the bathroom. The nomad turned his face away as if minding his own business. The two men snorted some cocaine and shouted a rude comment in Malay to the boyfriend and waitress. The boyfriend cursed back in Malay. The two men laughed and left the bathroom.

The nomad continued to stand at the urinal as the couple completed their rapture. The waitress came out first and saw the nomad standing at the urinal minding his own business with his face turned away. She walked to the sink and splashed water into her vagina and grabbed a paper towel from the dispenser and dried herself and straightened her dress and slipped out of the bathroom. The bathroom was now empty except for the nomad and the boyfriend. The nomad zipped up and walked over and slid a rubber doorstop leftover from the cleaning crew under the closed bathroom door and gave it a little kick to lodge it firmly. He removed his jacket and folded it and set it on the sink counter.

The boyfriend exited the stall and zipped up his pants. He came face to face with the nomad standing in front of the sink. The boyfriend cursed the nomad in Malay and pushed past him. The nomad pulled the homemade sap from his back pocket and hit him hard on the back of the skull. The boyfriend crumbled to the floor unconscious. The nomad dragged him back into the stall and sat him on the toilet. He could not be sure how long the boyfriend would stay unconscious. The nomad pulled the toilet paper roll off its hanger and peeled off several layers to make the roll thinner and squeezed the roll until the cardboard tube collapsed. He shoved the collapsed roll vertically into the boyfriend's mouth. The boyfriend still unconscious began to choke. The boyfriend woke and choked and saw the nomad's calm face. The nomad pressed the roll deep into the boyfriend's throat with the palm of his hand. The boyfriend struggled and grabbed the nomad's hand and tried to pull it away from the roll. The nomad was too strong and the boyfriend too weak from lack of air. There was a knock on the bathroom door as someone was trying to get in. The nomad pushed the roll further down into the boyfriend's throat. The boyfriend stopped struggling and went limp. More knocks on the door. The nomad pulled off the boyfriend's belt and threaded the belt through the back loop of the boyfriend's pants then cinched the belt around the toilet's flushing unit to keep the boyfriend's corpse from slipping down. The nomad locked the stall door from the inside.

He slid underneath the stall door and put on his jacket and kicked away the rubber doorstop. The nomad turned his face away as another man entered the bathroom. The man saw nothing out of the ordinary and moved into the unoccupied stall. The nomad straightened his clothes and hair and slipped out of the bathroom.

The nomad walked to the bar and bought a cigar from the bartender and walked back to the patio and sat at his table. He lit his cigar and listened to the young singer as she finished her set. The singer sat down across from him.

"You have a beautiful voice" said the nomad.

"Thank you."

"What would you like?"

"I'll just have a San Miguel Light."

"Beer? That's not a drink."

"Okay. Tequila shot."

The nomad ordered two tequila shots.

"Where you from?" she said.

"United States. Boston."

"Where Boston?"

"Do you know Disneyland? California?"

"Yes."

"It's not there."

They laughed together. The waiter brought the two tequila shots and set them on the table with a small plate of rock salt and several limes.

"Boston is above New York. You know New York?"

"I see New York on television. Times Square?"

"Yes Times Square where the ball drops on New Year's Eve."

"Dick Clark" said the singer.

"Well let's hope not. He's dead. That would not be a pretty sight."

She laughed. "You funny."

"I try."

The singer glanced toward the back of the club in search of her boyfriend.

"Are you looking for someone?"

She thought for a moment. "No."

"Well we best get to it."

He motioned to the two shot glasses. They each took a glass. She licked the top of her hand sprinkled some salt and picked up a lime.

"I see you've done this before."

"Yes."

"I thought Malaysians didn't drink?"

"This one drink."

"In that case, cheers."

"We say Yam Sing."

"What's that mean?"

"It mean finish drinking."

"Aaah. We say bottoms up!"

She looked confused. "Like bottom?" She pointed to her ass.

"Exactly."

They clinked glasses and she licked the salt on her hand and they drank the tequila and she bit the lime.

"So have you been to the new club?"

"Which new club?"

"In the old ship on the pier."

"Boat on pier has club?"

"Yes. Everybody is talking about it."

The nomad pulled a fake flyer from his jacket pocket, unfolded it and handed it to the singer. The flyer showed a nightclub and a drawing of the freighter.

"I'm going there later. You are welcome to join me."

"I can't. I have boyfriend. He give me ride home."

"Oh I see. Is that who you were looking for?"

"Yes."

"Well I understand. You could bring him. I will buy the drinks."

"I ask him."

"Good. I want another drink. How about you?"

She looked around again. No sign of the boyfriend. "Okay" she said and smiled.

Another hour had passed. The singer was much more relaxed after several more tequila shots. The nomad dumped his shot over his shoulder and let the tequila fall to the floor when she wasn't looking. The nomad gestured to the waiter for the check.

"Well it has been a pleasure meeting you."

"You go now?"

"Yes it is getting late and I still want to go to that new club."

"Yes you have fun."

"If you find your boyfriend maybe you bring him later?"

"Maybe."

The waiter gave the nomad the final bill. The nomad pulled out a thick wad of cash for the singer to see and paid the check.

"Are you going to be okay getting home?"

"Yes I okay."

"I could give you a ride."

"No my boyfriend take me."

"Of course. He must be around here somewhere. Well good night."

"Good night."

The nomad picked up his helmet and rose from the table and walked toward the entrance. She liked him. He was fun. She didn't want the night to end with her alone waiting again for a boyfriend who didn't really care about her. She knew in her heart her boyfriend was fucking other women behind her back. She knew.

"Wait!" said the singer.

The nomad stopped and turned. "Yes?"

"I go with you."

"Okay."

"I get my purse."

"I'll meet you outside."

She walked to the stage and knelt down behind the large speaker and grabbed her purse and took one last look for her boyfriend. Nothing. The nomad walked out of the club entrance and to his scooter. Billy spotted him first.

"Do you see him?" said Billy.

"Yeah I got him" said Eve.

The nomad opened the helmet compartment and removed the extra helmet and left the knife box concealed in the bottom. He closed the compartment and put his helmet on and climbed on the scooter. The singer walked out front with her purse and crossed over to the nomad's scooter.

"Who's the girl?" said Billy.

"I don't know. I haven't seen her before" said Eve.

The nomad handed the singer a helmet.

"I wouldn't want to scratch your beautiful face" said the nomad.

She put the helmet on and hopped on the back of the scooter.

"He's gonna kill her" said Billy.

"You don't know that and we've got no proof" said Eve. "He's not gonna kill everyone he meets."

"No but he's gonna kill her. I can feel it."

"There's no evidence Billy. It's our word against his and you are not exactly a pillar of credibility."

"Eve listen. He's—going—to—kill—her."

Eve looked over at the girl on the back of the scooter. "All right. I'll call the police" said Eve.

Eve hit a speed dial number on her phone. The nomad started the scooter's engine.

"So, do you want to go to your home or do you want to have a drink at the new nightclub first?"

"Nightclub for one drink. Okay?"

"Okay. Nightclub it is. Hang on tight."

She wrapped her arms around his waist and the nomad hung a U-turn and rode past Eve on the corner without noticing her.

"We're gonna lose him" said Billy.

Eve was still waiting for the police to answer.

"Come on goddamn it" said Eve into the phone. "Answer your fucking phone."

"I can't let this happen again" said Billy.

Eve watched Billy exit the store and jump on his scooter and start the engine. He pulled into traffic and followed the nomad and the singer. Eve stepped into the street and yelled at Billy as he rode past.

"Goddamn it Billy. Wait for the police."

Eve climbed on her scooter and followed the others.

Billy trailed the nomad by 100 meters. He gunned his scooter's engine to catch up. The nomad turned a corner and Billy followed. Eve saw Billy turn and she followed from far back. The nomad slowed for a construction site repairing old sewer lines. The construction crew used a backhoe tractor as a crane to lower a new pipe into a large hole on one side of the street. The nomad rode past the tractor and hole.

Billy approached and flagman signaled for him to stop. The tractor lifted a new pipe and a construction worker guided it to the hole in the street. Billy swerved past the flagman and the flagman cursed him in Malay. The heavy pipe moved over the hole and the construction worker guiding it could no longer reach it to keep it steady and the tractor lurched hard and the pipe swung out into the opposite side of the street. Billy swerved to avoid the pipe and his front tire clipped the edge of a stack of steel plates used to cover the hole between shifts. He continued after the nomad and felt the handlebars shimmy. He looked down—a flat front tire.

"Goddamn it" said Billy.

Eve was caught behind a line of traffic waiting to pass the construction site. She pulled out into the middle of the street and eased her way forward dodging oncoming traffic. Billy saw the nomad turn three blocks ahead. Billy sped up as fast as he dared and the handlebars shook violently. He leaned into the corner where the nomad had turned and hoped his weight would keep the scooter on track. It didn't. The front tire folded under and off the rim and bunched up in the forks. The scooter stopped abruptly and Billy flew over the handlebars and tumbled across the street and hit the curb hard with his shoulder and helmet. He was dazed but not unconscious. He looked down the street and tried to focus his eyes and saw the nomad turning again at the end of the street. In the distance he saw the lights of anchored ships in the harbor. He rose to his knees and then to his feet. He walked over to the scooter lying in the middle of the street. It was useless. He looked again down the street. It was empty. He could feel the pain in his shoulder—maybe broken.

"Eve I've lost him. He's down by the water" he said into his mobile earpiece. There was no response. "Eve?" he said again. Still nothing. Maybe it had been damaged in the fall.

Everything was on the line. Buck up you pussy. It ain't nothing you ain't felt before.

He started toward the end of the street where the nomad had turned. A slow trot at first and then a full out run.

Eve moved past the construction site and looked down the street. The taillight of Billy's scooter was nowhere in sight. She tried to raise Billy on the mobile link. Nothing. She sped up and rode down the street and looked at the side streets as she passed.

The nomad turned into the empty warehouses in front of the pier and slowed.

"Should be somewhere along here" he yelled back to the young singer.

Billy reached the end of the street and turned in the direction the nomad had gone and saw nothing but darkness. The nomad was gone. He slowed his run and walked not knowing where to go but refusing to give up.

The singer looked out at the dark buildings. Nobody was in sight. She felt uneasy. The nomad dialed his phone and triggered the remote switch. Inside the freighter hold, the CD player and the laser jumped to life. Music blared as multiple lasers shot up into the night sky.

Billy saw the lasers and heard the music in the distance. He picked up his pace and ran toward the pier.

The girl heard the music but still saw nothing.

"I hear music."

"Me too" said the nomad. "We must be close."

The nomad pulled past another dark warehouse and the girl saw the lasers coming from the ship.

"There it is" she said pointing.

"Oh you're right."

The nomad turned and parked at the edge of the pier. They both climbed off. The nomad took her helmet and opened the seat compartment. She watched the light show. The nomad pulled out the knife box and tucked it in his jacket pocket like a jewelry box. He placed her helmet inside the compartment and closed the seat. He set his helmet on the handlebars knowing there was nobody around to steal it. He gently grabbed her hand and guided her down the pier toward the ship.

"This cool" she said.

"I thought you might like it."

Eve rode down the street and saw Billy's scooter lying

in the middle of a side street with the taillight still on and the back tire slowly spinning. She turned and stopped and looked around for Billy. Nothing. She pulled out her phone and studied the locator app. Nothing. She continued down the street and checked each of the side streets and glanced at the locator app and hoped to see something.

Billy ran to the edge of the pier and saw the nomad's scooter. Billy bent over to catch his breath and turned to the ship and saw the nomad leading the singer up the gangway. He ran down the pier toward the ship.

The nomad and the young singer walked up the gangway and stepped onto the deck of the freighter.

"I no see any people" said the singer.

"They must be here somewhere. They're probably over there on the back of the ship. Where the lights are."

The girl nodded and climbed the ladder to get to the stern of the ship. He watched her legs rising up before him on the ladder. The need inside him swelled and he followed her up the ladder.

Eve rode down the street. She knew the odds were slim that she would find the nomad. She thought the best way was to cover multiple streets by taking a side street in the direction he was originally heading and hope to pick up something on the locator app or see something. She turned down a side street and rode two blocks and saw a blip on the phone app. It was in the direction of the beach street. She turned and stopped at the beach street corner and studied the signal on the app. It was in the direction of a pier. She looked up and saw the silhouette of a pier and a ship with lasers shooting into the sky. It had to be it. She turned toward the ship. Her phone was still on hold with the police station and the annoying music played in the background and was occasionally interrupted by a recorded voice speaking in Malay.

The nomad and the singer stood on the stern deck and looked down into the hull and saw the laser projector spinning but no people.

"I still no see people."

"No. No people. It's a private party. Just you and me. See?"

The nomad pointed to the crane. She turned and saw the crane and the rope hanging over the hull. She saw the ropes and harnesses and she knew she was in trouble. It was too late. The nomad pulled the homemade sap from his back pocket and smacked it across the base of the girl's skull. She crumbled to the deck unconscious. The nomad slipped the sap back into his pocket and scooped up the girl like a side of beef and hoisted her over his shoulder and walked toward the ladder leading to the rear deck and heard a voice.

"Hey shithead."

The nomad turned to see Billy standing below on the pier.

"Cowboy you have very poor timing."

"Do you want me to come up and kick your ass or you wanna come down?"

The nomad could see that Billy was breathing hard.

"You look tired. I'll come down."

The nomad set the girl down on the deck and walked back across the outer corridor and down the front ladder. He walked across the deck and stopped at the top of the gangway and reached inside his jacket. He removed the knife box, opened it and took out the boning knife. He dropped the empty box on the deck and held the knife with the blade pointed forward for stabbing. With his free hand he reached into his pants pocket and unsheathed his karambit knife. He slid his forefinger in the knife's safety ring and pulled it from his pocket and held it with the blade against his wrist ready to slash. The nomad walked down the gangway to the pier.

Billy reached into his boot and pulled out the greasing rag and unwrapped the fishing knife. He held the knife's handle with the blade point forward in a stabbing position and wrapped the rag around his free hand for protection. Billy knew that knife fights were not long affairs. He had seen a few. The first to be maimed was a dead man. One maybe two minutes tops and it would be over. One of them was about to die and if it was Billy, the girl would die too.

"You are really starting to annoy me cowboy" said the nomad.

"You always talk this much?" said Billy.

The nomad's face tightened as he moved toward Billy and closed the distance between them. Billy glanced down and saw several of the boards on the pier were loose with their edges sticking up. Not good ground. One slip and it would be over. Billy circled away from the nomad's boning knife and forced the nomad to follow the circle to keep away from Billy's knife hand. Their feet stumbled across the loose boards. The nomad took several playful slashes with each of his knives and probed Billy's reaction time. Billy was quick to move out of the blade's path without taking his eyes off the nomad. He stabbed back and forced the nomad to keep away.

Billy's boot caught on a loose board and he stumbled. The nomad slashed at Billy's face with the boning knife and Billy pitched backward to avoid the blade. His hands shot out in front to keep his balance and the nomad slashed with the karambit at Billy's knife hand and caught the flesh just below the thumb and cut a deep gash. Billy dropped his knife to the pier and knew he was a dead man without a weapon. The nomad stepped forward for the final stroke and heard the whine of a motor scooter engine coming up behind him. He turned and saw Eve speeding toward him on her scooter. He would slash her face as she passed. She laid down her scooter and it slid across the pier toward the nomad and she slid with it. The scooter knocked him off his feet and he fell. Eve skidded to a stop next to him. He swung the boning knife down at her and she rolled away to avoid it and the knife struck deep into the pier. He tried to remove it but it would not come free. Billy picked up his knife with his free hand and stepped forward. The nomad, still holding the karambit, climbed to his feet and faced Billy. Blood flowed from Billy's wound. The nomad slashed wildly at Billy's face and throat. Billy lunged and stabbed and found the nomad's side and the rusted blade hit rib and broke off and left Billy with a knife broken at the handle. The nomad was hurt but not out and moved forward again and slashed at Billy. Eve reached into her pocket and pulled her small can of pepper spray and flipped the safety top with her thumb and fired. The stream of dark liquid shot across the pier and hit the nomad in the face and eyes. He screamed in pain and stumbled unable to see and fell backward and disappeared off the side of the pier. Billy ran and looked over the edge into the blackness below and saw a circle of foam where the nomad hit the water. There was no sign of the nomad.

Billy ran over and pulled the boning knife from the pier and ran back to the edge of the pier where the nomad had fallen.

"Billy don't" said Eve.

Billy jumped. He landed boots first. The water was shallow and his boot stuck deep in the mud. He looked around at the hull of the ship with a large hole rusted through its side and the pilings supporting the pier—each a potential hiding place. He struggled to free himself before the nomad could attack from the darkness. But the attack never came. The nomad was gone.

CHAPTER 21

It was night. Billy sat and stared out the hotel window at the city below. His hand was bandaged and throbbed from the eight stitches that held close the knife wound. He had been fortunate that his shoulder was not broken and only badly bruised. The door opened and Eve entered. She walked over and stood behind him and stared out the window with him in silence.

"How did it go?" he said.

"Good. The police have set up checkpoints at the airport and ferry terminal and a roadblock on the only bridge off the island."

"It won't matter."

"No. It won't. He's gone."

She sat down across from him.

"But it looks like you're off the hook for Noi's murder. There is a lot of hard evidence plus the girl's statement. The police captain wasn't thrilled that we went after him on our own but he promised to call the Thai police and explain what happened. You'll still need to go back to Phuket and give a statement but it is highly unlikely they would still prosecute at this point."

"I let her down."

"You saved that girl."

Billy looked over at Eve and she understood.

"You mean Noi" said Eve. "Yeah. I see why you would feel that but it's not your fault. He's insane. He was going to kill someone."

"Yeah but not her. He killed her because of me. Because of what I did." Billy turned and stared out the window again.

"I've been thinking" said Eve. "I'm going to talk with the insurance company. If you come back with me now and give back the money, I think I can get them to drop all charges against you. You'd be free again."

"I'm not going back. It's not over."

"Billy we found him because he made mistakes. He won't make them again. He's gone."

"I'll find him."

"No you won't. Billy this is the best deal you're gonna get."

"I don't want a deal. I want him dead."

"I told you I'm not going to be part of that."

"I know and I respect your decision. But he has to be stopped. He'll kill again and again and he'll continue to kill until I find him and put an end to it."

"And what about your promise to me?"

"I'll give you the money."

"That's not the promise I meant. You said we'd turn him over to the police when we found him. Evil is a constant. Killing doesn't solve anything. It just perpetuates a vicious circle of violence."

"I could do without the lecture."

"I am sorry for what happened to Noi but from what you've told me about her, I don't think this is the life she would want for you."

"You need to shut up now."

Eve rose and walked out into her bedroom and closed the door behind her.

It was morning and raining. Eve sat alone in the hotel cafe. A full English breakfast sat before her untouched. Billy entered the cafe holding his boots and walked over.

"I'll be leaving now" he said. "I want to apologize for

last night. I know you tried your best and I appreciate it."

"Sit."

"What?"

"Sit. You gotta eat don't ya?"

Billy shrugged and sat. The waitress came over and Billy ordered.

"I may have a way."

"A way?"

"To find him. Well not find him. But make him want to find us."

"Okay. I'll bite."

"We take his money."

"His money?"

"He can't keep traveling without money. We cut off his cashflow and he's stuck."

"I agree that would piss him off. But why would he want to find us?"

"So he can kill us."

"For revenge?"

"More than that. Without being too obvious we let him know that if he kills us he also eliminates the block on his cash flow."

"How are we gonna do that? We have no way of reaching him."

"He'll reach out to us."

"It changes things a bit don't it? We being the bait."

"Certainly. But if we want 'im. That's how we get him."

"You have a plan?"

"I do. But the deal is the same as before. We find him and turn him over to the police."

"Goddammit Eve."

"I'm not gonna be part of killing Billy. If ya gotta kill 'im, good luck to ya. You can find him on you own."

Billy thought long and hard. Eve sat silent. Breakfast came and neither moved or said a word. The waitress poured Billy some coffee and left.

"Deal" said Billy.

Eve and Billy sat in their hotel suite. Eve took a deep breath and picked up her phone and dialed. The receptionist to a law firm answered.

"Mr. Martin please" said Eve.

"Mr. Martin is in court. May I take a message?" said the receptionist.

"Aye. Please tell Mr. Martin I will call again in one hour and that if he does not want to spend the next five years in jail, I suggest he take my call."

"Excuse me?"

"I think you heard me."

"May I ask your name?"

"You may not."

"Can you hold please?"

"Of course."

The receptionist put Eve on hold. After one minute Mr. Martin came on the phone.

"Who the hell is this?" said Martin.

"My name is Eve Donahue, Mr. Martin. You are the trustee for the Kyle Tanner estate, are you not?"

"What if I am?"

"Then you've been a bad boy Mr. Martin."

"You've got ten seconds to explain yourself or I am hanging up."

"Oh I doubt that."

The phone went silent. Eve waited ten seconds.

"Still there Mr. Martin?"

"What do you want?"

"You have been wiring funds to an account in the

name of Kyle Tanner."

"There is nothing wrong with transferring trust funds to the trustee's account. That's my job."

"Aye but Mr. Tanner is committed to a mental institution."

"So what?"

"So who has been withdrawing the funds each month?"

"I'm sure I don't know."

"I'm sure you do. I am also sure there are monthly wire transfers into your overseas account and that those amounts will correlate as a percentage of the trust transfers."

"How did you get this information?"

"I hacked your accounts. Actually I didn't hack them. I hired someone to hack them. He's very good."

"That's a felony."

"Aye it is. And so is embezzlement."

"How do I know you really have what you say?"

"I'm holding copies of the bank statements. Would you like me to email them to you? I think your email address is on your website."

"That won't be necessary."

"Wouldn't want that kind of evidence hanging around

on your server where it could be subpoenaed now would ya?"

"What do you want?"

"I want you to stop."

"That's it? Just stop."

"Aye. If I see one more dime transferred from the trust account beyond Mr. Tanner's monthly hospital bill, I'll send what I have to the FBI and your state bar association."

"And if you don't see any money transferred?"

"Then you won't hear from me again and you can go on living your life as if this phone call never happened."

"And that's it?"

"That's it. I know you won't agree over the phone. I could be taping this conversation and your consent could be used against you in court."

"Are you recording this conversation?"

"No. I don't need to. I've got enough to convict you and we both know it. So let's just say that if you hang up in the next three seconds, we got ourselves a deal."

Martin hung up.

"Why didn't you have him put us in touch with the nomad?" said Billy.

"He would never do it. It would directly implicate him in a felony."

"So what's next?"

"We wait until the nomad communicates with us."

"How?"

"I don't know but he will."Martin stood outside a courtroom and pulled out his wallet. He removed a prepaid calling card with an overseas phone number written in pen on the back. He walked into the phone booth and closed the door. He picked up the receiver and dialed the calling card number, heard a tone and dialed the overseas phone number written on the calling card.

The nomad with his eyes still red and puffy from the pepper spray lay on an examination table with his shirt off and surgical shields covering his side, chest and back. A doctor assisted by a nurse closed the 2-inch wound in his side with twenty-two stitches. The nomad's phone rang and he looked at the number on the screen and answered it. "We've got a problem" said Martin.

The nomad walked into a bookstore. His side was tender from the surgery and the local anesthetic was wearing off. He pulled a prescription bottle from his pocket, opened it, removed a pain pill and swallowed it without water and put the bottle back in his pocket. He studied a spinning rack of maps and selected one covering Southeast Asia.

The nomad entered his hotel room and closed the

door. He locked the deadbolt and walked over to a table. He unfolded the map and laid it out on the table top to study it.

Eve and Billy lay on lounge chairs by the hotel pool. Eve was in her bathing suit. Billy was fully clothed and wearing his boots and looked antsy.

"Where's your laptop?" said Billy.

"It's in the room. Why?"

"I want to check his credit card accounts again."

"Daesh is doing that."

"Yeah well what if he misses something?"

"He's not going to miss anything."

"People make mistakes."

"Not Daesh."

"How do you know?"

"Because I've worked with him for the last eight years."

"And you trust him?"

"Daesh is as solid as they get."

"Okay."

Eve turned over to tan her back. Billy noticed her figure and felt guilty like he was somehow betraying Noi by just looking at another woman.

"Never understood it" said Billy.

"Understood what?"

"How people could come all this way and just lay around all day."

"It's easy with the right amount of alcohol."

"Why not do something? Anything. It's a beautiful country. Better than sittin' soaking up skin cancer."

"Relax Billy. It's his move. Let him make it."

Eve's phone chimed. She picked it up and shielded the screen from the sun with her hand.

"Email from Daesh. We got a credit card hit."

"What is it?"

"Looks like he bought an airline ticket from Denspar Indonesia to a place called Pangkalan Bun Indonesia."

"On Borneo?"

"I guess. Do you know it?"

"Yeah I was there last year."

"So you know the area. That's good."

"Yeah but I don't get it. Why would he wanna see the orangutans?"

"Orangutans? Like at a zoo?"

"No. They're wild orangutans. There's a research

center and ranger stations with feeding platforms up and down the river. The orangutans go to feed during the dry season when their natural food supply is low."

"How do you know he's going there?"

"There's nothing else to do in Pangkalan Bun. It's a small town a few miles from Tanjung Puting National Park on Borneo. Tourists rent klotoks at the harbor. That's the only reason the town exists."

"What's a klotok?"

"It's like a two-story houseboat that comes with its own crew. People rent them and go up the Sungai Sekonyer River for a couple of days and sleep onboard."

"How many klotoks do you think there are?"

"Fifty maybe sixty."

"And they all go up the same river?"

"Yep."

Eve pulled up a Google map of the area around the national forest on her phone. There was a long river that started deep in the island and led to the coast.

"So we go up river and check out every klotok as we pass. He's got to be on one right?"

"Yeah but that's the thing. There's only one way up that river and there are no roads going in or out of the area. The rainforest is too thick. He goes up there it's a trap."

"No. It's an invitation" said Eve.

CHAPTER 22

The nomad stared out the window of a Boeing 737 flying over the emerald waters of the Karimata Strait that divided the two main islands of Indonesia. In the distance was a mountain of green—Borneo. Man carved out patches of civilization from the dense rainforests that covered the island but it was still a wild place, one of the few remaining on the planet. The equator divided the island, and the heat and humidity were unforgiving. The Boeing 737 jet touched down on a single runway surrounded by a thick rainforest. The out buildings that lined the runway were rusted from lack of maintenance with some abandoned from too little business.

The sky was blue and spotted with small bunches of white and grey clouds. The harbor had been excavated out of the surrounding jungle and had to be maintained monthly to keep the jungle from reclaiming what was once its own. A taxi dodged

muddy potholes and pulled up in front of the pier.
The nomad stepped out and collected his backpack.
He paid the driver and the taxi drove away. There was
no one in sight to greet him or help him with his
luggage. He lifted the backpack over his shoulder and
winced from the pain. He walked out onto the pier. It
was early in the afternoon and most of the boats had
already left with their passengers. He saw a two-story
houseboat at the end of the pier and a young
Indonesian man leaning against the top of a piling
asleep. He walked over and set his backpack down on
the pier and tapped the man's bare foot with his shoe.
The man woke and looked up.

"I'm looking for the Buaya Darat" said the nomad.

"This Buaya Darat. I guide" said the man. "You have
passport?"

The nomad handed him a passport.

"I make copy. Wait here."

The man disappeared inside an office. The nomad felt
the sun burning the back of his neck. There was no
shade on the pier. He thought about going on board
but decided to wait until asked. He needed the crew's
cooperation and didn't want to make trouble or raise
any suspicions.

He walked along the boat and studied its structure.
The klotok was made of ironwood and teak and was
painted blue and white. It had a rust red hull. The
bottom deck held the wheelhouse, the crew quarters
and the galley. There were several rectangular holes of
various sizes cut out of the walls that served as

windows and were purposely left open in hopes of a breeze. The top deck was an open-air patio with a solid wood roof with clear plastic tarps rolled up that could be unfurled to form see-through walls during a rainstorm. On the back of the top deck was a small dining table with chairs and in the center of the deck were two twin beds turned into couches for afternoon naps. On the front of the top deck were two lounge chairs that gave guests a commanding view of the river and surrounding rainforest. There were two ladders on either end of the top deck leading below to the stern and the foredeck of the boat. A roofless and windowless wooden box that served as the outhouse and shower was built on the back of the lower deck. Inside the outhouse a large tub of water was filled twice a day from the river and used by the crew and guests to flush the toilet. The nomad saw the name Buaya Darat neatly painted on the stern. A woman's head popped out of the galley window. She was Indonesian and had an attractive face.

"Are you guest?" said the woman.

"Yes."

"I cook. Very hot. You want water?"

"Is it bottled?"

"Yes. Very clean and cold. We have Coke and beer too."

"Water."

The cook's head disappeared back through the hole and she reappeared from the galley's doorway holding a cold bottle of water. She handed it to the nomad. He opened it and drank half.

"Where you from?"

"America."

"America good but too many war. You have wife?"

"No."

He motioned to the name on the stern of the boat. "What does it mean Buaya Darat?"

"Land crocodile but mean like woman chaser."

"We say playboy in English."

"Ah playboy. That funny."

"Will the captain show me how to pilot the boat?"

"Yes. I think he show you."

"Good."

The cook stepped off the boat and picked up the backpack with ease and slipped her arms through the straps. She was surprisingly strong.

"Come. I show you boat and meet captain."

The nomad followed her onto the boat and up the stern ladder.

The Buaya Darat chugged down the wide river. There was no visible shoreline along the river. The rainforest was pushed to the edge of the water and then some. The water was a dark blue with occasional patches of green vegetation that had broken loose from the plants growing along the banks and were now floating down the river.

In the wheelhouse the pilot instructed the nomad on operating the throttle and steering the vessel. The nomad practiced steering. The throttle was older than the boat and had been recycled from an older boat that finally met its demise. The throttle had two levers but only one side worked since there was only one engine, a 100 hp diesel with a top cruising speed of 9 knots. It wasn't fast but it was reliable.

"Not hard steer in big river. Not easy steer in jungle. More broken tree in water. If go under boat break prop. Very bad. Much money fix" said the pilot.

"Where are we now?"

"Here" the pilot said and pointed to a map. River go straight to ocean. "We turn here into jungle river and go up to see orangutan."

"Only one way in and out of jungle river?"

"Yes. All tourist boat go. Everyone want to see orangutan."

The Buaya Darat approached a tributary into the wide main river. The water from the tributary was light brown like coffee with too much cream. Where the two rivers met the dark blue water of the main river and coffee-colored water of the tributary mixed creating a murky grey color. The nomad steered the klotok upstream into the tributary river leading into the jungle. The edges of the river closed to four boat widths in most places and wider in others. The jungle was impenetrable, a solid mass of dark green. The occasional honey bee tree with its smooth grey bark shot up from the tangles and towered over the rainforest and gave the animals a safe perch to nap in the afternoon breeze. The nomad could smell the rotting vegetation in the still air. The heat was held captive by the forest wall on both sides of the river and the sun reflected off the water raising the temperature even further. The only relief from the heat was the breeze created from the motion of the boat.

It was early morning. Billy and Eve exited the small airport of Iskandar. Annisa—an attractive Balinese woman wearing Ray Bans left behind by a tourist— saw Billy and immediately rushed over.

"Mr. Billy. I was so excited when I hear you come back" Annisa said and gave him a big hug.

"Thanks Annisa. I'm excited to see you again. I want you to meet Eve. She'll be with us on the boat."

Annisa gave Eve a big hug.

"You very lucky girl be with Mr. Billy. He good man."

"No. We're not—" said Eve.

"She's just a friend Annisa" said Billy.

Annisa give them an incredulous look.

"Friends? That how you do in America?"

"Yeah just friends. Listen we are looking for someone."

"Another friend?"

"No. I mean…yeah we'll say he's a friend. He is on one of the other klotoks. We need to find him. Okay?"

"Sure. We go where you want."

Eve pulled out the photo of the nomad and showed it to Annisa.

"Have you seen this man?" asked Eve.

"No. He handsome. He American too?"

"Aye. He's American."

"We find him. All klotoks go same place."

"Good. We pay extra big tip if we find him" said Billy.

"No no. Not necessary. We help you find your friend. No extra charge. You good customer Mr. Billy."

"Thank you."

"Taxi over here. Where your bag Mr. Billy?"

"I don't have a bag Annisa."

"Oh you share bag with friend" Annisa said and nodded knowingly.

"No. It's not like that. I just—oh nevermind" said

Billy.

Annisa grabbed the bag from Eve's hand and loaded it into the taxi. Annisa climbed in the front seat next to the driver and Billy and Eve climbed in back. Billy looked at the driver in the rearview mirror as he drove out the parking lot. It was a face that had seen fighting with several scars.

It was a short ride to the pier. The taxi pulled to a stop and Annisa jumped out and grabbed Eve's bag from the trunk. Billy and Eve stepped out of the back of the taxi and looked at the flurry of activity. The klotoks were stacked three deep against the pier. The crews were busy loading their passengers and supplies. Billy motioned for the driver to wait five minutes. The driver nodded.

"I take it those are klotoks?" said Eve.

"That's them."

"This way please" said Annisa holding Eve's bag and leading the way to the pier.

"I can carry that" said Eve.

"Better not. It's her rice bowl" said Billy.

"What?"

"It's her job. The Balinese take pride in serving. You don't want to insult her."

Billy pointed to the third klotok on the left side of the pier with the name Mau Ke Mana written on the stern. The boat was painted red and white with a grey hull.

"That's us. Last one."

"What's it mean—Mau Ke Mana?"

"Loosely translated 'Where do you want to go'?"

Billy and Eve followed Annisa as she stepped over the wood railing onto the gunwale of the first boat. Billy and Eve cautiously looked into the depths of the first klotok and searched for the nomad.

"He not here. No guest arrive for this klotok until this afternoon" said Annisa.

"How about the next one?"

"I not sure. Maybe he there. I ask."

"No. It's better we look for him."

"You want surprise for him?"

"Aye. Surprise."

"Okay. You look. Crew not mind."

Eve and Billy stepped over the railing onto the gunwale of the second boat. Billy searched the lower deck while Eve and Annisa searched the top deck. No one was aboard. A large brown rat scampered across the deck in front of Eve.

"Rat" said Eve slightly alarmed.

"Yes. But not like dirty city rat. It jungle rat. Clean. They drop from tree in forest as boat pass under.

Sometime swim to boat and climb up rope from anchor."

"Rats swim."

"Yes. Very good at swim."

"That's comforting."

"They no hurt. Just want food for babies."

"Why don't you get a cat?"

"We do. But rat eat them."

Eve climbed down the ladder and met Billy on the stern.

"You see anything?"

"Yeah a very large rat."

"Sorry. I should've warned you."

"Anything else I should know?"

"Mmm…no swimming once we leave the main channel. Crocodiles."

"Good safety tip."

They stepped over the railing onto the gunwale of the third boat. It was tied up tightly to the second boat and cushioned by used car tires lashed to both sides.

"Annisa I have a couple of errands that I need to run before we leave" said Billy.

"What errand?"

"I need to buy some things. Toothbrush and deodorant. I'll be back soon. In the meantime if you could show Eve the boat."

"I give her good tour."

"Do you want me to go with you?" said Eve.

"I think one of us should stay here and keep an eye out."

"Aye. You're right."

"Do you need anything?"

"No. I'm good."

Billy climbed through the boats and onto the pier. He jogged over to the waiting taxi driver and climbed in the back. The taxi drove out of the harbor parking lot and onto the road.

Annisa introduced Eve to the other two members of the crew. The pilot was the second son of his mother and therefore named Kadek as was the tradition with the Balinese. He rarely wore a shirt or shoes and his dark skin was almost impervious to the sun. His manner was relaxed and confident. He spoke little English. It was hard work piloting a klotok. He was the captain and deckhand and mechanic all rolled into one. Even though everyone tried to pitch in, they were usually more trouble than they were worth and it was simpler to do the job himself. That way he knew it was done right. He took great pride in being a klotok pilot. It was a good job that paid well for a Balinese at ten US dollars a day—enough money to support his mother, wife and two children.

Hani the cook was the oldest member of the crew at 42. She was Malaysian and a Muslim and wore a traditional hijab over her black hair. She didn't like grilling the bacon for the tourists' breakfast. It was pork and a sin but she had a family to support so she kept the evil meat at a distance by using long metal tongs. She cooked traditional Indonesian and several European dishes but her favorite were the Malaysian dishes that her mother and grandmother had taught her. Cooking was her life and she loved hearing Annisa read guest comments on TripAdvisor as they complained about gaining five pounds because the meals were so delicious.

Annisa gave Eve a quick tour of the klotok and demonstrated how to flush the toilet by tossing a small pale of river water into the bowl and how to climb into the hammock slung between two patio columns on the top deck. She showed Eve the boat's English lending library which had nine novels and a Lonely Planet guide for Southeast Asia. Eve reminded her that they would want to get a good look at each klotok that they passed on the river. Annisa said she had already spoken to Kadek and that she should not worry—they would find her friend.

The taxi rolled through a poor part of town judging by the size of the potholes. The stores and houses were mostly made from rusted tin sheets scavenged from billboards and road signs. The taxi came to a stop in front of a bar and Billy and the driver got out and went inside.

The bar was unusually busy for a morning and the customers were a rough crowd talking in small groups at tables. The driver crossed to the bartender and said something in a language Billy did not recognize. The bartender studied Billy and then nodded to the driver. The driver went through a doorway and motioned for Billy to follow.

Billy followed the driver into a back room filled with boxes of appliances stoves and air conditioners all of them stolen or smuggled to avoid import taxes. A man sat at a table counting money. He glanced up briefly at Billy and the driver but seemed uninterested. The driver gestured to Billy to show the man his money. Billy pulled a fold of $100 US bills from his front pocket. The man looked up again and saw the bills and was more interested. He conversed in the unknown language with the driver and yelled something to another man hidden somewhere in the stacks of boxes.

The second man appeared holding a heavy metal box and set it on a bench near the table. He pulled out several old pistols and set them in a line on the table. Guns in Indonesia were illegal, rare and expensive. Billy picked up the pistol he thought was in the best shape—a 1962 British Webley Revolver. There was some rust on the barrel and the cylinder but nothing that couldn't be scrubbed off with a pad of steel wool. He pressed the release and broke open the cylinder and barrel from the firing mechanism in the handle. It was empty—a precaution black market arms dealers took to prevent being shot by their own merchandise during a deal. He could see by the file markings that the bullet chambers had been modified to take .45 ammunition. He spun the cylinder to ensure it wouldn't stick and could see by its easy movement that it had been oiled recently. He closed the cylinder and dry-fired the weapon twice. The springs in the firing mechanism were still strong and the hammer snapped closed with ease. It was an old pistol but it had been maintained and worked well.

"How much?"

The man at the table held up 7 fingers. Billy held up 4. They settled on 6 which included a box of .45 shells. Billy counted out $600 US and handed it to the man. The man put the gun and box of ammunition in a bag and handed it to Billy. Billy nodded his thanks and left with the driver.

Billy stepped back onto the Mau Ke Mana holding several plastic bags and informed Annisa they were ready to go. Billy climbed the ladder to the top deck and walked across to Eve already sitting in one of the two lounge chairs overlooking the bow.

"Did you get everything you needed?"

"Yeah. I couldn't find an electric toothbrush."

"Too bad. So where is the gun you bought?"

"What?"

"The gun?"

Billy looked back over the top deck for anyone

watching and lifted his shirt and pulled the revolver from his belt behind his back and handed it to Eve.

"It's loaded" said Billy.

"Wouldn't be of much use if it wasn't."

She inspected the pistol. "Bit old don't ya think?"

"It was the best I could do on short notice."

She broke open the pistol and checked the cylinder and noticed the modified chambers and the marking on the bullets.

"A modified .45?"

Billy nodded.

"If the police catch you with an unlicensed firearm you'll see a jail cell for sure."

"So I'd better not let 'em catch me."

She nodded and closed the gun and handed it back to Billy. "You made a promise Billy."

"And I'll keep it but he's not getting away this time."

Eve nodded and lay back in her lounger.

"Aim for his knees" said Eve.

CHAPTER 23

With Billy and Eve tucked into the loungers on the top deck, Kadek cranked up the engine and cast off the lines from the neighboring Klotok. The boat chugged into the river and headed down river with the current. Billy used the boat's high-powered binoculars and Eve used the long zoom on her surveillance camera to scan each klotok they passed. Most of the guests on the boats were seated on the top deck like Billy and Eve.

"What if he's inside the boat's lower cabin? We won't see him" said Eve.

"I suppose it's possible on the main channel here but once we get onto the tributary and head upriver into the rainforest the temperature will rise. I doubt anyone would stay inside for long. It's just too damn hot without a breeze. You'll see" said Billy.

They passed a slow moving barge loaded down with hundreds of steel drums.

"What's in the drums?" said Eve.

"Palm oil from the plantations up the main river. They're responsible for most of the deforestation on Borneo."

"So why don't they outlaw it?"

"How do you tell a farmer that trees and orangutans are more important than feeding his family?"

Annisa peeked her head out of the pilot's cabin and gave Billy and Eve a questioning thumbs-up. Billy and Eve each responded with a return thumbs-up. Satisfied her guests were happy she disappeared below deck. Annisa had an uncanny sense of when to join her guests and when it was best just to leave them alone. It was part of what made her a good tour guide. She spoke good English. Her vocabulary was not big but she spoke clearly and enunciated each word making it easy to understand her even with her heavy accent. She was smart and thoughtful for only being 22 years old.

The Mau Ke Mana slowed as it came to the junction of the two rivers. Kadek cranked the wheel and goosed the throttle bringing the bow of the boat into alignment with the jungle river. The boat entered the narrow mouth of the tributary. The sides closed in and the green wall of vegetation grew thicker and taller. Giant palm leaves arched over the light brown water. The air stilled and the heat climbed. Eve and Billy felt the heat and sweated heavily.

"Oh my God. You were right. You can really feel the heat" said Eve.

"Yeah. It takes a little getting used to. If it gets too much you can take a shower in the outhouse. It's clean water but there isn't that much so you have to make it quick. I usually take one in the evening to clean off the stickiness. It helps me sleep at night."

"I can't imagine sleeping in this heat."

"Bourbon helps."

Annisa poked her head up from the foredeck and pointed.

"Starboard side up in trees" she said.

Eve aimed her camera and spotted a group of twelve proboscis monkeys with their long flat noses and reddish-brown hair. They were resting in the shade of the branches. A baby clung to her mother as she climbed higher in the tree to get away from the potential threat of intruders. The group leader—a large alpha male—watched the boat approach.

"They're pretty big for a monkey species, especially the males" said Billy.

"The babies are so cute" said Eve.

Annisa climbed the ladder and moved up beside Eve.

"They called proboscis monkey. We call them long-nose monkey. They only live in Borneo. They live in groups of ten to twenty but only one adult male in each group. Females have hierarchy in group. Alpha female is queen bee and the boss of other females. They are endangered so rangers protect them in national park" Annisa explained in very clear English, having practiced this particular speech over and over again. She pointed to the starboard side of the river. "This side is park" she said. "The other side is private. Monkeys only live on park side. They know poacher not come to park side. Very smart."

"What do they eat?" said Eve.

"Mostly leaves and fruit. Sometimes small insects. You want to feed them banana?"

"Is that allowed?"

"It okay. They like banana."

"Do we have time?" said Eve to Billy.

"It'll only take a minute or two."

Annisa ducked her head over the edge of the top deck to talk with Kadek through the wheelhouse window. Kadek called back to the galley and Hani carried a bunch of small bananas up to the top deck, broke them into two clumps and handed them to Eve and Billy. The boat slowed to a stop just below the monkeys. Annisa used a gaff to hook a heavy branch and pull the boat closer to the bank. Several of the monkeys climbed down the tree and swung themselves through the bushes to the side of the boat. Billy and Eve tossed them each a banana. The younger monkeys chewed the bananas with the skins still on and used their fingers to pick out pieces of fruit. The older monkeys simply squeezed the banana until the fruit popped out.

An adventurous teenage male boarded the boat and scampered over to Eve and stole the remaining bananas from her hand. Hani chased him off the boat and threatened to hit him with the boat's gaff hook.

"It's okay. Please don't hurt him" Eve said.

"Bad monkey. He thief" said Annisa.

"I think he's just hungry" said Eve.

"Yes but he not share with others. Eat all for himself. You want more bananas Miss Eve?"

"No. I'm okay."

"Okay. We go now Mr. Billy?"

"Let's go. We're burning sunlight" said Billy.

Annisa leaned over the front of the deck and told Kadek in the wheelhouse that they were ready to leave. The Mau Ke Mana carefully pulled away from the jungle and steered back into the center of the river and Kadek throttled up the engine and the klotok headed upriver deeper into the rainforest. Villages with 50 to 60 families dotted the edge of the river. Each village had a pier with long-tail fishing boats tied up to it and nets hung out to dry. Eve watched as they passed a group of women repairing broken nets and fishing gear.

"Where are they men?"

"Probably sleeping. Women do most of the chores

around the villages."

"Hardly seems fair" said Eve.

Children played on the pier and dangled their feet in the cool water but dared not swim for fear of crocodiles and water snakes. They shouted and waved to the klotoks and struck funny poses for photos as the tourists passed. The peace sign sometimes turned into rabbit ears behind the head of a friend or sibling was the favorite pose. Billy and Eve waved at the children as their boat passed.

"They seem so happy" said Eve.

"I suppose they are" said Billy. "Fish and fruit give them plenty to eat. Their houses are made of wood and dried palm leaves from the jungle. Fish in the morning then sell your catch at the local market before lunch and take a long nap in the afternoon when it's hot. Not a bad life."

"Until a panther eats your cat."

They shared a laugh.

"So how do you know all this stuff?" she asked.

"I find it interesting" said Billy. "How people live. What kind of problems they face. Life."

"You miss home?"

"Wyoming? Yeah I miss it. Seasons don't change much here. I miss the fall."

"And the winter?"

"Have you ever been to Wyoming in the winter? It's bone cold. Nobody misses a winter in Wyoming."

"But it must be beautiful. The mountains and the trees covered in snow."

"That it is."

The Buaya Darat chugged up the river. The water changed from milky brown to a dark tea color. The banks along the river were a tangle of mangrove trees with thick roots rising from the water and forming the tree trunks. The nomad steered the boat and felt confident behind the wheel. The pilot watched the river and searched for floating tree branches large enough to damage the hull or prop.

"Not many birds or monkeys in this area" said the nomad.

"No. This black water. Many crocodile" said the pilot.

"I'd like to get a photo of a crocodile."

"No easy. Crocodile hide in mangrove."

"Is there a place where there are many crocodile?"

"Yes but very dangerous. Many tree."

"I would pay extra to see crocodiles."

"How much you pay?"

The nomad pulled out two $100 US bills from his money clip. It was more money than the pilot made in two weeks.

"We go see crocodile" said the pilot.

The nomad stepped aside and the pilot moved behind the wheel. The Buaya Darat slowed as it approached a narrow side river. The pilot pivoted the boat and lined it up with the narrow passage, throttled the engine down to a slow speed and carefully guided the boat deep into the mangroves.

It was dark under the mangroves and the sun was choked out by the thick canopy of leaves and branches—only small patches of light dappled the boat. They traveled a few hundred feet to a small open area and the pilot slowed the boat to a creep and turned the boat around by pulling forward and backward until the bow of the boat was pointed back the way it came. The pilot tied up the boat between two trees and disappeared into the crew quarters.

The nomad stared out into the mangroves. No human could survive this. The mangrove roots would surely snap an ankle of anyone stupid or desperate enough to traverse the grove. It seemed strangely peaceful.

The silence was broken by an argument in Balinese between the cook, the guide and the pilot. The pilot emerged from the back of the boat with a bowl of raw chicken that he took from the galley.

"You get camera" said the pilot and pushed past the nomad to the foredeck.

The guide emerged from the crew quarters and yelled at the nomad. "You talk to me when you want something. Not pilot. Not supposed to be here.

Ranger give big fine they catch us feed crocodile" said the guide. "Very dangerous."

The guide pushed past the nomad and exited the wheelhouse to continue the argument with the pilot. The pilot ignored the guide and chummed the water with the raw chicken. The nomad slipped back through the crew quarters and into the boat's galley. The cook was still seething from the argument and was in no mood to deal with the stupid tourist that wanted to see the crocodiles. She climbed out of the galley onto the stern deck and pushed into the wooden outhouse and slammed the door behind. The nomad searched the galley drawers until he found what he wanted. A carving knife. He checked the edge for sharpness. The blade had several nicks and wasn't to his standards but it would do. The nomad rolled down his sleeves and carefully slide the knife tip first up his right sleeve so the hilt of the knife rested in the palm of his hand.

He climbed out of the galley and up to the top deck where he retrieved his camera from his bag. From the top deck he could already see the first crocodile swimming toward the chicken parts floating in the water by the bow of the boat. It was a 10-footer. The nomad climbed down the front ladder onto the foredeck. He took several photos of the crocodile snapping up the chicken. The guide cursed and the pilot tossed several more pieces of chicken at two more crocodiles. The nomad turned to the guide and straightened his arm and let the knife slide into his hand.

"You're ruining the moment" said the nomad.

The nomad slashed the guide's throat in one swift stroke. Blood spurted across the deck and onto the nomad's shirt. The nomad pushed the guide over the opposite side of the boat. The splash caught the attention of the pilot. He turned and met the nomad's eyes staring at him. The nomad plunged the carving knife into the pilot's chest and quickly slit the blade downward. He pulled the knife out and slashed the blade across the base of the pilot's stomach forming an upside down T. The pilot looked down to see his bowels fall onto the deck. The nomad pushed him backward over the side railing and into the water below. The crocodiles swarmed and tore at the pilot's remains.

The Nomad looked down at several pools of blood on the deck. He climbed up to the top deck and crossed to the stern ladder. "Cookie I've made a mess. Do you have a mop?" The cook emerged from the outhouse with a mop in her hand. The nomad climbed down the ladder to the stern deck and turned to face her. She saw the blood on his shirt and her face filled with fear. He was pleased by her expression and wanted to play with her now that the others were no longer a threat. He gently took the mop from her hand. "Thank you" said the nomad.

CHAPTER 24

The Mau Ke Mana chugged into a clearing with two piers on either side of the river. Nine boats were tied up to the pier on the park side. Billy and Eve saw a large female orangutan sitting on the deck under a wooden gazebo next to the pier. Her hair was orange-reddish brown and long and fine.

"Oh my God. It's just sitting there" said Eve.

"That Queenie" explained Annisa. "She like to sit by pier and watch boats. She was alpha female. But now too old and no have baby. No can be alpha female without baby. You can take photo with her later. Now we need to go to feeding orangutan. We a little late."

"I never realized they were so beautiful" said Eve.

"I felt the same the first time I saw one. Still do" said Billy.

Kadek steered the Mau Ke Mana next to one of the boats already tied to the pier. Annisa tossed a thick rope from the Mau Ke Mana to the pilot of the boat tied to the pier. Kadek cut the engine and grabbed another rope at the bow of the Mau Ke Mana and jumped onto the neighboring boat. Both pilots pulled the Mau Ke Mana up close and lashed their ropes around the deck pillars supporting the top deck and tied them off securely.

Annisa prepped Billy and Eve on the stern deck. "Park rangers say no touch orangutan. They very similar to human. We no want to give them disease. Stay on path and close to me. Feeding area one half kilometer from pier. No talk when we get close. If your friend there you say hi later when we back on pier."

"You packing Billy?" said Eve.

Billy nodded.

"If you see wild boar no run" said Annisa. "Just stand still. If he come close you put hands over head so you look bigger and he go away. You see snake tell me. If I not near you run other way. Cobra and coral snake very poisonous and kill tourist. You put on mosquito juice?"

Eve and Billy both nodded.

"Good. Please you wear hat. Sun strong. I have water if you thirsty. Okay we go now."

They each stepped over the side rail and through the neighboring boat to the pier.

"We want to see inside the other boats for our friend."

"If he here at feeding area we go see him there."

"Aye but we still want to see inside the other boats. It's important."

"Feeding start soon. You going to miss."

"We won't be long" said Eve.

"Okay" said Annisa.

Eve and Billy walked along the pier and looked into each boat. The boat crews were busy doing chores and taking baths using river water or napping while their guests were away. No sign of the nomad. Billy and Eve returned to Annisa waiting by the boardwalk that led into the jungle.

"He's not here" said Eve.

"We   go   now?"   said   Annisa.
"We go" said Billy.

Queenie watched them walk down the boardwalk and disappear into the rainforest. Eve looked down at the boardwalk made of ironwood planks greyed from the sun and built on pilings over a one-foot deep swamp. Sunlight dappled the boards. The swamp water covered everything as far as the eye could see except for the heavy mangrove trees. The leaves and branches in the overhead canopy were backlit and looked black and choked out most of the sun and air. Tiny fish swam through the grass and plants growing from the muddy swamp bed. The muffled snap of a tree branch brought Billy's and Eve's heads around. There was a faint rustling of leaves in the treetops above but nothing was visible through the dense vegetation.

"Orangutan" said Annisa.

Annisa loved the orangutan. They provided her with a good living. She felt responsible for them and always encouraged her guests to keep the rules when around them. Even after years of seeing them in the jungle she was still amazed by their playfulness. They were just like human children.

The boardwalk ended as the swamp turned to leaf-covered dirt. A well-worn path was cut through the trees and cleared of bushes. They exited the rainforest and came to a clearing of chest-high grass. An abandoned lookout station towered over the clearing. The boards on the station were greyed and broken in several places and abused by high winds and by bored tour guides throwing rocks. Several of the lower rungs of the ladder that were used to climb up to the station had been removed by the rangers to prevent accidental falls in an area far from any hospital.

Eve and Billy studied the tall grass that could hide anyone or anything just a few feet away from the footpath. Billy put his hand under his shirt and around the gun handle so he could draw quickly if the need arose. It was the perfect place for an ambush and there was little they could do to protect themselves except to push on.

At the edge of the clearing, the footpath once again plunged into a carved-out tunnel through the trees. The leaf-covered ground was soggy and slippery from poor drainage. Tree roots crisscrossed the path and made each step a potential ankle-breaker. Eve's boot sank into a puddle of mud and she started to fall when Billy caught her and helped her pull her wet boot free. They heard an unseen ranger bellow an orangutan call through the rainforest.

"Ranger call orangutan to eat" said Annisa. "We be very quiet now."

They continued through the rainforest and carefully stepped around and over the exposed tree roots and shallow streams and mud holes. It was slippery going. There was more rustling in the treetop. Annisa gestured for them to stop and look up.

"Their coming" Annisa said with a child-like smile.

Billy and Eve looked up into the canopy above and saw the silhouette of a teenage orangutan with its orange hair backlit giving it a strange and unearthly glow. He used his 8-foot arms and legs to swing from tree to tree and moved effortlessly through the rainforest.

"Cool huh?" Billy whispered.

Annisa raised her finger to her pursed lips and shushed him and waved them forward. They stepped into the feeding area—a wooden platform covered with papaya, bananas and mangos and built between four trees three feet off the jungle floor. Thirty tourists watched and snapped photos as twelve orangutans descended from the trees.

The orangutans had a hierarchy. The alpha male and the alpha female descended first and had first crack at the food on the platform. The others waited in the trees above. One of the teenage orangutans slowly lowered to the platform. It only took a glance and a grunt from the huge alpha male to send the empty-handed teenager backup to the safety of the trees above. A baby clinging to the alpha female of the group dropped down to the wooden platform and picked up a banana then climbed back up to its mother. One hand holding the mother's chest hair and one hand holding the banana, the infant chewed the banana and spat out the parts he didn't want.

The tourists had their backs to Billy and Eve and prevented them from seeing their faces. Billy motioned for Eve to check one side of the group of tourists while he checked the other. They moved off to both ends to get a better angle on the group without drawing attention. They scanned each face carefully and waited for a camera to drop down or a head to turn slightly. No sign of the nomad. Half relieved and half disappointed they met again at the back of the group. Eve shrugged, raised her camera and snapped some photos of the orangutan.

The alpha female and her baby had their fill and climbed back up into the trees. The alpha male continued to gorge himself. The next female with a baby in the group's hierarchy descended and took up a spot just out of reach of the alpha male so there were no mishaps from a male feeding. She and the baby dug into the pile of fruit. The orangutan finished their meal and disappeared into the canopy above. Billy, Eve and Annisa hiked back the way they came. The sky darkened and it began to rain. Eve removed her backpack and pulled out her raincoat and re-slung the backpack in front of her chest to protect it from the rain using her coat. She pulled on her coat over the backpack straps and zipped it partway and left the straps and the backpack partly exposed. They walked down the boardwalk toward the pier.

"I need to help Katek with the rain tarps so your things no get too wet. Klotok just ahead one hundred meters. You remember which one?" asked Annisa.

"Yeah. We'll see you in a few minutes" said Billy.

Annisa took off jogging down the boardwalk toward the pier. Billy and Eve continued at a slower pace. They saw Queenie sitting on the boardwalk holding a tree branch covered in leaves above her head to shelter against the downpour.

"Poor thing" said Eve.

"She probably likes the rain. Imagine wearing a fur coat like hers in this heat" said Billy.

They walked past Queenie and she reached out with her long arm and grabbed the strap of Eve's backpack.

"Hey" said Eve.

Billy turned to see Queenie grab the other strap and pull Eve closer. Eve pulled back.

"Do you have anything in the backpack?" said Billy.

"Just a couple of water bottles and a Snickers."

"She smells it. Give her the backpack."

"I'm not giving her my backpack."

"Give her the damn backpack."

Eve tugged back. Queenie wasn't taking no for an answer.

"I-am-not-giving-my-backpack-to-this—Oh shit!"

Queenie pulled Eve over and Eve dropped to her knees on the boardwalk deck.

"Okay. She can have the backpack."

Eve tried to remove the backpack but her coat was over the straps.

"Pull your jacket off" said Billy.

Billy grabbed one of Queenie's massive hands and pulled it off one of the straps. Queenie gave him a shove and sent him back onto his ass. Queenie grunted and grew angry and flashed her teeth.

"Billy don't let her bite me" said Eve.

Billy yelled for Annisa and Kadek in the direction of the boat. Kadek and Annisa were busy unwrapping the rain tarps on the top deck and turned to the sound of Billy's voice and saw the danger. They jumped down the ladder and through the neighboring boat and hit the pier at a dead run. Kadek cursed.

"No Queenie" yelled Annisa.

Eve pulled hard against the straps and tried to keep away from Queenie's teeth. Billy grabbed Queenie's hand again and pulled her fingers from a strap. Queenie snapped at him with her teeth and barely missed his fingers and warned him to back off.

"Oh shit" said Billy.

I think the Snickers is in the front pocket" said Eve.

Billy reached over and unzipped the front pocket. Queenie batted his hand away and reached inside and pulled out the Snickers bar. She released Eve. Eve was leaning back and tumbled backwards off the boardwalk and fell into the swamp water below. She landed on her ass and the mud cushioned her fall. Billy looked over the edge of the boardwalk and down at Eve sitting in a foot of muddy water. She laughed. But Billy didn't laugh with her.

"Well it's better than getting bit" said Eve.

"Ah yeah but I'm not so sure your gonna feel that way in a few minutes."

Eve quickly glanced around alarmed.

"What is it? Crocodiles?"

"No. Leaches" said Billy.

Eve scrambled for the boardwalk and grabbed for the edge and tried to pull herself up. Billy reached down and grabbed the back of her jeans and pulled her up onto the deck.

"What do I do?"

"Let's get back to the boat."

"Oh God! I feel something on my leg!" Eve pulled her pant leg up to reveal an ugly black leach. "Oh God. Oh God. Get it off! Get it off!"

"I can't. Not yet."

"Why not?"

"If I pull it off and the head breaks off it'll get infected."

"So what do I do?"

"Like I said we get back to the boat quickly."

Annisa and Kadek arrived out of breath and looked at the leach on Eve's leg.

"That big leach" said Annisa.

Billy scooped Eve up into his arms and carried her down the boardwalk and back to the boat. Annisa turned to Queenie sitting on the edge of the gazebo and eating the Snickers bar with the wrapper still on.

"Bad Queenie" said Annisa.

Queenie turned her back to Annisa and shit off the end of the pier.Billy carried Eve into the crew quarters and laid her down gently. She stared at the leach growing bigger as it sucked the blood out of her leg.

"I'll be right back" said Billy.

Billy passed through the doorway in the galley and looked through knives and picked out a carving knife and checked the blade for sharpness and turned to Annisa.

"Do you have any rubbing alcohol?"

"What rubbing?"

"Alcohol for medicine."

"Yes. In first-aid box. I get."

"And iodine."

"What iodine?"

"Never mind just bring the whole box."

Annisa crossed the galley and went through the doorway into the crew quarters toward the wheelhouse where the first-aid box was kept.

"Everything be okay Miss Eve."

"Oh God. Hurry. I think it's getting bigger" said Eve.

Annisa disappeared into the wheelhouse. Billy entered the crew quarters holding the carving knife and a roll of paper towels.

"What's that for?"

"I've got to remove the leach."

"Yeah but I thought you were getting salt or vinegar or something."

"Nope. This is the best way. Salt or vinegar will kill it for sure but it will probably barf into your wound before it dies and it'll get infected."

"Barf into my wound?"

"Yeah they do that."

"I think I'm gonna be sick."

"Probably not a good idea. Just close your eyes."

Annisa entered with the first aid box and set it down next to Eve. Billy reached in and pulled out a bottle of rubbing alcohol and opened it and poured alcohol on his hand and over the knife. He slid the edge of the blade between the leach and Eve's leg and carefully pried the leach free and grabbed it with a wad of paper towels and studied it. Eve's leg was left with a small round hole oozing blood.

"It still has its mouth."

"Oh good. I wouldn't want to see the poor thing hurt."

"If it has its mouth then it's not still in you."

"Well that is good."

Billy poured alcohol over the wound. Eve yelped.

"Son of a bitch."

"Sorry. No iodine."

Eve felt something higher up in her pants. "Oh shit. Oh shit. Oh shit."

"You okay?" said Billy.

"I think there's another one."

"Where?"

Eve pointed at her crouch.

"Oh shit" said Billy. "Okay. Pull off your pants and let's have a look."

Eve didn't move.

"I didn't mean let's have a look at your—"

"I know what you meant goddammit. I'm afraid."

"Yeah well unbutton your jeans and lay back. You can close your eyes. I'll look for you."

Eve unbuttoned the top of her jeans and lay back closing her eyes. "Okay do it" she said.

Billy pulled her jeans off. A leach sucked on her inner thigh just inches away from her vagina.

"Do you see something?"

"Lay back and keep your eyes closed."

"Oh God. Oh God. Oh God."

Billy didn't waste any time and used the knife to pry off the leech and studied its mouth.

"It's okay now. It's gone" said Billy.

Eve sat up and looked at the blood filled hole on her inner thigh. Billy poured rubbing alcohol on the wound and was surprised to see her eyes well up with tears and was caught off guard by her vulnerability.

"Hey. It's okay. It's over" said Billy.

Billy wrapped his arms around her and she wrapped her arms around him. They held each other and she cried. Eve sensed Billy smelling her hair. She stopped crying. Billy let go of her.

"Let's get you cleaned up. You smell like a swamp" he said.

They both laughed.

The sun cast long shadows across the river as the Mau Ke Mana chugged along. The afternoon rain was late. Billy and Eve sat in the loungers on the top deck and enjoyed the artificial breeze created by the motion of the boat. They passed other klotoks already tied up for the night and Billy used the binoculars to inspect each boat until he got a good look at each of the occupants. Still no sign of the nomad. Eve picked at the bandages on her leg and inner thigh and tried to peek at the wounds beneath.

"Why do they itch so much?"

"You don't want to know."

"Yeah you're probably right. Ignorance is bliss."

Kadek searched for a good spot to tie up for the night. The Mau Ke Mana glided past an opening in the mangroves.

Deep in the shadows of the mangroves the nomad sat on the top deck of the Buaya Darat peering through binoculars at Billy and Eve as they passed the entrance to the mangroves on their boat.

It was going to be a long dark night. The nomad smiled.

CHAPTER 25

The boat traffic on the river slowed to a trickle as the crews secured their vessels for the night and prepared dinner for their guests. Kadek had piloted the Mau Ke Mana to one of his favorite spots below a tree he knew had a group of monkeys. The tourists would wake in the morning to the monkeys calling one another and they could feed them the leftover fruit from their breakfast. Kadek liked making the tourists happy and not just for the tips. He wanted them to love his country the way he loved it. He slowed the Mau Ke Mana to a stop and tied up between two trees along the edge of the river. The monkeys lounged in the safety of the tree and groomed one another and picked off fleas and ticks and ate them. The jungle was silent and still and the heat was still strong but waned as the sun lowered to the horizon and the shadows grew longer.

The sun finally set and Billy and Eve dined in the twilight on the back of the top deck. They were surrounded by citronella candles that kept the mosquitos at bay. It was a romantic setting that made both Billy and Eve slightly uncomfortable.

"I could eat the twelve apostles" said Eve.

Hani brought plate after plate of traditional Indonesian dishes. There was stir-fried nasi goreng noodle, Balinese green bean salad, beef rendang with dried chilli and egg stew. Not to mention the jasmine rice, local fruit salad and Balinese grilled fish that came with every meal. As was tradition it was all served as one giant course family-style—a table full of color and aromas. Billy and Eve dug in and filled their plates. While their guests dined, Annisa and Katek lowered a canvas tarp from the patio roof that divided the dining area from the sleeping area.

In the twilight Billy and Eve finished their meal.

"Oh God" said Billy pushing his plate away. "I can't move."

Eve laughed. "I told you not to finish the beef rendang."

"It would have been a crime to leave it."

"Said the man as his gut burst."

"True."

"I admit I might have overdone it a bit" said Eve. "But unlike you I need the extra energy to recover from my wounds."

"Said the three-hundred-pound fat lady."

Annisa and Katek rolled up the tarp and revealed a white gauze mosquito net hung from the ceiling like a Persian tent covering a queen-sized bed with flowers arranged in a heart shape displayed on the white sheets. Annisa smiled pleased with her creation. Eve saw it first.

"Billy didn't you tell her two beds?"

"Yeah. Why?"

Billy turned around and saw the bed. "I don't think she listened."

"Obviously not. Look don't say anything" said Eve. "They'd feel embarrassed. It's just one night. We'll pull the beds apart once they turn off the deck lights."

Eve and Billy smiled at Annisa and Kadek. Hani climbed up the ladder with a platter of sweet coconut rice balls and Getuk lindri finger pastries.

"Coffee or tea?" said Hani.

Storm clouds drifted in front of the moon and extinguished its reflection on the river. Eve exited the outhouse wearing a t-shirt and shorts. She climbed the ladder to the top step and saw Billy already under the mosquito net. He didn't notice her as he pulled off his shirt. His body was tight and muscular and had a few scars from his years on the ranch. She wondered how he kept so fit while traveling. Billy heard steps on the wooden deck and turned. Their eyes met for a moment and Eve turned away.

"I don't know about you but I'm really knackered" said Eve with a yawn.

"You need to make sure there are no mosquitos on you before you climb under the net" said Billy. "Otherwise, we'll wake up in the morning looking like we have chicken pox."

"Okay so what do I do?"

"Just brush your hands up and down your clothes and any exposed skin."

Eve rubbed her hands up and down her clothes, arms, legs and neck.

"That's good. Now get on your knees and duck under quickly. Mosquitos are sneaky little bastards."

Eve knelt down and Billy picked up the edge of the net and let her duck under and quickly closed the net.

"Good. No mosquitos."

"So how are we going to do this?"

"Just lay down."

Eve followed his instructions.

"Annisa. We're ready to sleep now. You can turn off the deck lights" said Billy.

The deck lights blinked out.

"Christ almighty it's dark" said Eve.

"Your eyes will need time to adjust. You'll be surprised at how much you can actually see."

Billy turned on the flashlight on his phone. He slid the queen bed apart and made two twin beds under the net.

"You take the top sheet. It's too hot for me anyway" said Billy.

"Thank you. Nice to see chivalry is not dead."

"Not in Wyoming."

They both climbed into their respective beds with Eve under the sheet. Billy turned off his phone flashlight. The jungle was a wall of black. Slowly Eve's eyes adjusted. She could see the silhouette of the trees and the monkeys above against the night sky. A flash of lightning illuminated everything around them and then vanished leaving only a ghostly outline that slowly faded.

"It's coming" said Billy. "Can you smell it?"

"Smell what?" said Eve.

Billy didn't respond. A soft whack hit the patio roof and another hit the tarp on the jungle side of the deck and then another and another. The sky opened like a fire hydrant and drops smashed down in hard sheets on the deck and patio roof and sounded like a snare drum as they pounded away. The black river churned under the downpour. It was the hardest Eve had ever seen it rain and she felt frightened. She looked over at Billy lying on his bed peaceful and unafraid. His eyes closed. She felt alone.

"Billy are you asleep?"

"Almost. What's up?"

"The bite on my leg really itches."

"I've got some cortisone in my backpack. It should help."

Billy turned on his phone flashlight and fished out the tube of cortisone. Eve pulled back the sheet revealing her legs. Billy carefully pulled off the bandage and dabbed some of the cream on the wound.

"That's nice" she said.

"Yeah it works quick. Modern medicine."

"My mom always kissed it better."

Billy laughed and playfully kissed her bandage and screwed the cap back on and moved to put the tube away in his backpack.

"Billy?"

"Yeah?"

"The other one is starting to itch."

Billy stopped for a moment to play back and decipher what he had just heard. He pulled the tube back out of his backpack and moved to her side. Eve slipped off her shorts and pulled up her t-shirt to reveal the bandage on her inner thigh and her panties. Billy carefully removed the bandage and dabbed on the cream. Eve could see that his fingers were shaking. He put the bandage back down over the wound. His head rose to meet Eve's eyes. Lightning flashed again and again followed by the thunder. She reached over and gently pushed his head back down. He kissed her on the bandage and moved upward and kissed her softly. Eve reached over and turned off the light on this phone and laid her head back down and stared at the net above as the lightning and thunder grew. Her chest heaved as Billy nuzzled and kissed her panties. He no longer needed her permission. She reached down and cupped his head with her hands and pulled him up to her lips. They kissed deeply. She pulled off her t-shirt and pulled his head down to her breasts. He kissed and bit her nipples gently. She unbuttoned his pants and pulled them off with his briefs. He pulled off her panties. They fell back to her bed tangled in each other's arms and legs and kissed deeply. She pulled at him with a hunger. Billy thrust inside her. Lost in the moment Billy stared out into the darkness.

Lightning flashed again and Billy saw the dark silhouette of man standing on the foredeck with sheet of rain pouring down on him.

Billy jumped off Eve and scrambled for his phone.

"Billy what is it? What's wrong?" said Eve.

Billy turned on the flashlight and pointed toward the foredeck and heard a loud clap of thunder. The silhouette was gone. Sheets of rain pounded down bouncing reflections from the flashlight.

"Billy what is it?"

"Nothing. It was nothing."

Eve put her hand on his chest.

"Oh my God. Your heart is pounding."

"I'm okay."

"Dammit. I'm sorry. I'm an idiot" she said. "I knew it was too soon after—"

"No. No. This is great."

Billy had interrupted her not wanting to hear Noi's name, not wanting to ruin the moment any more than he already had. Billy bent down and kissed her forehead.

"Really great" he said.

He kissed her deeply. She smiled and kissed his neck softly. Billy took once last glance at the foredeck and turned off the flashlight. She moved down to his chest and kissed him and moved lower and Billy closed his eyes.

The air was hot and thick. The jungle still and silent. The lightning storm had passed. Eve slept with her head nestled in the crook of Billy's shoulder. A faint orange shadow flickered across the mosquito net and slowly grew brighter. Eve's eyes cracked open and stared at the orange flicker. She didn't think anything of it, closed her eyes and drifted back to sleep. She heard the chug-chug of a boat engine and thought she might be dreaming. The chug-chug grew louder. She stirred and opened her eyes again and looked up at the net now flickering yellow and orange then out at the surrounding trees with the orange flicker dancing across them. She looked in the direction of the sound of the boat engine and saw a houseboat with the words Buaya Darat painted on the stern. It headed down river and disappeared into the darkness.

She nudged Billy. He stirred.

"Billy?"

Billy opened his eyes to see her face illuminated by the orange light. He smiled. She didn't smile back. *That's strange* he thought. *Is she angry? Did I do something?* She pointed to the trees and the flickering orange light.

"Look."

Billy looked out, his face confused by what he was saw. Slowly he realized the meaning and sat up.

"Fire" he said.

He pulled his pants on and clawed his way out of the mosquito net and stumbled to his feet.

"What? Where?" said Eve.

"I don't know."

Billy crossed to the end of the deck and stepped down the ladder. He turned to the lower deck doorway and saw Annisa completely consumed in fire climbing out of the doorway. The oxygen around her was sucked up into the flames and she couldn't breathe or even scream. Billy was stunned by the site and stumbled backwards and tripped and fell to the deck and stared at her unsure of what to do. Annisa was unable to see through the flames and reached out and felt her way to the side of the boat and tried to make it to the river. The pain overwhelmed her and she fell to her knees and moaned. Billy snapped out of his shock and crossed to the outhouse and grabbed the bucket of flushing water and tossed it onto Annisa and the flames died down and steam rose up. Her skin crackled and popped. Billy ripped down a canvas tarp and covered Annisa and extinguished the remaining flames.

Eve climbed to the bottom of the stairs and looked into the inferno of the crew quarters. The heat pushed her back. She remembered the fire extinguisher in the wheelhouse but there was no way to reach it through the flames. She scrambled up the stairs and crossed the top deck. The varnish on the deck bubbled from the heat. She ran across the hot deck and down the front ladder to the wheelhouse. She opened the door and retrieved the fire extinguisher. She pulled the safety pin and kicked open the front door to the crew quarters. Flames burst through the doorway hungry for oxygen. She pitched to the side and shot a blast from the extinguisher inside the room and pitched to the other side and shot another blast. The flames retreated and she stepped inside the room blasting the extinguisher as she moved. Eve kept low below the heavy layer of smoke near the ceiling. She saw the bodies of Kadek and Hani tangled in their hammocks and consumed in flame. Their struggle was over. Both were still. Kadek's hammock snapped and his corpse fell to the floor. Eve doused them both with white powder from the extinguisher until the flames died. She put out the rest of the flames and coughed from the smoke and smell of charred flesh. The fire was out and she climbed out the back doorway to see Billy holding Annisa.

Eve moved forward and gasped as she saw Annisa's face burned beyond recognition and her beautiful hair gone. Her clothes had melted into her skin making it impossible to distinguish between the two. She was still alive and mumbling something in Bahasa Indonesia and her breathing labored.

"Oh God. Billy?" said Eve.

Billy's eyes were fixed on Annisa's face. Her eyelids had burned off and she looked up helpless and in pain.

"I don't know what to do" he said.

"Kill me" croaked Annisa her larynx burnt from the smoke and fire.

Billy eyes filled with tears and he looked up from Annisa and met Eve's eyes. They were helpless. The closest hospital was still hours away. Annisa convulsed.

"Billy please help her" said Eve.

Billy steeled himself and placed his hand over what was left of Annisa's nose and mouth. He pushed down and her skin cracked from the pressure. She suffocated and the convulsions stopped and Annisa was dead. Eve knelt and cried. Billy was grateful that Annisa was at peace and the pain gone forever. The fact that he was now a killer didn't register at first. That would come later when there was time to think. At the moment it just wasn't important.

CHAPTER 26

It was dawn. The rainforest awakened. A veiled mist hung over the river and the smell of burnt flesh and charred wood loomed in the air. Billy and Eve sat on the stern deck and stared at the three bodies each wrapped in a tarp.

"You were right" said Eve. "We should have killed him."

Billy nodded and rose to his feet.

"We should get going" said Billy.

Eve nodded and rose to her feet.

"We should keep the bodies out of the sun" said Billy.

They carried the bodies into the crew cabin and set them down on the deck.

"Why do you suppose he didn't kill us?" said Eve.

"He should've. Probably thought the fire would get us."

"He wants us to suffer for what we did to him."

"Hard to tell what he's thinking and I don't really care anymore. Next time I go straight at him."

"We go straight at him."

"All right. We go straight at him" said Billy. "Do you think you can get the engine started?"

"Aye" said Eve.

"I'll pull the anchor."

Billy stepped through the doorway into the galley and out onto the stern. Eve stayed a moment longer with the bodies.

"I'm sorry this happened to you" she said to the silent crew.

Eve crossed into the wheelhouse and used a rag to wipe the soot from the windshield and turned the ignition. The engine cranked and sputtered to life. Billy pulled up the anchor and untied the mooring lines from the trees. The vessel floated free into the river's current. Eve throttled the engine to half speed and cranked the wheel. The boat moved down the river. Billy stood quietly on the deck in front of the wheelhouse. Eve steered the boat. He reached back through the doorway and offered her his hand. She took it. It was comforting feeling the touch of another human after so much suffering.

The sun was two hours higher in the sky and the morning glow was gone. The heat rose as the day marched on. Billy took his turn at the wheel and dodged floating islands of water hyacinth with their purple flowers and tree branches broken by monkeys swinging from the trees that lined the banks of the river. Even with two sets of eyes it was difficult to spot submerged logs that could break the boat's single propeller and strand them on a river that they did not know and in a place they did not understand.

The river bent back and forth like a snake and each turn exposed a new stretch that seemed surprisingly similar to the last and denied travelers a sense of progress. Tedium grew as the temperature rose and the day wore on. Eve sat on the top deck and stared at the river before her. Her sense of wonder was gone. The breeze was hot and humid. Her clothes stank of smoke and sweat. She thought about taking a shower but couldn't muster the energy. She could live with the grime.

Billy wanted to be rid of the smell of death that stalked the boat. He could not stop thinking that all of this death was his fault and that his actions long ago had triggered some unstoppable chain of events like a mirror shattered. What good had come of his life? What value did he still bring to humanity? He was just taking up space on the planet and using up precious resources. Everything and everyone he touched was ruined.

The Mau Ke Mana approached the river junction to the main channel. Eve stepped down the ladder to face Billy through the wheelhouse window.

"So what's the plan?" she said.

"We go back to the dock. I call the police and explain what happened and hope to God they believe me."

"You mean we go back."

"No. You're on the next flight out of here."

"That's not your decision."

"Eve I know you feel responsible and you want to help. But I can't help but feel that there is something bigger going on here. It's like the world is out of balance and it has to be set right. A price has to be paid and I don't know what it is."

"That's bullshit Billy. He's just a man, not a demon sent to torment you."

"That may be but whatever he is I'm the one who has to stop him. I don't want anyone else hurt especially you."

"I'm not leaving Billy."

"It's not an option."

"Who died and made you God? I've got a stake in this too."

"You mean the finder's fee."

"I mean you. I mean us."

"There is no us. There never was."

Billy knew his words stung her like a slap but he also knew they were a gift—her way out from the hell he created. Tears welled up in Eve's eyes.

"You think you're a bad guy God wants to punish. But you're just another fuckin' wanker who doesn't know his head from his ass. And that's why I feel sorry for ya."

She climbed back to the top deck. Billy spun the wheel and steered up river as the boat entered the wide channel. The river widened and the air thinned bringing relief from the heat.

The remainder of the trip down river passed in silence. The Mau Ke Mana approached the pier. It was early afternoon and storm clouds were already gathering on the horizon and moving over the rainforest. Most of the boats had already picked up their guests and left the dock. Only one boat remained. Eve studied the lone klotok from a distance. It was familiar. She picked up her camera with the powerful zoom lens and focused on the words Buaya Darat painted on the stern. Eve lowered her camera and her mind pressed to remember the boat pulling away into the darkness with only the flicker from the flames illuminating the boat's name. Eve climbed down the ladder to face Billy in the wheelhouse.

"I think that is the boat that was leaving when the fire started."

"Are you sure?" said Billy.

"No. Not absolutely. It was dark and I only saw it for a second."

Billy pushed the throttle all the way forward and the engine knocked under the load and the boat picked up speed. Eve crossed the wheelhouse and stepped into the crew quarters. She stepped around the bodies of the crew, entered the galley and searched the drawers. She pulled out the carving knife and walked back to the wheelhouse. Billy reached under his shirt and pulled out the pistol and pressed the release. He opened the cylinder and checked that it was fully loaded and spun the cylinder to make sure it worked properly and closed it.

The Mau Ke Mana chugged toward the pier. Billy and Eve watched for any sign of the crew or the nomad. Nothing moved on the boat or pier. Billy throttled back the engine and the Mau Ke Mana slowed. He steered parallel to the pier behind the Buaya Darat. He reversed the engine and cranked the wheel and forced the stern of the boat into the pier. Eve jumped off with the bow line and pulled the boat until the tires on the side compressed and she tied off the line to one of the pilings. Billy killed the engine and moved back to the stern and passed the bodies in the crew cabin and emerged from the galley onto the back deck. He picked up the scorched aft line and stepped off the boat onto the pier and tied it off. He moved up beside Eve.

"I'll have a look" he said. "You stay here and—"

"We both go" she said.

"Okay but we stay together. I have the gun so I take the lead" said Billy.

Eve nodded. They walked cautiously toward the Buaya Darat. Billy stepped onto the stern deck of the Buaya Darat and Eve followed. He checked the outhouse first and pushed the wooden door open with his free hand and looked inside. It was empty.

Eve stepped to the galley doorway and peered into the darkness. Nothing moved. She turned to Billy and shook her head. Billy motioned to the ladder leading to the top deck. Eve stepped up the ladder and peeked over the edge of the top deck and saw everything all the way to the bow—nothing moved on the top deck. She looked down at Billy and shook her head. Billy motioned to the galley doorway leading into the lower part of the vessel. Eve nodded. Billy moved into the doorway and checked both sides of the galley before entering all the way. Nothing. He stepped forward into the crew quarters and again checked both sides before entering. Eve followed and kept an eye on the back of the boat as they moved forward. Billy entered the wheelhouse. It was empty. Eve moved up behind him. Billy stepped out onto the foredeck. The blood from the guide and pilot was gone. The deck and wheelhouse exterior were clean. Eve followed Billy onto the foredeck and stepped up the bow later to recheck the top deck. Nothing.

"He's gone" said Eve.

Billy nodded.

"Where do you suppose the crew went?" she said.

"No idea."

"We'd better tell the port authority what happened before the other boats pull in for the evening and their crews see the bodies. The harbor master can contact the police."

"Let me go" he said. "I don't want you involved."

"Billy just cut the shit" she said. "I'm staying with you until we finish what we started. End of story."

"You sure?"

"Aye I'm sure. I'm going to find the harbor master."

Eve stepped off the boat and walked down the pier. Billy tucked his pistol behind his shirt and finished tying up the Mau Ke Mana. He heard a muffled scream and a thud from the pier. He couldn't see beyond the buildings and warehouses at the start of the pier. He pulled out his pistol and ran up the pier and searched for any sign of Eve or the nomad. He rounded the corner to the first building and saw an open door slowly swinging outward. He moved cautiously and checked both sides before going into the building. It was a warehouse full of palm oil drums. He moved down an aisle of stacked drums. At the end of the aisle he saw Eve's feet sticking out and he ran forward. Eve was on the floor facedown not moving.

"Oh God please no" he said.

Billy knelt down beside her and turned her over on her side. No blood. That was a good sign. A sap hit him from behind at the base of his skull. He crumbled unconscious and landed on top of Eve.

"Hello Cowboy" said the nomad standing over them.

CHAPTER 27

Billy slowly woke to the sound of an engine cranking to life. He had trouble focusing. His head felt like the inside of a thunder cloud with streaks of lightning blinding his vision. He could hear a voice. It sounded like Eve but he couldn't make out what she was saying. "Billy wake up" or something like that he thought. He opened his eyes. The sun was too bright. He closed his eyes and opened them slower. There was a boat in front of him. He saw the words Buaya Darat painted on the stern and puffs of exhaust bubbling up from the water. He was on the foredeck of another boat. He didn't know which boat. That was too much to figure out at the moment. He was sitting in a chair and he could not move his hands and feet. Something kicked him in the ankle. It hurt. He heard Eve's voice again and it was more clear.

"Goddammit Billy. Wake up" she said.

He looked down. It was Eve kicking him. He was happy to see her. Her hands were tied with a heavy rope with one end disappearing over the bow and her feet were tied too and the excess rope was coiled on the deck with the end tied to his chair. Things were slowly registering in his mind. He tried to move. No good. He was tied up too.

"For God's sake Billy. Do something" she said.

Billy saw the nomad appear on the stern of the boat in front of him. He knelt and picked up the end of the rope tied to Eve and wrapped the end of the rope around a cleat on the stern of his boat and tied it off so it was secure. He rose and stepped on the gunwale and onto the pier and walked over and stepped onto the boat where Eve and Billy were tied and stood in front Billy.

"Are you awake?" said the nomad. "Do you understand? It's important that you understand."

Billy looked up at the nomad.

"I understand you're a piece of shit" said Billy.

"That's good. I want you to fight. You should never take life for granted. You know cowboy, I was disappointed to see you take on a new lover so quickly. I thought Noi meant more to you than just another piece of Thai pussy. You really fooled me and her."

"I'm going to watch you die" said Billy.

"No. You're not. But you are going to watch your new bed buddy die. In fact you're going to kill her."

"You're a fucking coward" said Eve.

"Stop interrupting" said the nomad. "The men are talking." He kicked Eve in the stomach and knocked the wind out of her.

"Women can get so emotional. I probably should have gagged her. If you want I can just give her a kick over the side right now. The end result will be the same but it'll be a lot quieter."

"Rot in hell you bastard. I hope you suffer when they catch you" said Eve.

"What do you think cowboy? No? Okay. I'll respect your choice. I'd explain how this whole set up works but honestly it's getting a little late and I've got a flight to catch."

The nomad leaned close to Billy's face.

"You fucked with the wrong guy cowboy. I win. You die."

"If there's a hell I'll be waiting for you" said Billy.

"We should be so lucky" said the nomad.

The nomad stepped off the foredeck and onto the pier and walked back to the Buaya Darat. He stepped onto her foredeck and disappeared into the wheelhouse.

Eve cried and pleaded for Billy to do something. But

there was nothing he could do. It was so simple. The Buaya Darat would pull Eve into the water when it left the pier. If she was lucky she would drown before the coiled rope ran out and Billy and his chair were pulled off the bow into the water. He would be turned into a water anchor and surely pull Eve apart.

Billy was angry and he knew it was clouding his judgement. There was no time. He had to think clear. He closed his eyes and let the anger go and started thinking about the situation. He was sitting in a chair. A cheap wood chair that was screwed together. The kind his father hated because they don't last. He twisted violently from side to side and forced the legs of the chair to scrape across the deck.

Billy heard the engine of the Buaya Darat throttle up and watched it pulled away from the pier. Eve screamed. Billy tried to focus. *Stay on task* he thought. *It's her only hope.* Several more hard twists and he could feel the chair pulling apart. He grabbed the bottom of the seat and twisted with his shoulders. Gaps widened at the connecting points between the seat and the legs. The chair was breaking apart. Billy saw the rope from the back of the Buaya Darat rise up out of the river. He looked down into Eve's eyes filled with tears. The rope snapped taught and she was swept from the foredeck.

Eve plunged into the water and was pulled behind the Buaya Darat. The coiled rope at Billy's feet uncoiled faster and faster. Billy twisted as hard as he could. The chair broke apart and the pieces fell to the deck. The rope tied around Billy sagged. Billy wiggled out of the ropes and watched as the coil grew smaller and finally disappeared. The last of the rope caught Billy by the feet and tripped him and he fell to the deck with a thud. The rope pulled free of his legs and fell into the water and pieces of the chair fell with it. Eve was stilled being dragged by the Buaya Darat and disappeared under the surface of the river.

Billy crossed into the wheelhouse and fired up the engine and pushed the throttle forward but the boat didn't move. The boat was still tied to the pier. He throttled down, stepped out of the wheelhouse, jumped onto the pier and untied the bow line. He ran back for the stern line and untied it. He ran back across the pier and jumped onto the foredeck, entered the wheelhouse and gunned the engine. The boat chugged away from the pier and slowly picked up speed and headed out into the river and after the Buaya Darat. The Buaya Darat pulled Eve underwater and the additional drag slowed it down. The Mau Ke Mana gained on it quickly.

"Come on you bitch. Move" said Billy.

There was nothing he could do to make it go faster. He needed a way to grab the line so he could pull Eve back to the surface and aboard the boat. He searched the wheelhouse and grabbed a long gaff hanging above the doorway. The point on the gaff hook was sharp. He would need to be careful to hook the rope and not Eve.

The nomad peeked out the wheelhouse to check on Eve's progress. He saw the Mau Ke Mana following from behind and Billy in the wheelhouse. The nomad twitched and pushed the throttle all the way forward but there was nothing left. The Buaya Darat was going as fast as it could. He looked out again and saw that Billy was gaining on him. He could cut Eve loose. That would give him more speed. But that was what Billy wanted and not an option he would consider further.

The Mau Ke Mana was almost even with the stern of the Buaya Darat. It was as close as Billy dared without running over Eve with the boat and cutting her with the prop. He eased on the throttle and matched the Mau Ke Mana's speed to Buaya Darat's speed. The nomad appeared from the wheelhouse and raised the pistol that Billy had bought and fired. Four bullets hit the Mau Ke Mana's wheelhouse and splintered the wooden wall panels and shattered the windshield. Billy ducked down and counted each shot and knew he had to stay under cover until all six were fired or he would be wounded or killed and Eve would die for sure. Two bullets were left in the gun. Billy peaked through the doorway and the nomad fired another round that zinged but an inch from Billy's face. Billy ducked back into the safety of the wheelhouse. Only one more bullet but Eve was running out of time.

The nomad readied himself. Billy lunged through the doorway with the gaff pole in hand and landed on the foredeck. The nomad took his shot. The wood on the foredeck splintered from the last bullet. The nomad threw the useless pistol into the river.

Billy used the gaff pole and reached out for the line dragging Eve. The pole wasn't long enough. Billy tried again and again. It was too short and he couldn't reach the line without running over Eve. Billy reentered the wheelhouse and threw the throttle all the way forward and the engine revved and the Mau Ke Mana gained on the Buaya Darat. He ran back to the galley and grabbed the only knife left—a short paring knife—and tucked it into his belt and ran back to the foredeck.

The Mau Ke Mana's foredeck and the Buaya Darat's stern deck were now even and only a few feet apart. The nomad could see that Billy was going to jump on board his boat and attempt to cut Eve loose. The nomad cranked the wheel hard and turned his boat into Billy's boat. The Mau Ke Mana rammed the side the Buaya Darat and Billy was knocked off his feet. The Mau Ke Mana slowed. The boats separated. No time. Last chance to save Eve. Billy threw the gaff pole to the stern deck of the Buaya Darat and jumped.

Billy landed short and hit the port side of the Buaya Darat and grabbed the gunwale and pulled himself up and turned to see the nomad exit the galley doorway with the carving knife in his hand. Billy lunged across the deck and grabbed the gaff pole and swung it into the nomad. The nomad was knocked off balance and slammed against the outer wall of the galley. The nomad regained his balance and lunged at Billy with the carving knife and Billy pitched to one side. The nomad slashed at Billy's hand holding the gaff and cut him. Billy dropped the gaff to the deck and pulled out the paring knife from his belt and faced the nomad.

The pilotless Mau Ke Mana rammed the side of the Buaya Darat and the nomad and Billy lost their balance and fell to the deck. Billy lunged at the nomad and swung the paring knife down at the nomad's face and the nomad shifted his head only catching the point of Billy's knife down the side of his cheek. The nomad screamed in pain and blood flowed from the gash. Billy's paring knife plunged deep into the deck. The nomad grabbed his carving knife and swung it into Billy's back and hit in the shoulder blade and the tip of the knife's blade skidded along the bone but did not break it. Billy rolled and forced the knife stuck in his back from the nomad's hand. The nomad grabbed Billy's paring knife stuck in the deck but could not get a good grip on the small handle and the short blade would not budge. Billy reached back and pulled the nomad's knife free from his shoulder.

Both men climbed to their feet. Billy had the carving knife and the nomad was weaponless. They both turned to see the Mau Ke Mana once again about to ram the Buaya Darat. Billy stepped toward the nomad. The nomad turned and stepped on the gunwale and jumped to the foredeck of the Mau Ke Mana as it rammed the Buaya Darat. Billy was knocked off his feet.

Billy watched the nomad stumble into the Mau Ke Mana's wheelhouse. The nomad would get away if Billy didn't jump on the Mau Ke Mana. He glanced back at the stern of the Buaya Darat where the rope to Eve was still tied to the cleat and taught. There was no more time and he chose. Billy watched from the deck of the Buaya Darat as the nomad cranked the wheel and steered the Mau Ke Mana away to safety.

Billy ran forward into the wheelhouse and pulled down the throttle and the engine sputtered to a stop.

He ran back to the stern and pulled in the line tied to Eve. Billy saw Eve appear from underneath the water. She was limp. He pulled her up onto the deck.

He knew he had to get air into her brain but her lungs would be filled with water. He reached two fingers into her mouth and cleared debris from her throat and mouth and rolled her onto her stomach and straddled her back and pushed down hard on the back of her chest. Water spurted from her nose and mouth. He pushed down three times until most of the water was out and flipped her onto her back. He breathed into her mouth twice. Her chest expanded as it filled with air but her body remained limp. He let her chest deflate and breathed again into her mouth twice. Still nothing. He felt her neck for a pulse. Nothing. He placed his hands over her chest and pumped thirty times and breathed into her mouth again twice and watched her chest expand each time. He checked again for a pulse. Nothing. He pumped on her chest thirty times again. He kept at it refusing to give up.

It was sunset. Birds flew across the water. Monkeys climbed to the safety of the highest branches. The Mau Ke Mana had drifted into a clump of trees along the river bank. It was quiet. Billy sat on the deck and cradled Eve's head in his lap and brushed her hair gently away from her face. Her eyes were closed and her body limp. She was dead.

Billy felt lost and stared out at the river and watched the water glide by. The heavens had finally exacted a toll for his sins. He knew there would be no joy in his life now and only pain. It was just.

CHAPTER 28

It was morning in the sheltered bay of El Nido in the Philippines. Waves massaged the crescent-shaped beach. Limestone cliffs with long vines hanging down their shear rock faces towered over the seaside town. The water in the bay was turquoise and dotted with dozens of traditional paraw boats. The paraw boats equipped with double outriggers were used to ferry tourists to the 45 islands in the Bacuit Archipelago.

The nomad sat in a seafood restaurant with tables made of bamboo and a sand floor. He didn't like it. It seemed dirty and unsanitary but TripAdvisor had given it four stars and the restaurant specialized in grilled tiger lobster which he thought would be safe to eat. A white bandage covered the side of his bruised face and the stitches underneath throbbed. He swallowed a 400 mg tablet of ibuprofen and chased it with bottled water. He looked out the open walls of the cafe. The cafe was built at the top of the beachfront and had a nice view of the boats bobbing in the morning surf. Tourists gathered along the shoreline waiting for instructions from their Filipino tour guides.

Things could be worse. Not a bad place to recoup from his wounds. A few weeks on the beach sipping San Miguel beer and eating fire-roasted lobster and he would be ready to go again. But slower this time. No need to rush things. It was rushing that almost got him caught. He would learn from his mistakes and plan better and be more prepared and be more patient. Patience was never his strong point but if that is what it took to keep going then that is what he would do. He would feed his need. It was fun and made him feel alive. It gave him purpose.

He watched a young Filipino waitress lean over to reveal her cleavage as she cleared a table. She glanced over and noticed the nomad. She finished cleaning and walked toward him. He knew he looked bad with his bandage and bruised face but maybe she didn't care. He was rich and white.

A drop of blood landed on the white placemat in front of him. The passing waitress pointed to her cheek and then at his cheek. The nomad touched his bandage. It was wet with blood. *Fucking cowboy* he thought.

"Toilet?" he said.

She pointed to the alley beside the restaurant. The

nomad grabbed the bottle of water and picked up his shoulder bag and headed to the alley. The alley was compacted dirt and smelled of sewage like most alleys in the Philippines. He walked to the men's room and entered.

He looked in the old bathroom mirror that had lost most of its silver backing. He was a mess. He pulled out a package of gauze and cotton pads, a small bottle of hydrogen peroxide and a roll of medical tape. He washed his hands using the water from the bottle. He peeled back the bloody bandage and revealed the stitches holding together a long gash of swollen cheek flesh leading all the way back to his ear. He was nauseated by the site of his future scar. He had no problem seeing other people's pain and suffering but when it came to himself, he was actually a bit squeamish. He opened the bottle of hydrogen peroxide and soaked several cotton pads with the liquid and used them to clean the wound. The wound bubbled white killing bacteria and liquefying the puss. He opened the gauze package and pre-taped the sides of the gauze bandage covering his wound. He scooped up the medical waste on the counter and looked for a trashcan. It was full. *Savages* he thought. His hands were full and he used his foot to kick open the toilet stall door and threw the waste in the toilet and flushed it. It clogged and started to overflow. *Fuck 'em if they can't even empty the damn trashcan* he thought.

He turned to exit the stall and saw the ka-bar knife plunge into his chest just below his left shoulder. It was a powerful stroke and drove him back into the stall and he fell to the toilet seat. The 7-inch blade shattered the second rib from the top of the left side but only reached a depth of 5 inches before it hit the nomad's shoulder blade. It had missed all his vital organs and arteries and was an inch and a half away from the aorta and the pulmonary artery at the top of his heart. A hand was still wrapped around the handle of the knife. It was Billy's.

Billy repositioned his hands, both covered with bandages from his wounds where the nomad had cut him. He put his left hand near the knife's crossguard to keep the blade from popping out and placed the palm of his right hand directly under the knife's pommel. The nomad realized what Billy was about to do and reached into his pocket and slipped his finger into the ring guard of the karambit. He used his thumb to flip off the leather sheath and pulled the knife out of his pocket. He would only get one shot at Billy and he wanted to distract him if only for a moment.

"If you kill me they will never stop hunting you" said the nomad.

"Yep" said Billy.

Billy pushed up hard on the knife's pommel and the blade inside the nomad's shoulder pivoted and the edge of the blade sliced down through the nomad's aorta and into the top of the heart. Blood flowed and soaked the nomad's shirt. The nomad tried to raise his hand holding the karambit but his brain was no longer receiving blood and incapable of issuing commands to his body. His eyes seemed confused and then lifeless. The nomad was dead.

Billy walked out onto the beach. His shirt was spotted with the nomad's blood and he pulled it off and set it beside him as he sat down in the sand. There was a small breeze coming in from the bay and it felt good on his skin. He had stitches in the back of his shoulder from the wound the nomad had given him and his shoulder was stiff and he felt old and tired. He stared out at the horizon and watched the dark clouds rolling in over the distant islands. *The monsoons are coming* he thought.

MONSOON RISING

ABOUT THE AUTHOR

David Lee Corley grew up on a horse ranch in Northern California, breeding and training appaloosas. At 28, he packed up his family and moved to Malibu, California to write and direct motion pictures. His movies have been seen by over 50 million viewers worldwide and won a multitude of awards, including the Malibu, Palm Springs and San Jose Film Festivals. At 56, he sold all his possessions and became a nomad. After three years of wandering the globe, he started writing novels based on his travels. He has circumnavigated the world three times and visited 56 countries. David is still a nomad and loving it!

His motion picture credits include "Solo," starring Adrien Brody and Mario Van Peebles, "Executive Power," starring Craig Sheffer and John Heard, "Angel's Dance," starring Jim Belushi and Kyle Chandler and "Second in Command," starring Jean-Claude Van Damme.

Dear Reader,

I hope you enjoyed Monsoon Rising as much I enjoyed writing it. Look for Billy Gamble to return in Book 2 of The Nomad Series. I will give a little hint as to his whereabouts... he's in Meteora, Greece running from a team of mercenaries sent to capture him. Who the hell hired mercenaries and why? The stakes are higher in the sequel and the madman Billy will hunt is much more dangerous. It's gonna be good... you have my word on it.

In the meantime, if you are so inclined, I would really appreciate a review of Monsoon Rising. Loved it, hated it, I'd benefit from your feedback. It makes me a better writer and, honestly, if it's a positive review, it helps promote the book. Reviews are hard to come by these days and now more than ever potential readers use them in their decision-making process. You, the reader, have the power to make or break a book. So, here is the link to my author's page on Amazon: https://www.amazon.com/David-Lee-Corley/e/B073S1ZMWQ Just click on the cover of Monsoon Rising and you will find the reviews button under the yellow stars. Once you land on the reviews page you can select the Write a Customer Review button and you are ready to write your review. It's pretty simple.

Thank you for your consideration and I hope to hear from you.

In gratitude,

David Lee Corley

Made in the USA
Columbia, SC
04 November 2022